SWORD OF
VALOR

Books by Tom Willard

SWORD OF
VALOR

Book Five of The Black Sabre Chronicles

Tom Willard

A TOM DOHERTY ASSOCIATES BOOK
New York

SWORD OF VALOR

Copyright © 2003 by Tom Willard

Title page illustration by Ellisa Mitchell

This book is printed on acid-free paper.

A Forge Book
Published by Tom Doherty Associates, LLC
175 Fifth Avenue
New York, NY 10010

www.tor.com

Forge® is a registered trademark of Tom Doherty Associates, LLC.

Library of Congress Cataloging-in-Publication Data

Willard, Tom.
     Sword of valor / Tom Willard.
        p.   cm.—(The Black sabre chronicles ; bk. 5)
     "A Tom Doherty Associates book."
     ISBN 0-312-87385-9
     1. United States. Army. Airborne Division, 101st—Fiction.
2. African American soldiers—Fiction.   3. African American
families—Fiction.   4. Women helicopter pilots—Fiction.
5. Persian Gulf War, 1991—Fiction.   I. Title.

PS3573.I4445S95   2003
813'.54—dc21
                                                        2003041764

Printed in the United States of America

0   9   8   7   6   5   4   3   2

For Don Johnston, Las Vegas, Nevada, educator, musician, father, husband, friend, and fraternity brother of Sigma Tau Gamma. He served in the elite Air Commandos of the U.S. Air Force. When I came back from Vietnam, he spent hours in front of the fireplace with me at the frat house listening to my catharsis.

His patience was—will always be—greatly appreciated. He passed away during the writing of this novel.

Fades the light;
And afar
Goeth day, cometh night,
And a star,
Leadeth all, speedeth all,
To their rest.
—"Taps," author unknown

Lieutenant Colonel Michael R. Chambers, his wife, Regina, and their children, Ray and Michelle.

Colonel Frank Wiercinski, his wife, Jeannine, Commanding, Task Force Rakkassan, (Afghanistan) 3rd Brigade, 187th Regiment, 101st Airborne/Air Assault . . . A SOLDIER OF THE NATION!

And Heather Ohlhauser . . . a future author.

Acknowledgments

The author wishes to acknowledge the following people for their overwhelming support and assistance in the writing of The Black Sabre Chronicles:

Julian Bach Literary Agency/International Management Group, especially Julian Bach, Carolyn Krupp, and Ann Torrego. Thanks, guys . . . you were terrific!

Editors Harriet McDougal and Dale L. Walker. Assistant editors Lisa Wiseman, Stephanie Lane, and William Smith. The best of the best. Their patience is greatly appreciated.

For support and assistance, The U.S. Army Center for Military History, Brig. Gen. Jack Mountcastle, Chief Historian; Gen. William C. Westmoreland; Gen. Colin Powell; Gen. Ron Griffith; Gen. Eric K. Shinseki; Lt. Gen. Gerald Johnson; Maj. Gen. Larry Jordan; Maj. Gen. Richard Cody; Col. Ted Crozier, Clarksville, Tennessee, Fort Campbell Historical Foundation; Col. John Rosenberger; Col. James Hurd, Jr.; Col. David H. Hackworth; Col.

Thomas H. Taylor; Col. Thomas Smith, and his wife, Christine; Warrant Officer 4 Charlie Musselwhite, and his wife, Jacquelene, St. Petersburg, Florida; Lt. Col. Robert Schroeder; Lt. Col. Nasby Wynn; Lt. Col. Michael Chambers; Lt. Col. Lawrence C. Hannan, Fort Riley, Kansas; 1st Lt. Travis B. Smith, 3rd. Bn., 502nd Inf. Reg., 2nd Bde., 101st Airborne/Air Assault Division; Command Sgt. Maj. Leo B. Smith, my "1st Shirt" in the 101st Abn.; Bryan Hall Jackson and Chuck Knowlan, National Medal of Honor Museum, Chattanooga, Tennessee; Command Sgt. Maj. Russ McDonald, "C" Company, 1st Bn. 327th Abn. Inf., 1st Bde., 101st Airborne Division, Clarksville, Tennessee; Command Sgt. Maj. Harve Appleman, and his wife, Molly, and "Candy," 1st Bn. 327th Abn. Inf., 1st Bde., 101st Airborne Division, Military Order of the Purple Heart, Clarksville, Tennessee; Sgt. 1st Class John (Dynamite) Hughes, Tiger Force, 1st Bn. 327th Abn. Inf., 1st Bde., 101st Airborne Division, Nashville, Tennessee; staff and personnel at the Buffalo Soldier Monument, Fort Leavenworth, Kansas; Mary Williams, Park Ranger and Historian at the Fort Davis, Texas, Historic Site; Jerry Johnson, Alpine, Texas, and the Friends of Fort Davis.

First Sergeant Monty Ohlhauser, North Dakota National Guard, his wife, Judaine, their children, Heather, Brandon, and Tiffany.

Daniel and Travis Usselman, Bismarck, North Dakota, friends forever.

Most important, my wife, Laura, our children, Sean, Ryan, Allisa, and Brent. Thanks for putting up with the old man as "deadline" neared.

And . . . all the others I may have forgotten.

Where is the prince who could so afford to cover his country with troops for its defense as that 10,000 men descending from the clouds might not in many places do an infinite deal of mischief?

—*Benjamin Franklin*

Preface

The Vietnam War taught the United States many painful lessons; most important, the military learned that a foreign war could not be fought without the support and involvement of the American people. Army Chief of Staff General Creighton W. Abrams, Jr., who succeeded General William Westmoreland as commander of forces in Vietnam, encouraged the involvement of the nation as a whole in any foreign military conflict. He believed the best possible method to achieve this goal was through a strong National Guard and reserve readiness.

The "Weekend Warriors," as they were referred to by the regular military, became a powerful military tool. Not a reserve force to draw from; rather, a force that could be committed to the field as a vital, well-trained, and sophisticated fighting force that would equal any regular American unit.

Unlike in the Vietnam era, when the draft caused young men to suddenly disappear from their hamlets, towns, or cities, American communities are now an integral part of the total commitment through the use of guard and reserve units. The full gamut of military requisite stood ready and waiting, from cooks to fighter pilots, air defense units to armor, Navy SEALs to Army Special Forces.

The "Abrams Doctrine" relied on the fact that the country would be more supportive of an overseas military confrontation if everyday "citizen soldiers" were involved, thus including the very fabric of the nation. Local bankers, gas station owners, teachers, ministers, professionals, and blue-collar workers, their call-up would rally the country to stand behind the troops and, unlike Vietnam, would hasten the government to a swift and decisive victory. Sons and daughters of veterans and nonveterans would fight with the support of the nation at their backs, while they did the job that lay ahead with the confidence that they would not be left stranded on faraway battlefields, or return to a country that did not appreciate their sacrifice.

Drawn from the all-volunteer regular military, national guard, and reservists, the fighting force of the land would not be uniformed by conscripts; rather, by those who stepped forward, wanting to defend their country. The concept of a professional military within all the services was more successful than dreamed of initially. Men and women served alongside each other in basic training, advanced individual training, and in all units, including combat support. In some cases, women were allowed to serve aboard ships in the Navy, which, along with the Air Force and Army, gave women the opportunity to enter flight programs that included flying combat aircraft.

This integration would be of tremendous value toward the close of the twentieth century, when the democratic world was faced with one of its greatest international challenges.

On August 2, 1990, the small, oil-wealthy Arab state of Kuwait was invaded by the air, ground, and sea forces of Iraq. This act of invasion and occupation brought the wrath of the world community down upon Iraqi president Saddam Hussein. United Nations forces rallied immediately with Operation Desert Shield, which began with the rapid deployment of United States troops to Iraq's neighboring nation, Saudi Arabia, for fear the Saudis' rich oil fields might be Hussein's next target.

This operation would mark a significant chapter in the history of the African-American in the United States military: The Persian Gulf War was the first declared war in which African-American women officers would lead men and women of all races into battle.

Unlike their predecessors, the WASPs—Women Army Support Pilots, who were only permitted to fly replacement aircraft to rear areas of both theaters in World War II—women pilots in the Persian Gulf would fly in combat in support of Allied air, sea, and ground forces. Women had served close to battlefields in American history, but primarily as medical, clerical, and administrative personnel, never on or above the FEBA, the "forward edge of the battle area." The contribution of women officers, noncommissioned officers, and enlisted personnel during the Persian Gulf War will perhaps never be fully recognized for its record of heroism, sacrifice, and dedication to service and nation. A large percentage of that contribution was the work of African-American women, serving at all three echelons of rank.

The performance of women was remarkable, operating in extreme desert heat by day, freezing in the cold of the desert night, constructing and defending the vital base camps, highways, air bases, that would ultimately form an intimidating and formidable wall of defense between Saudi Arabia and Iraq.

During the initial phase of the war—Operation Desert Shield—troops and matériel were shipped by air and sea to buy precious time for the Saudis and other neighboring Arab countries. All branches of the United States military participated at breakneck speed, leaving family, friends, and jobs to protect vital foreign American interests.

Operation Desert Storm began with the "Air Campaign," when Lieutenant Colonel Richard Cody, 101st Airborne/Air Assault (now Major General, Division

Commander), fired the first Hellfire missile from his AH-64 Apache attack helicopter, destroying the first cog in Iraq's western radar fence. On the FEBA, black women pilots and ground personnel were already geared up to go to war.

The "Ground Campaign" found women in the teeth of the battle, some killed, some captured and forced to endure the feared mistreatment that American society considers its strongest argument in opposing women in the combat arms.

Yet, ten years later, women in uniform have not been given the full opportunity to succeed in the vastly male-dominated community. Difficult issues have risen—sexual discrimination, harassment, acceptance into the academies and military colleges, the disparity in the officer corps, and the opportunity for advancement in the enlisted ranks.

This novel attempts to shed light on the valorous performance of women in the Persian Gulf War, whatever their color or ethnic origin, and whether they are officers, noncommissioned, or enlisted.

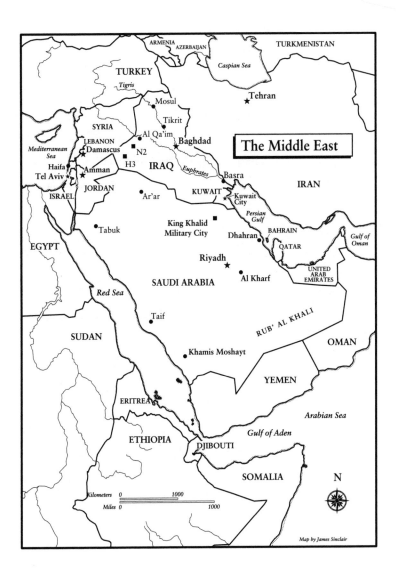

ARMENIA
AZERBAIJAN
TURKMENISTAN
TURKEY
Caspian Sea
Tigris
Tehran
Mosul
Tikrit
SYRIA
Al Qa'im
Baghdad
LEBANON
Damascus
N2
Mediterranean
Sea
H3
IRAQ
Euphrates
Haifa
Amman
Basra
Tel Aviv
IRAN
ISRAEL
JORDAN
Ar'ar
KUWAIT
Kuwait
City
Persian
Gulf
King Khalid
Military City
Tabuk
Dhahran
BAHRAIN
Gulf of
Oman
QATAR
EGYPT
Riyadh
UNITED
ARAB
EMIRATES
SAUDI ARABIA
Al Kharf
Red Sea
Taif
RUB' AL KHALI
OMAN
SUDAN
Khamis Moshayt
YEMEN
ERITREA
Arabian Sea
Gulf of Aden
ETHIOPIA
DJIBOUTI
SOMALIA
N
Kilometers   0   1000
Miles   0   1000

The Middle East

Map by James Sinclair

Miss Marie

|

Della Liberty—Moss Liberty

Jonathan Sharps (Virginia)

|

Patricia Bennet

|

Jonathan Sharps Bennet

The Sharps Family

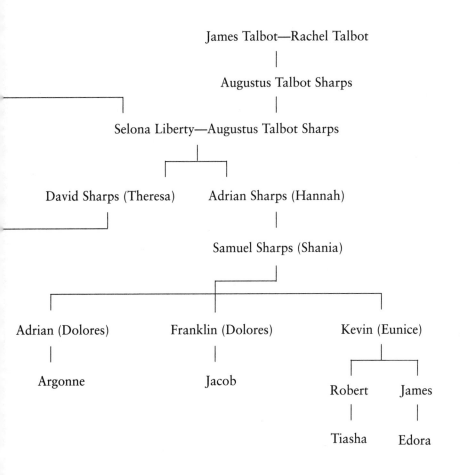

PROLOGUE

*　*　*

At Sabre Ranch, Dr. Franklin LeBaron Sharps sat at his ormolu desk, uninterested in his daily mail, with the exception of one letter that had arrived that morning from Argonne. At forty-seven, he was still sapling-lean, his physique strong and durable, like that of a long-distance runner. He continued to wear a paratrooper hair-cut, his scalp shaved two inches above the ears and close-cropped on top. He allowed himself a narrow mustache. He wore a light blue jumpsuit.

When he finished reading the letter, sudden movement from outside the house caught his eyes. He rose and walked to the French doors and watched a dozen antelope walk lazily through the front yard, ignoring his sudden appearance as he studied them through the glass.

He watched for several minutes, then returned to the letter, read it again, then glanced to the wall and slowly swiveled his leather chair as he studied a panorama of family photographs, awards, and decorations, all of which swelled him with pride. But it was his medical degree that gave him the most satisfaction, earned at the University of Arizona, after he was discharged from the army.

Life had been good to him and Dolores, whom he had married in the fall of 1967. Their son, Jacob LeBaron Sharps, was now a first-year medical student at the University of Southern California. An orthopedic surgeon, Franklin practiced in Phoenix, where he commuted daily in his private airplane.

He scanned the wall carefully, ultimately pausing on one particular frame that reminded him of one of the saddest days of his life.

Captured in the frame was a piece of paper the size of a dollar bill bearing the name ADRIAN AUGUSTUS SHARPS II. The paper reminded him of a lightning storm at night, what with the brilliance of the name at the center, then the surrounding dark shading from the lead pencil he used to transcribe his older brother's name from the Wall at the Vietnam War Memorial. There had been other names on the Wall he had recognized on that first—and only—visit, in 1983. But his brother's was the only one he had framed. The more than dozen others he had brought back lay within the cover of a book in the bookcase. The book was titled *About Face: The Odyssey of an American Warrior*. The author was Colonel David H. Hackworth, Franklin's former commander in the 101st Airborne.

He had visited the Memorial with Dolores; his father; his younger brother, Kevin, now an attorney working for the NAACP in Atlanta; his stepdaughter, Lieutenant Argonne Sharps, a graduate of West Point, who was the daughter of his brother Adrian; and his son, Jacob.

Instinctively, his eyes drifted to another photograph on the wall, this one taken six years ago at Argonne's graduation from West Point. She stood at attention, wearing the uniform of a cadet, saluting with her drawn sabre. Beside her photograph was a picture of his dead brother, wearing an identical uniform, the same sabre salute.

"Tradition," Franklin whispered softly; almost reverently.

Then he heard the front door open and Dolores's voice calling—sounding frightened. He hurried toward the liv-

ing room, where he found her standing in front of the
large front window. She turned, and he could see the
worry on her face. He put his arms around her and felt
her trembling body weaken against his. "What is it, sweetheart? Aren't you feeling well?"

"You haven't heard? It's just been announced on the
news."

She went to the television and pressed a button on the
remote, quickly switched the channels until she found
CNN.

From Baghdad, correspondent Bernard Shaw's voice
rang with excitement as the greenish picture, filmed with
night-vision cameras, showed the night sky of the Iraqi
capital aglow with the tracer etchings of antiaircraft fire
pouring upward from the ground.

He sat heavily on the couch. "The air campaign has
begun."

"My God, Franklin, Argonne! Her unit is on the front
lines in Saudia Arabia!" Dolores's words were shrilling
with fear.

Within seconds he was on the telephone to his father,
who now lived in Falls Church, Virginia. Franklin wrote
down numbers of several influential military men at the
Pentagon, called them all, but ran into the expected blank
wall of military silence.

For the next few hours, like most Americans, he and
Dolores sat in front of their television set, knowing their
daughter and other sons and daughters were now jour-
neying in harm's way.

"Good, God. Our boys are tearing them apart," said
Franklin.

Dolores was almost angered by the sound of glee in his
voice. She stared at him coldly. "Your daughter might be
in the middle of that fighting right now."

He reached and patted her hand. There was no hiding the
fear on her face or in her voice. "Sweetheart, she's in combat
support. That means she's rear-echelon. Besides . . . this is

an air campaign. Obviously ground-support troops have not been deployed into the fight."

Forcing herself away from the greenish report from Baghdad, Dolores went to the telephone. "I'm going to call Patricia."

Franklin shook his head. "She won't know any more than what we're learning from the television. You know the media has been locked out of this from the beginning. We wouldn't be seeing this if it weren't for CNN reporting from Baghdad."

Dolores was not dissuaded by that fact. The ringing seemed interminable until she heard the sound of Patricia Sharps, a distant cousin who lived in Phoenix.

"Patricia, are you watching CNN news?"

There was the immediate sound of fear in her voice. Her son was a Navy fighter pilot aboard the USS *John F. Kennedy* aircraft carrier. The two mothers spoke for ten minutes; then she hung up and returned to the television and did not move until past sunrise.

PART 1

WINDS OF WAR

1

☆ ☆ ☆

As a child, Lieutenant Argonne Sharps had heard all the stories of her family's more than 130 years of honorable and dedicated military service to the United States. While little was known of the centuries of tragedy suffered by her ancestors during the period of slavery, she did know Sharps history since the end of the Civil War. She had thrilled to the stories of her great-great-grandfather, charging on horseback, his sabre at the ready, fighting in the Indian Wars on the western frontier as a buffalo soldier; of her great-grandfather, one of the Sable Doughboys, in the mud and blood of no-man's-land in World War I; of her grandfather Samuel, now retired, one of the first of the "Tuskegee Airmen" in the skies over Europe; and her father descending into the hatred of the Vietnam War.

She had stood in awe at her first sight of the arch at Tuskegee Institute, Alabama, where she had visited in her childhood, and stared in silence at the statue of Booker T. Washington. She recalled the red clay, brick buildings that nurtured men like Washington and Martin Luther King, and women like Barbara Jordan and Harriet Tubman, who were her heroes.

Now, on August 7, 1990, sitting in the briefing room of the 2/17th Cavalry, she was no longer a child. She was an officer, a Kiowa helicopter pilot, wearing the patch of the "Screaming Eagles" of the 101st Airborne, considered the fiercest fighting unit in the world. The 101st was the leading edge of the United States' rapid-deployment force, standing "airborne and air-assault ready" to begin transporting a full brigade of troops, helicopters, and equipment to the other side of the world in six hours. The full division could be prepared to follow within seventy-two hours.

Maps of the Middle East lined the walls; a large overview of Kuwait stood on an easel, marked with red, green, and black ink. A senior officer entered, followed by his staff. They appeared confident, but there was no doubting the weight of the moment.

The officers rose, shouted in unison: *"Air Assault!"* The officer motioned them to their chairs.

"Gentlemen," he began, then nodded at Argonne and another female pilot, "and, ladies . . . I'm certain you're aware of the situation in the Persian Gulf. The division has been put on alert for deployment. Commencement has begun for permanent overseas replacement. Our mission is to move as rapidly and efficiently as possible to provide support to the Saudi Arabian defense forces."

There it was, thought Argonne. The air had been thick with expectation since the invasion of Kuwait. Now it was POR time.

"You'll need to get all your people processed . . . shots, dental needs, eyeglasses checked for proper fit in gas masks, and final wills. Equipment maintenance will begin immediately. Forget about sleep and get your personal matters in line. Until we deploy there will be a constant vigil. Give your married personnel as much time with their families as possible, but stay with the program. We will be ready when the balloon goes up. Questions?"

"What about personnel on leave?" asked a warrant officer.

"Bring them back. All leaves and passes are canceled," the officer said. He looked around, knowing there were many questions, but figured few would be asked at the moment. The major points would arise as POR moved forward. "That is all, for the moment."

The soldiers quietly stood and left to rejoin their units. She trailed in the rear, hearing the near-electrical buzz that filled the air, the buzzing of a thousand simultaneous thoughts.

At her squadron hangar, Argonne found her crew chief, Specialist Five Desmond Baker, a short, muscular African-American, wiping oil from his hands. He wore a sheepish grin on his face, as though he knew some great secret. "We gearing up for the Iraqis, Lieutenant?"

She eyed him warily. A twenty-two-year-old hip-hop kid from Chicago, Baker was razor-sharp in his uniform, conscientious in his job, and had a street-smart perception of everything that affected his world. "What makes you think that, Baker?"

"I heard the 'word' in the mess hall."

Typical way it works, she thought. She recalled her father telling her that in 1965, the officers' wives knew about the 1st Brigade's deployment to Vietnam before the battalion commanders. While the chain of command was designed to release information in an orderly fashion, clerks throughout the army were generally privileged to the most sensitive material.

Within an hour the hangar was filling with troops awaiting a special meeting. The mood was upbeat, and except for the expected adrenaline of nervousness the sky soldiers appeared eager. Unlike in Operation Just Cause— the invasion of Panama nine months before, when the 101st was battle-ready, assembled on the tarmac for deployment that would never come—in what the division now called Operation Desert Destiny, the Screaming Eagles knew there was no way they would be kept from the fight.

She heard a voice whisper from behind, using her radio call sign, saying, "Looks like this is the real deal, Six Gun."

Warrant Officer Matthew "Monty" Ohlhauser, from Denver, Colorado—Argonne's copilot—was new to the unit, but aggressive, cool, and eager to learn. He had come up through the ranks, receiving his warrant officer's commission at the U.S. Army helicopter training center at Fort Rucker, Alabama. With blond hair, green eyes, and stocky build, he had been a champion bull rider in college, but chose the military over the professional rodeo circuit. His call sign was "Buckaroo."

Argonne smiled. "Was there ever any doubt?"

"Just glad to finally get to see some action. We've trained for this so long we know the drill in our sleep."

That was true. The Screaming Eagles were the sharp point of the military's bayonet, trained to thrust and drive through the enemy, not sit in the rear and wait for the fight to be joined.

"You better call Jenny." Argonne knew that Monty's wife was pregnant with their second child.

He shrugged. "It can wait until I get home. Besides, she probably already knows."

Her thoughts went to her parents. They wouldn't know, but would probably suspect she was going to war.

She checked her watch. "Have to go to the dental clinic. I'll see you in the morning." She left, pausing to look at her Kiowa. The two pilots would spend a lot of time in the aircraft the next few weeks. While they didn't know each other that well, by the time the unit deployed they would be as close as brother and sister.

2

That afternoon, Argonne went to her apartment, showered, and ordered pizza. While waiting for the delivery, she dialed a number from memory. It seemed the phone would ring forever, but finally she heard a familiar voice.

"Hi, Mom. How are you?"

There was a strained pause; she could hear her mother's breathing, giving her a momentary fright. "Hi baby," Dolores answered. "I'm watching the news and thinking about you. How are you?"

"Busy, and tired," Argonne said. "Mom, maybe it's not such a good idea to watch the news. It might only make you upset."

From her living room in Bonita, Arizona, Dolores answered with a question: "Are you going to Saudi Arabia?"

Argonne figured her mother already had the answer. "The division was alerted today for deployment."

"What does that mean? I want you to tell me everything you can. Your father and I have a right to know what's happening to our child." Her voice was stern and strong.

"I can only tell you that we've been alerted. Which

means we are preparing for shipment. The entire division. Several officers on the division staff have already left Fort Campbell."

She thought she heard a whimper; then her mother's voice seemed to calm. "When do you think you'll be shipping out?"

"Not certain at this moment. There's so much to do in order to be prepared. Several battalions in the division have to be brought back from various assignments. Equipment has to be prepared for transport. The troops need to get processed for the deployment. It won't happen overnight." She envisioned her mother sitting in the living room, her face twisted with worry.

"Maybe it'll be over before you get there." There was hope in Dolores's voice.

"That's not likely. Saddam Hussein now has control over some of the most important oil fields of the world. Not to mention the vast wealth of the people of Kuwait City. He won't give that up without a fight."

Dolores sighed. "Can you come home?"

"Yes. But I don't know when. Or for how long."

Dolores thought about the family history. She saw her first husband, David, go to Vietnam and return in a coffin. She saw how that war nearly destroyed the Sharps family. Now another war loomed, and she could feel the dark clouds once again closing around her family. "At least we'll have some time together before you ship out." Her voice sounded weak to Argonne. But she seemed to be trying to understand.

Argonne tried to console her mother. "This is what we've trained for, Mom. Hussein's army might be the fourth-largest in the world, but in today's world size means nothing. We've got the training, the technology, and the support of the world."

"But," her mother said, "it's on the other side of the world. In the desert, for God's sake. You know what the desert can be like. Fighting in that sand will be a nightmare."

"We're trained to fight in the desert, Mom. That's why we train at Fort Irwin, in Death Valley. This has not come as a total surprise. We'll be up for the fight if it comes. And we will win."

Dolores laughed. "Well, at least you're not lacking in confidence. That makes me feel better. Not much, but more than when you called. I know your father is quite concerned, especially about the possibility of your getting captured. Those Iraqis are monsters to civilians . . . I don't want to think of what they'd do to a female enemy soldier."

"I won't get captured, Mom, I promise." She had already considered that possibility and decided she would fight to the death before enduring that nightmare. Then the doorbell rang. "Pizza's here, Mom. Gotta go. Love you. I'll stay in touch."

She hung up and took her pizza and ate by the pool of her apartment complex, staring at the stars, thinking about family, not about impending war.

3

That August in 1990, Michelle Martinson was twenty-two, tall and trim, with long blond hair, and deep blue eyes framed within a freckled face. "Mickey," as she was known by her friends, was preparing to enter her senior year of nursing college at the University of Mary, in Bismarck, North Dakota. She was at Miami International Airport, having returned from Jamaica with her family, when the television sets blared the news of the invasion of Kuwait.

She felt her gut tighten and her mouth turn dry as all her concentration focused on the unfolding events in the Persian Gulf. She glanced at her father, who looked nervous, as though reliving another dark moment from his past. A combat veteran of Vietnam, Calvin Martinson knew what the invasion could mean to his family.

Mickey Martinson, specialist fourth class, North Dakota National Guard, served in a unit that provided one of the most precious commodities in a desert war: water. Assigned to the 144th Quartermaster Detachment, their mission was to distribute potable water to corps and theater army units, whether behind or beyond enemy lines.

Calvin Martinson sat down beside his daughter. "Looks like Saddam Hussein has finally gone completely nuts."

Mickey smiled. The Iraqis had been a focus of the United States for many months. "That should come as no surprise to anyone."

Both knew the warning flags had been flying over the tiny oil-rich nation of Kuwait for months. Now the storm had hit the sands of the Gulf with a raging fury.

"I need to make a call." She stood and went to a pay phone and dialed a number; the voice that answered was familiar, and, she noted, tinged with a sound of excitement.

"This is Captain Elaine Crager. How may I help you?"

"Captain Crager, this is Specialist Martinson. I just heard the news."

Mickey listened as her company commander explained that the unit was not officially on alert, but she expected they would be one of the first should the American government commit ground forces to the Gulf. "It's what we've trained for, Specialist Martinson." Mickey heard the rustling of papers in the background, then listened as her commander said, "I've scheduled a unit meeting for this coming Saturday, zero-eight-hundred hours. Report with full field gear . . . including your chemical-warfare equipment."

Mickey's heart jumped. "I'll be there, ma'am." She hung up and returned to her family. Her mother, Jean, and brother, Wally, a high-school senior, sat waiting with her father.

"Well?" asked her dad.

She shrugged. "Special formation this Saturday. Full field gear."

Calvin's mouth and jaw muscles tightened. "Damn. I was afraid of that."

Her mother looked stunned. "Cal, you're not seriously suggesting that Mickey might have to go over there, are you?"

He nodded gravely. A petroleum engineer for Amoco,

in Mandan, North Dakota, he fully understood the global ramifications of the Kuwaiti—and possibly the Saudi Arabian—oil fields under the control of Saddam Hussein.

"The United States—the world, for that matter—won't sit by and let this continue." He looked at his daughter. He had seen war and knew its horror; his wife had lived and suffered along with him as he dealt with the memories of Vietnam. Now his little girl might become caught in the maelstrom sure to follow. He checked his watch. "Let's get to the departure gate. We can discuss this when we get home."

Jean refused to be quieted on the subject. "I want to discuss it now. We're talking about our baby going to war. You know that they'll be one of the first units sent there. Water is priceless in the desert, the rarest natural commodity in that part of the world."

He knew she was right about that. Water would be precious, and in great demand. Her unit would no doubt operate near the front lines, if not directly in front of the enemy on the forward edge of the battlefield. "You make it sound like they'll be dumped into the middle of this mess and be left without any kind of security. The fact their job is so critical to the whole mission gives me a greater sense of confidence that they will be given every protection available. There'll be paratroopers, air assault, Marines, air support. Not to mention the Navy and Air Force of the United States and the United Nations." He patted his wife's hand. "Don't worry. She'll be fine. Besides, there's no certainty yet that her unit will even be sent to the Middle East."

"I suppose you're right," Jean said.

Mickey had listened from the seat behind her parents. Her mind was already traveling at Mach 1, but not out of fear. She now found the thought of going to war exhilarating; to see a foreign country in turmoil and be a part of the saving of its people. Not like a tourist trap like Jamaica where only dollars were important. But to war!, where she could make a real contribution.

*   *   *

The family flew to Minneapolis, then to Bismarck. Throughout the entire flight, not a word was spoken by any member.

After unpacking, Calvin went to his private office in his home, poured a large drink of bourbon, and sat looking at the wall. A shadow box displaying his decorations from Vietnam was his point of focus. He raised the glass, toasted the medals, then fell asleep in his chair, the sounds of war echoing in his brain.

4

"Tango Golf Six Niner, cleared for straight-in landing."
The voice of the air-traffic controller snapped Franklin
Sharps back to reality. His thoughts had been consumed
by his daughter and the events in Kuwait. The news reports from CNN had graphically portrayed the Iraqi Republican Guard overwhelming the small Kuwaiti army
and air force. Rumors of atrocities were surfacing, including ejecting newborn babies from incubators only hours
after their birth.

He eased back on the throttle, set in twenty degrees of
flaps, then descended to the flight pattern above Phoenix
International Airport. On final approach, he lowered the
landing gear. Nothing happened. The light indicating
whether the gear was down and locked remained red.

"Damn." Taking the radio, he said to the tower, "Phoenix approach control, this is Tango Golf Six Niner. Re-
questing a flyby to have you check my gear. I'm not
getting a green light."

"Roger, Six Niner. Will scope you out" was the reply
from the control tower.

Franklin flew past the tower at fifty feet, where he could

clearly see one of the controllers studying the undercarriage through binoculars.

"Negative on the gear, Six Niner. Get back in the pattern and recycle your gear. I'll keep watching."

Franklin increased power, cleaned up the flaps, and eased back on the yoke, bringing the aircraft to pattern altitude. On base leg he cycled the gear again, heard the whirring, and felt a reassuring bump from the undercarriage. He glanced at the gear light. It was green.

"I'm in the green and down and locked, Phoenix. Thanks a lot for your help."

When the aircraft touched down, he taxied to a tiedown area and found the mechanic who worked on his airplane. After describing the problem, he hurried to a car he kept at the parking lot, then drove to his clinic.

Patients sat waiting, and he was met by a rush from his receptionist, secretary, two nurses, and Dr. Todd Thornton, a young orthopedic surgeon who specialized in sports medicine.

He went directly to his office. The others followed. He was quickly briefed on the status of the patients he would see that morning, and discussed an afternoon surgery with Thornton. He concluded the meeting by telling them about his daughter coming home on leave before deployment to Saudi Arabia.

"I'm going to need some time off during that period of time." He could see them shift uneasily in their chairs. "I'm sure you all understand. I'll be available, but I need to spend some time with my daughter." His eyes drifted to the wall, to a photograph of Argonne in her flight suit.

"Is it for certain she'll be sent to Saudi Arabia?" Thornton asked. He was tall, with blond hair, and green eyes, and Franklin considered him a brilliant knee surgeon.

"Yes," he said. "Her division is always the first on the list. Especially in this type of situation."

"How's Dolores taking it, Franklin?" asked one of the nurses.

"She's torn apart. You all know Argonne's natural father was killed in Vietnam. I don't think she ever dreamed that her daughter would wind up in a war on the other side of the world."

"We'll handle the office and patients," said Thornton. "I know the time will be important for you and your family."

Franklin nodded. "OK. Let's get to work. I'll be there in a few minutes."

They left and he was left with his thoughts, which focused on the night before, after Argonne telephoned. It was not one of his more pleasant remembrances.

5

Franklin was a student of the world situation, had even predicted in private conversation with his father that Saddam Hussein would do something dramatic in the Middle East. But the invasion of Kuwait was more than a surprise; it spelled national suicide for the Iraqis.

After talking with her daughter, Dolores stormed out of the house and headed for Selona's Bench, in the family cemetery. She stood staring at the shiny weapons hanging above the entrance. Four cavalry swords were suspended from the archway, all joined at the center. Each represented a generation of Sharps family men who had gone to war for the United States. All but David, who lay in France.

Franklin stepped beside her. His hand slid around her waist. He felt her body tremble as she quickly pulled away, and in the darkness he could see the fire in her eyes. "Don't touch me. I hold you responsible for my baby being in this situation."

It took him a few moments to recover from the heated statement. "I didn't start the war. We both knew that in this time of world terrorism that she might be called on to serve."

Dolores crossed her arms angrily. "No, but you encouraged her to go to West Point. She could have gone to medical school, like Jacob. But no, not her. She's a Sharps! And you of all people had to have known that this very situation would occur one day."

"I couldn't have stopped her even if I had put her in a locked room. She made her choice. You know that, baby."

He was probably right, she thought. Argonne was a headstrong young woman. "You could have been more supportive of me and my feelings. I lost one loved one in war. Now I might lose another."

"No. I won't hear that kind of talk. You know the policy of women in combat. She'll fly support missions. I doubt that she'll even hear the gunfire if there is a shooting war."

He was lying, but it was the only thing he could think of to say. He had never seen Dolores so upset in the nearly three decades of their marriage. He patted her softly on the shoulder, and whispered, "She'll be fine. You'll see. Besides, once the United Nations get involved, Saddam will back down. He's crazy, but he's smart."

Again her eyes flared. "He is insane. Otherwise he wouldn't have invaded Kuwait. He knows our interests in that part of the world would force us to stand by the Kuwaitis. He wants to pull us into another Vietnam." Then she stopped. "Oh, dear God."

"What?"

"He has chemical and biological weapons. There's rumors he even has nuclear weapons. What if he uses those monstrous tools? That insane bastard could set the whole world on fire."

That was the thought plaguing most of the world. What if Saddam had developed nuclear capability? It was just a few years ago that the Israelis had blown up a nuclear reactor in Iraq over the same fear. Now he had Russian

Scud missiles, and fanatics who could slip across the border carrying suitcase atomic devices.

"He murdered thousands of his own people with chemical gas. I read the newspaper, Franklin. I watch the news. You know what he did to the Kurds." She was becoming hysterical. "He doesn't have to defeat our army. All he has to do is kill forty or fifty thousand and we'll run like frightened rabbits."

Franklin shook his head. He was trying to calm her, but she was making sense. "He won't resort to that type of destruction. He knows what the retaliation will mean. I think he's bluffing. I wouldn't be surprised if he withdraws his troops in the next couple of weeks." Again he lied.

"You better hope so, Franklin." She pointed to the empty grave of his uncle killed in the Great War. "I better not see another grave here."

He turned and walked to the grave of his mother. She had watched his father go to war and waited in pain and agony, hoping the telegram informing her of his death would never be delivered by an army officer and accompanying minister.

"We've got another situation, Momma. And I know you just heard all about it. I wish I knew what to say to Dolores, but I don't. How do you calm a mother worrying that her child might be killed on some foreign ground? I don't know the right words to say." He sighed. "But, she's right. That is one helluva mess over there. A lot of young men and women could come home in body bags. I can't imagine our nation going through something like that again. I wonder what you would say to her?"

6

There is no moment more intense in a person's life than to go to war. To spend every moment fighting to stay alive. To save comrades. To kill strangers. To hone the primordial skill of survival. Even to risk life and limb when there is no certainty of why one is placed into harm's way. Each moment of preparation becomes gripping, bearing onto the warrior like a dark, hovering tempest approaching.

That intensity was forever etched onto the faces of the 101st troopers as they stood in long lines, moving in lock-step through Permanent Overseas Replacement processing at post gymnasiums, mobile medical clinics, the hospital, athletic centers, and designated areas. The troopers were in high spirits, but none were excited about the moment: shots were annoying, dental exams, vision tests, complete physical examinations to insure each soldier was physically fit for the arduous task that lay ahead, were all a pain in the ass.

Problems of training, logistics, supply, sighting weapons for accuracy, classes on the Saudi culture, were confronted and resolved in order to produce the finest individual human fighting machine on Earth. The unit training was grueling and nearly nonstop, repetition necessary to shape the units into a single-minded fighting group that would instinctively learn as much about their buddies as possible. That can often be the deciding factor in a fierce fight: How well do you know the soldiers at your elbows and back?

But there was another problem: Units of the Screaming Eagles—America's first strike in the rapid deployment of troops to a foreign battlefield—were undergoing jungle warfare training in Panama; more than a thousand were serving as aggressor and cadre units at West Point; while hundreds were assigned across the United States to reserve and National Guard units. As one officer noted, "Most of the division will have to redeploy back to Fort Campbell in order to deploy to Saudi Arabia."

A difficult task, but one not unheard of in the history of the Screaming Eagles. From Carentan on D-Day at Normandy to Market Garden at Eindhoven, Holland, Bastogne, Dak To, Tuy Hoa, and Hamburger Hill, the 101st had woven into its division flag a history of having to "go first," on short notice and, too often, not fully prepared. To hold the ground, knowing that the others would soon follow with more behind them.

Argonne realized early on that no one could journey through Fort Campbell without noticing the constant reminders of the division's heritage: obelisks in front of battalion headquarters bearing names of Medal of Honor recipients; the presence of tens of thousand of retirees living in the area; the constant cadence of troops on long runs; and, the grove of 248 maple trees donated by the Canadian government in rememberance of the troopers killed in the 1985 aircraft tragedy at Gander, Newfoundland, while returning from joint military training operations in Egypt.

Heritage, history, indelibly etched into the division flag and guidons; streamers depicting battles fought to defend the nation. With that came a sense of foreboding as well, as Argonne Sharps watched soldiers spending long days in preparation, then hurrying home to be with their families for a few precious hours before turning in for the night. Then, the whole thing began anew the next day after reveille, and a ripple effect began to build to a surging wave of excitement as D-Day approached: Deployment Day.

Fort Campbell wasn't the only military installation gearing up for the desert. Across the United States, reserve and National Guard units were enduring the same basics of the POR. At Fort Irwin, California, the OPFOR (opposing force) of the 11th Armored Cavalry Regiment was training as aggressors in the Mojave Desert, sharpening the skills of units from all services in mock combat against the finest armor unit in the world. Every aspect of the nation's fighting forces, support, and logistics was agonizingly building up to speed, all hoping that Saddam Hussein would not cross into Saudi Arabia until the Allied forces were in place and ready to go to war.

In the cockpit of her OH-D-58 Kiowa helicopter, Argonne sat wrapped in a shroud of darkness. Her right hand gripped the collective, which controlled the rotors; with her left hand on the throttle, her feet firmly planted on the rudder pedals, she imagined the rise and fall of the aircraft, maintaining level flight while preparing to fire one of her weapons systems.

Instinctively, she switched on the chopper's guns and fired four quick bursts at an enemy aircraft's glowing engines. The opponent banked hard; she adjusted and stayed on his tail. Then she went to missiles, heard the "tone" of locking up the target, and squeezed the trigger, sending a heat-seeking Stinger missile at the MiG-31. The deadly weapon tracked through the black night, changing course with each evasive move of the enemy aircraft.

Her jaw tightened as the sky lit up from the MiG's magnesium flares, a countermeasure designed to protect the fighter.

"I've got you, big boy." she said aloud, as the missile

struck the starboard engine of the evading airplane.

A ball of fire erupted and the enemy fell from the sky.

Argonne sat back, removed the blackout cover over her helmet visor, and allowed her eyes to adjust to the bright sunlight filling the cockpit on the tarmac of the flight line. Sweat poured down her face, and her muscles ached from the exercise. She did this often, replicating a "blackout flight," in the event her night-vision capability were to go down.

One thought burned in her mind hotter than the sun: If she was going to war, she would be ready for any contingency. There would be no mercy shown to her; she would show none to the enemy.

7

On the flat, lush farmland of North Dakota, the 144th Quartermaster Detachment was conducting training and preparations for the deployment to the desert of the Middle East. Giant "blisters," which would hold thousands of gallons of precious water, were checked and rechecked for worthiness; mechanics worked on the tractors that would transport the precious cargo from key water points to the troops in the desert. Vehicles were worked on with a driven passion to make the equipment as perfect as possible. Weapons were checked, as was every item issued by the U.S. government.

The state was buzzing from all corners as the young men and women serving as guardians of the nation's security sweated and bled beneath the grueling heat in preparation for transport to one of the hottest lands on the face of the planet.

Cando, North Dakota, a small farming community in the north central part of the state, tingled with curiosity and pride as the 144th prepared for transfer to Camp Ripley,

Wisconsin, the first of many military installations the troops would visit on their journey toward Saudi Arabia.

Captain Elaine Crager, the detachment commander, sat in her office, reading the endless communiqués arriving by fax or telephone. A native North Dakotan, she was a single parent, and while she was deluged with requests for everything imaginable, her thoughts were foremost occupied with the most important person in her life: her five-year-old daughter. Where to keep the child while she was on assignment? How long would she be farmed out to parents or friends? And what if something happened to her in the desert? What would become of her child?

Her mother had agreed to take care of the child on their family farm near Devils Lake, but that meant they would not winter in Arizona as they did every year after the fall harvest. The child needed the stability of home and school, the continuity provided by a stable environment.

The phone rang, and she knew it would be her father. She envisioned him taking off his CAT tractor baseball cap, revealing a bronzed face and a beautiful, strong smile. "Hi, Daddy."

His gentle voice was comforting to her. "Your mother and I talked. It's important that you know that Alissa will be well taken care of while you're gone."

Tears welled in her eyes. "I know this is a hardship for you. I'm really very sorry."

"Don't be," he said. A veteran of the Korean War, he understood that when the bugle blows, the call from the nation must be answered. "We can weather this with no problem. The hardship is on you and we want to help as much as we can."

A clerk interrupted, laying a fax on her desk. She scanned it quickly, her father's words obscured by what she was reading. "Dad, I have to go. I'll come by tonight and we'll work out the details."

She hung up, read the communiqué again, and realized there would be little time to spend with family. CENT-COM—Central Command—was turning up the burners, wanting the "water boys" to hasten to the battlefield.

Time was running short; the desert was getting closer.

That night, SP/4 Mickey Martinson called home, telling her father in Mandan, "We've been ordered to transport to Camp Ripley, Wisconsin, in two days. I don't have any idea what will happen from there or how long we will be at Ripley. I doubt it will be very long."

The long pause from her home was heart-wrenching. "We'll drive up there tomorrow. Your mom and me want to spend some time with you . . . what little time there is left."

"Maybe you shouldn't," she said, not really understanding why she spoke the words.

"We're your family. Believe me, once you get to Saudi Arabia, it will be a good memory to have and fall back on. There will be times when it may be the most important moment of your life. Trust me. I know. I've been there."

She straightened, wiped at a tear. "I'll see you tomorrow."

Suddenly she realized, *This is no longer a game!* All the barracks talk and gung-ho bravado was being narrowed to sharp reality. She was being ever-so-purposely moved toward a situation she thought would never come about. Weekend warrioring at Camp Grafton and a few beers afterward was one thing. But now . . . her head spun and her stomach tightened as though being gripped by a giant vise.

She walked out into the hot sun, stared for a long time at the blue, cloudless sky, oblivious of the noise of trucks and equipment moving in and out of the depot. When she joined the Guard she saw it as an adventure, an exciting way to serve her country, receive educational benefits, and have an experience unlike others her age.

Studying the sky, she realized she never thought the commitment would take her so far from home and country. And she wondered: Had she made a mistake?

8

Major Robert "Jerome" Moody stood at the rear of a Hercules C-130, dressed in desert camouflage fatigues. The Special Forces soldier wore a helmet, night-vision goggles, and a HALO free-fall parachute. Behind him, seated along the hull of the massive transport, forty men of his elite group, all dressed in similar garb, sat in the red glow of the jump light mounted at the exit doors.

Gripping the anchor-line cable threading through the center of the "Herky," as the aircraft was affectionately known, he walked along the line of combat soldiers, checking each man, looking for loose straps, or weapon gurneys not properly connected to their parachute harnesses.

He was pleased by what he found, and, smiling, his cinnamon-colored features appeared demonic in the red light. A former football player at Indiana University, he was stocky, muscular, a combat veteran of Panama, where the lessons of special operations were learned the hard way, always recalling the fate of the Navy SEALs decimated in a deadly ambush.

He paused by a surly, flat-faced master sergeant putting

on gloves. The tattoo of the Green Berets was on the man's wrist, "De Oppresso Liber" engraved on the skin beneath the emblem of two crossed arrows.

Moody motioned for his men to join him. Taking a map, he unfolded it on the deck and went over the mission a final time.

This was the night for perfection.

He looked at the team leaders, telling them, "After I deploy with my group, you'll continue north and drop at Shatt al-Arab, Samarra, then Kirkuk. Each team will be met by friendlies. You know what to do."

Master Sergeant Michael Donalson shook his head. Like the others, he was concerned about the extended line of insertion. "That's a lot of ground to cover, Major. One end of Iraq to the other. We don't have tactical escorts for this mission. I'd hate for MiGs to get on our asses."

Moody grinned. "The Iraqis are keeping their radar turned off to prevent our AWACs from learning their exact locations. And since the Iraqis don't have airborne radar platforms, they are blind. We won't be spotted. Any ground observer will simply assume it's an Iraqi transport."

The sergeant nodded, though he didn't appear convinced. He had heard that before on other special ops, and invariably something went wrong. "OK, Major. But if you're wrong, our asses will be hanging out like Macy's parade floats."

Moody slapped the sergeant's shoulder, saying, "I'm not wrong, Sergeant. Let's get them up and ready."

"Yes, sir," the tough Green Beret replied as he motioned the other soldiers to their feet.

Moody looked at the other team commanders. The force was broken into three "A Teams," each led by a captain. His unit of four men had been designated a different "need to know" mission. While the other teams would set up in the desert, his small group would penetrate to the very heart of the enemy's position. He looked at them grimly, then smiled. "You know your assignments. I expect you to succeed. If you fail—you're on your own. Questions?"

There were none.

The red light blinked twice, the signal from the pilot that the aircraft was reaching the first point for the airborne drop—where Moody and his men would step into the darkness above Kuwait.

Making a fist, the sergeant slipped on his oxygen mask, adjusted his helmet, then raised his hand and was joined by his men as the rear ramp lowered. One soldier carried a large radio pack, their lifeline to SOCCENT—Special Operations Command of Central Command.

Looking through his NVGs, Moody saw the water of the Persian Gulf turn to desert. He nodded and the five men hunkered in close to him. When the hull suddenly glowed green from the jump light, the five men fell silently off the tail.

From 32,000 feet, the Green Berets fell through the darkness, hands joined in a "star" formation. At 500 feet they separated, fell to 300 feet, and opened their canopies. Checking his parachute, Moody saw that the square-shaped canopy was inflated. He released the slider, then gripped the toggles.

Down they floated in the pristine quiet above the captured oil fields of Kuwait.

When he saw the ground coming up, the major pulled down on the toggles, planing up the leading edge of the canopy, breaking his descent to the point that the flared touchdown was almost imperceptible.

On the ground, he and his men wrapped up their parachutes and scurried for an outcropping of rocks, where they buried the canopies, then formed a defensive perimeter and sat waiting. Moody checked his watch. It was 0105. "The contact will meet us in twenty-five minutes," he whispered.

At 0130, they heard the scraping of leather sandals

against the hard sand. Peering through his NVGs, Donalson made out the shape of a lone man walking toward
their position.

As the man neared, Moody slipped forward in a low
crouch and hid behind a large rock. He gauged the sound
of the footsteps in the sand, tightened on the handle of his
knife. As he passed, the man didn't see the commando rise,
but he felt the harsh grip around his neck and the sharp
edge of a knife at his throat.

"Who are you?" Moody said. He could see the man
was not wearing an Iraqi uniform.

"I am Suleiman. I was sent to guide you to a safe
place." He stepped back and in the moonlight he became
more clear. He carried an AK-47 and wore a kaffiyeh
wrapped around his face. The traditional headdress had
been made internationally famous by PLO leader Yassar
Arafat, always seen wearing the traditional cloth of the
Arab bedouin.

The Green Beret judged him to be an old man by the
sound of his voice and the thick carpet of hair on his face,
but he recognized the name given him before departure at
King Fahd Airport, near Dhahran.

The five shadowy figures followed the resistance fighter
toward the faint lights of Kuwait City. In every direction
fires burned from oil-drilling sites, giving the landscape a
hellish appearance. Sweat poured down Moody's face and
neck; the heavy equipment straps cut into his shoulders as
his feet sank into the sand from the heavy burden he carried.

As they approached the outskirts of the city, Suleiman
led them to a sewage outlet that meandered beneath the
captured city. This made Moody nervous. Surely the Iraqis
would have the system monitored, he thought. "Are you
certain this route is secure?" He leaned forward and whispered into Suleiman's ear. He didn't like using spoken

words while infiltrating an enemy position; his training called for silent hand signals.

The old man shrugged, slung his automatic weapon with ease and grandeur. "Yes, *fiendi*. It is secure. The Iraqis are too busy looting the city to concern themselves with crawling through the sewer." He chuckled as he moved forward through the miasma that was now a protective cocoon for the Green Berets.

Moody said nothing; he merely followed the green glow of the Arab through the stench of the underground labyrinth.

9

In Kuwait City, sporadic machine-gun fire broke the eerie silence of the curfew imposed by the Iraqis. Despite the danger, Muhammad Reza Mustafa slipped quietly through the darkness looming over the burned-out shops and buildings along Fahed Al-Salim Street, or rather, what had once been called Fahed Al-Salim. The name had since been changed, like the Al-Sabah hospital. Everything was changing or would be changed. Including the people. The only pride a man had left was to die fighting the invaders.

What was most difficult was ignoring the arrogant Iraqi soldiers sitting in their armored personnel carriers and Russian-built TU-72 tanks. But he did ignore them, knowing this was not the time to stare the Iraqis in the eyes; it was a gesture many Kuwaitis had paid for with their lives since the invasion. Especially the women, who fell prey to the monsters like sheep to a lion.

The Iraqis didn't like the loathsome leers of the people they had annexed in the name of Saddam Hussein's Arab revolution. There were many things the intruders didn't like, but they loved the wealth. The coffers of banks throughout the world overflowed with the money gained by the Kuwaiti people's hard work, commitment to their culture, and the blessings of Allah.

Mustafa wanted to vomit at such a thought. It was the wealth of the nation the Iraqis needed to replenish the war chest that had been badly drained during the war with Iran. Saddam now stood alone in the Arab world with his foot squarely planted onto the back of his once loyal neighbor.

Along the street were the constant reminders of the brutal Iraqi presence in the capital city.

Bullet holes marred the buildings; windows were broken; automobile showroom floors stood empty after the pillaging invaders swooped down and stole the plush cars from their rightful owners.

Allah! They have even removed the lampposts!

A far worse reminder lay on the sidewalk where Mustafa walked. The maggoty corpses of young men, their hands and feet bound, littered the streets and alleys.

Where are the Americans?

That was what had swept through the underground in those first few days. After a week the cry became a murmur until it was no longer heard. That was when Mustafa, and others, took action, as he was doing now in the late hours of the night.

His photographic mind was taking pictures of each Iraqi position; the number of soldiers was being mentally recorded. He would transcribe the information later on a detailed map he was preparing.

Preparing for whom? he suddenly asked himself.

"Halt!" a loud, gruff voice called.

Mustafa froze.

"Raise your hands and stand against the building." A soldier was approaching from across the street. In the dim light from the moon, he could see that the soldier wore the red beret and pipings of the Republican Guard—the dogs who invaded in the early hours of the attack.

"I have nothing of value," Mustafa pleaded. It was difficult to hide the anger he felt.

"What are you hiding?" The soldier was pointing at Mustafa's pocket; his left hand was thrust deep into to pocket of his coat.

"Nothing. My word to Allah."

The soldier raised his weapon. The coldness of the AK-47's barrel was nearly as chilling as the look on the Iraqi's face.

"Remove your hand . . . slowly," the soldier ordered.

Mustafa's hand came out slowly. The soldier's eyes widened.

"Are you a thief?"

A shiny, steel hook protruded from the artificial arm covered by the sleeve. Mustafa nearly laughed. In Iraq, the hands of thieves were still severed when they were caught stealing, but not in Kuwait. He wanted to tell the soldier that if thievery were punished by amputation every soldier in Saddam Hussein's army would return with both hands missing, as well as their feet.

"No. I'm not a thief. I'm an oil worker. I lost my hand in an accident."

"Take it off. It will make an interesting toy for my children."

Take my arm! Shamoot! *You've taken my country, taken my nation's wealth. Now you want my arm!*

A coldness settled over Mustafa. "Yes. For your children. My arm will make a wonderful gift."

In the next instant the soldier's eyes widened as Mustafa's left arm sliced upward, the open hook driving toward the Iraqi's throat. Two highly sharpened stainless-steel hooks speared into the soldier's throat, straddling each side of the larynx.

A gush of dark blood pulsed as the Kuwaiti turned the sharpened steel, severing the carotid artery and slicing through the vocal cords.

Holding with all his strength, Mustafa kept the soldier at arm's length, standing upright while jerking his neck, forcing the life to flow faster from Saddam's pig.

In what seemed an eternity, he felt the soldier go limp,

then allowed the body to pitch forward. He dragged the man into an alley and there, in the darkness, he tried to compose himself.

His mind raced. When the body was found, the Iraqis would seek revenge on his people. The resistance in the city was killing Iraqi soldiers by the score. For each Iraqi killed, twenty Kuwaitis were executed in their place.

Then the breeze brought him the answer—the foul smell of bodies rotting in the streets, butchered by the Iraqis and left to be feasted on at night by the rats that now swarmed the city.

In that instant he knew what to do. He stripped off the man's uniform and undershorts until he was naked. Taking the laces from the boots, he tied the soldier's hands behind his back, then bound the feet.

He whispered to the dead man, "By tomorrow morning when you're found, the rats will have taken your face away. No one will recognize you. Not even your mother. The soldiers will think you're just another Kuwaiti killed by your army."

He hawked and spit onto the dead man's face.

Moving silently, he trudged back to the street, hugging the shadows until he reached a burned-out shop on the bottom floor of a building. His shop.

He slipped through the open window now devoid of glass and went to the rear of the shop. A walnut-paneled wall was all that remained. Everything else had been stolen. He took a small plastic remote from his pocket and pressed a button. An electric whir followed as the wall opened. He slipped the remote into his pocket and removed a pistol from the waistband beneath his shirt. One could never have too many weapons in Kuwait City.

Beyond the wall lay a small anteroom. Another door, much larger, made of shiny steel, separated the anteroom from the heart of Mustafa's secured walk-in vault—a vault that had more features than merely to protect the coins he sold in his shop.

Muhammad Mustafa was an international arms dealer.

An arsenal of automatic weapons, grenades, ammunition, and rocket launchers was stored on the other side.

He carefully dialed the combination, opened the door, and walked into the vault.

The coolness of the room was pleasing after the heat. He rested for a moment, then looked up. What greeted him was fear—and the muzzles of four M-16 rifles; behind the weapons were faces clearly not Arabic.

Mustafa's dear friend Suleiman—the only other to have access to the vault—stepped forward. He eased down the barrel of a gun held by a tall, black soldier wearing civilian clothes. "*Inshallah!* It is all right, my brother. Allah be praised. We have been sent help."

The black man extended his hand. "I'm Major Jerome Moody, Tenth Special Forces Group, United States Army. We have come to help train your people to fight the Iraqis."

Mustafa collapsed into Jerome's huge arms and muttered, "*Praise be to Allah . . . the Americans have come to help. We will fight to death!*"

10

Following the initial orders for deployment, Campbell Army Airfield became one of the busiest airports in the world. Huge C-5A transports lined the tarmac, their front fuselages yawning open as trucks, Humvees, and tons of equipment were gradually consumed within their vast bellies. C-17 and C-141 cargo planes arrived, returning troops from other locations, preparing to gyro out laden with more supplies targeted for the desert.

One of the phenomena of the journey to Saudi Arabia was the transportation of aircraft, vehicles, and supplies to the seaport at Jacksonville, Florida. An endless stream of trucks moved from Fort Campbell, passing through cheering crowds lining the interstate highways along the route. Draped with banners and flags, the troopers became instant heroes to the people along the route, who set up welcome stations at rest areas, offering the soldiers food, soda pop, and other libations. Television crews filmed their exodus as the convoy snaked southward, ever closer to the waiting ships that would convey the equipment by sea to Saudi Arabia.

The aviation battalion flew to Fort Blanding, Florida,

where their choppers would be readied for storage aboard
a ship departing for the Persian Gulf.

Argonne Sharps and Monty Ohlhauser had left just after
dawn, and now she felt the warm sun against her face as
the trees of western Georgia passed beneath her scout helicopter. The squadron flew in a long line, bobbing from
the rising thermals, giving them the Wagnerian appearance of the attack helicopters in the movie *Apocalypse
Now*.

"How's your wife taking all this, Monty?" Argonne
said.

He turned from the right seat. "Alice is scared out of
her mind. What about your family?"

"The same. Especially my mother. And my stepdad."
She saw him look curiously at her, as though she had
revealed a secret. "He is my natural father's brother. My
natural father was killed in Vietnam."

He nodded. "Helluva war. Did you know Alice's father
was captured? He spent three years in the Hanoi Hilton."

"I didn't know," she replied. A chill swept through her
body.

"Do you think about that . . . capture?"

All pilots going into combat worried about getting shot
down, being alone in a foreign land, captured by the enemy. The torture, brutality, and degradation came with
the territory. For a woman, it could be horrifically worse.
"No," she said. She knew it was a lie before the word
issued.

Ohlhauser patted her gloved hand. "I'll look after you,
little lady."

She smiled and said nothing. If there was one thing for
certain, she knew how to look after herself. She had been
raised to be a lady, but she could fight as well as any man
and, if necessary, was prepared to prove that with guns,
knives, teeth, and claws.

*   *   *

Their flight plan called for a fuel stop at Fort Benning, where she landed around noon, removed her helmet, slipped from the cockpit, and walked to flight operations to check on the weather.

The post was buzzing with the excitement of the impending war; the talk was cheerful; bravado and boot stomping ruled the atmosphere. She wondered about that: Why did the guys in air assault always stand around stomping the floor? Childish to her. Manly to them?

Argonne immediately caught the eye of the other pilots. All were male, which came as no surprise. She had learned to live with the whispers and snickers that always confronted her when in the presence of men she did not know. She wasn't treated that way by the men in her squadron. She had earned their respect with cool professionalism, dedication, and a driving desire to come out the winner.

"Looks like we're in for a bumpy ride to Blanding." Monty Ohlhauser was holding a printout of a weather satellite report. He ran his finger along the isobars trying to figure the storm's ferocity.

Argonne's eyes studied the computer screen where weather radar indicated a front moving through southwestern Georgia. "The bumpier the merrier, Monty," she replied laughingly. "If you get scared . . . you can hold my hand. I'll lead you in."

"Yeah, right. Cocky, aren't you?" He flashed her a big grin, ready for the response he knew would follow.

Her eyebrows rose seductively. "Have to be in this woman's army."

"Let's take Fort Rucker as an alternate," he said.

She agreed. "Roger that call." Which reminded her she had something important to do. She stepped off to the side and went to a pay telephone. She punched in a telephone number and waited. No answer.

"Let's grab a bite to eat at the mess hall," said Ohlhauser.

They caught a ride on the shuttle bus in front of Operations and found the dining facility. The chow tasted good, better than either would know in the future, how-ever long that might be.

Stepping off the bus, she heard a whistle, a crisp *wheet-wheer* . . . the kind a man uses to show his appreciation of a woman. Argonne did not feel appreciated. A group of young black enlisted men were giggling nearby; two high-fived each other.

She walked over, remaining calm, and watched as the smug grins on their faces began to evaporate.

"What's your unit, soldier?" she snapped to the one wearing the biggest grin.

He looked ready to deliver a smart reply; the cold, hard stare in her eyes changed his mind.

"You stand at attention and salute when addressing an officer, soldier." Her face was hard as set concrete when she looked at the others, saying, "All of you!"

They snapped to attention, braced their shoulders, gave a resounding "Yes, ma'am," and sounded off with their units. "Next time you act like soldiers, not trash on some street corner. Dismissed," she said.

The soldiers hurried away and the two pilots went into the mess hall. Not a word was mentioned of the incident, but Ohlhauser was ready to bust a gut.

After the meal, Argonne made the phone call again. This time there was an answer.

11

Dolores Sharps had just returned from the garden, picking the last of the tomatoes beneath a hot Arizona sun, when she heard the telephone. She checked the caller ID, smiled, and answered quickly, saying, "Where are you, young lady? I've been calling you all morning."

"I'm at Fort Benning, Mom."

"What are you doing there?"

"Fueling up at the moment. Then, off to Florida. That's where the unit's helicopters will be transported to Saudi Arabia."

There was a long pause from Arizona, then, "You're really going, aren't you?" She had hoped it would have ended by now. That the madman Saddam Hussein would have realized his folly and spared the world the horror certain to follow.

"Yes, Mom. We're really going. I'll drop off my chopper, then fly back to Fort Campbell in a couple of days. Then . . ." Her voice trailed off. "Can't tell you much more at this moment. We're not on a secured line."

Dolores understood.

"I've been given seven days' leave. I already have my reservations made and will leave the morning after I get back to the fort." Unlike most of the soldiers in the 101st, she didn't take her two weeks' leave. "I can't wait to see you." She felt her heart suddenly being tugged by emotion. "How's Daddy taking everything?"

"He's not taking it very well, sweetheart. Matter of fact, he's contacted Paw-Paw to see if he can pull strings and get you reassigned to another unit."

"Paw-Paw" was her grandfather, retired Major General Samuel Sharps, former Tuskegee Airman, hero of World War II, Korea, and Vietnam. Her ire boiled at the thought.

"Don't let him do that, Mother. I'm a soldier, not his little sorority-house baby. I know my job, and I do it damned well. Better than any man I know."

While not consoled by this, Dolores understood her daughter's commitment to her career. "I can't stop him. I suggest you not try. It might make our visit uncomfortable."

"Our visit will not be uncomfortable, Mother. It'll be a wonderful time. But, please try to make him understand my feelings."

Dolores's eyes roamed the markers in the cemetery. "I will. But you know how he feels about the military."

Argonne's voice tightened. "I know his feelings. But he raised me to believe that people do have choices. I made my choice. I like the position I'm holding. It's one I've trained and worked hard for since entering the academy." In the background, Argonne heard her aircraft number called over the intercom at flight operations. "I have to go Mom. Tell Daddy I love him, and I can't wait to see you guys this weekend."

"We love you, too, baby. Be careful."

Argonne gave her best Screaming Eagle response: "Time to ride. Love to you both."

She hung up and started for her helicopter. Something

jabbed at her and she put her hand into her leg pouch. She held the object to the sunlight and smiled, recalling the significance of the miniature sabre that had been given to her father before he left for war.

12

The family tradition was that the Sharpses always went to war carrying the buffalo soldier's cavalry sword, which now hung on the wall at Sabre Ranch. Her father had given her the miniature he carried in Vietnam, where he served at the same time as his father. Samuel, then a brigadier general, carried the original.

She thought about that as she slipped into the cockpit of her helicopter and started the engine.

Franklin Sharps's journey to war would begin the same way as his father's and grandfather's: standing on the railroad platform at Willcox, Arizona. Now it was his turn. He had learned to overcome fear, to confront fear.

He was twenty, a high-school dropout, and, to some extent, an embarrassment to his father, Brigadier General Samuel Sharps, one of the original Tuskegee Airmen fighter pilots.

Franklin, a paratrooper, was lighter-skinned, which he attributed to his mother's Cherokee blood.

She stood beside him on the platform. "You'll be fine. Just don't go trying to be a hero."

He smiled that boyish smile she adored. "I won't. One's enough in the family."

"You know your father would be here if he could."

"Maybe we'll run into each other in Vietnam."

"Don't fill your heart with anger, baby. It'll only make things worse for you."

"How can you say that about him? After what he did to you? To our family? With another woman!"

She had not forgotten the betrayal. "That's between your father and me. You and your brother are both grown men, starting your own lives. Don't let his mistake destroy a lifetime of love and respect."

"Respect? He was carrying on with another woman! His secretary, for chrissakes! He betrayed us all. And him, always talking about honor. I despise him."

She began to cry but wiped her tears, reached into her purse, and handed him a miniature replica of a cavalry sabre. "All Sharps men go to war carrying a sabre. Your daddy has your grandfather's. This one is for you."

He recognized it. It was the same sabre that had been returned with his brother Adrian's personal effects six months ago. A West Point graduate, Adrian had been killed by the Vietcong at an overrun Special Forces camp in the Central Highlands.

He slipped the sabre into his pocket, gave no thought to the possibility it might bring him bad luck. He felt the kinship bleed into his soul.

He would look at it later, on the train, and remember those moments that bring so much pain to the healing heart. He would remember.

And God help the sonsabitches who killed his brother. He was going to balance the books!

Argonne knew it had been a time of great strife in her family. One that had nearly destroyed the Sharpses. Her uncle Kevin became a war protester and made plans to avoid the draft by fleeing to Canada. Franklin was bitter about his part in the war. Then his mother died of brain cancer.

The family survived. Franklin married Dolores; Kevin was injured by her grandfather's thrust of a rusty sabre through his knee, rendering him draft-exempt. The wounds healed and in time the family became whole again.

She touched the pocket on her flight suit. The presence of the replica had always given her a sense of confidence, of focus on who she was, where she came from, and what was expected of her.

13

*T*he rifleman, perched atop a mound of huge boulders, had been told that the best hunters were those with gray eyes; that gray eyes, like the color of fur on a wolf's throat, were the keenest.

At twenty-two, Samuel Sharps, the second son born to Adrian and Hannah, knew that wasn't true as he cammed the stock of his Sharps .50-caliber rifle against his shoulder. His black-diamond eyes gleamed as he eared back the hammer, sighted the target, and squeezed the trigger.

Four hundred yards away an antelope kicked upward slightly, took one step, then fell dead on the slope of Mount Graham, five miles north of Bonita, Arizona.

The tightness in his mouth loosened as he watched the blue-gray cloud of smoke clear, saw the dead antelope, and knew that what mattered most was the heart of the hunter.

Moments later, he walked to his tethered horse, slid the rifle into the carbine boot on the McClellan saddle, and stepped into the stirrup. As he climbed aboard, he felt the presence of the saddle and rifle's original owner.

Like his grandfather, Samuel loved the McClellan. Even

though it was old, the open slot in the seat allowed his butt to join with the horse's spine, giving him a sense of partnership with the animal, as though both horse and rider were joined as one. The way the Sharps felt when the weapon joined his shoulder.

He resembled his grandfather, who had been killed in a riding accident shortly before Samuel's birth: narrow at the hip, broad across the shoulders, and heavily muscled at the chest. He was strong as a bull and had a voice that was deep, but gentle until riled.

When he reached the antelope he sat for a moment looking at the animal, pleased that the bullet cut a clean groove through the animal's heart. None of the meat would be ruined; steaks and tenderloin on the spine would be intact. Which meant more money for him when he sold the meat to the local restaurant.

Thirty minutes later, with the antelope dressed and tied to the horse's back, he rode down from Mount Graham toward town.

The air that April morning was still and quiet, except for the slow, steady drum of the horse's hooves cracking against the hard ground, and the distant drone of a Stearman carving its path through the clear sky approaching a vacant strip of flat land outside of Bonita. The sound was alluring, pulling him toward a dream the way metal is drawn to a magnet, a dream he had never shared with any other person, not even his mother, who was standing on the front porch of the family restaurant in Bonita as he rode up with the antelope strapped behind the saddle.

At forty-nine, Hannah Sharps was still trim and lithe, her skin the color of dark molasses, her eyes dancing with pride as she watched her son haul the antelope from the horse.

"Clean shot?" His mother always asked Samuel that, in a teasing sort of way, knowing he always shot clean.

"Clean through. Took him down at four hundred yards," Samuel said as he stepped onto the porch and carried the antelope inside, through the dining area, past the

kitchen permeated with the wonderful smells of lima beans, roasting corn, and other vegetables cooking on the two huge stoves. He went out back, where he had a skinning rack, a block-and-tackle system that he used to hoist the carcass off the ground. There he stood for a moment, studying the animal, feeling pride in doing the job masterfully, the way he had been taught.

Hannah followed with a sharp skinning knife, a bone saw, and a meat cleaver. She raised her hand to shade her face from the the sun.

"Tomorrow I'll be expecting a dozen sharp-tail grouse," she said, handing him the knife.

Samuel nodded. "I'll get up early. You'll have them by the noon meal."

"Use the shotgun. I don't want that old buffalo gun tearing up the meat."

"I'll take them at a hundred yards, Momma. That way I can build me a stand and not have to walk them hills all morning." Then he paused for effect. "The shots will be clean. Just the head will be missing." He glanced at her. "You don't cook the heads, do you, Momma?"

"Just your head if you bring back nothing but feathers and feet!"

He took the knife and she watched him in silence, a slight smile on her mouth, recalling when she was a young girl during the Great War, working on a processing line in a slaughterhouse in East Saint Louis, Illinois. She had taught Samuel how to process deer, antelope, cattle, any kind of creature, with swiftness and ease, never losing an ounce of prime meat. He had always been amazed that her hands, so small and delicate, could move sharpened steel with such speed and strength.

An hour later Samuel had finished the butchering, cutting steaks, roasts, and filets, using every part of the animal except the hooves and horns. He carried the meat into the rear of the kitchen and loaded the game into a meat larder, then washed his hands.

"I believe I owe you a piece of money," Hannah said.

His fingers trembled as he reached for the coins she always paid him for providing game to her restaurant. She dropped five silver dollars into his palm. "What are you going to do with this?"

He knew it was time to let the cat out of the bag, so he spoke without looking into her eyes, caution in his voice. "That barnstormer pilot is charging five dollars for a ride in his airplane."

She looked at Samuel as though he had lost his mind. "Ride in an airplane! You got to be crazy! If God had meant for you to fly, you'd have been born with wings. And if you go off in that airplane, you'll probably get a pair. Angel wings!"

"It's important to me, Momma."

She shook her head in dismay. "You're going off to college next fall. You could use that money to buy you a new pair of boots. Or a hat. Not waste it on flying around the sky with some crazy man."

"Don't worry, Momma, it'll be all right. The pilot has lots of experience. What's more, he's a Colored man. He needs the business. He's working his way east by stopping in little towns and selling rides."

Hannah had met the pilot—Sparks Hamilton—the day before, when he arrived in Bonita and had lunch at her restaurant.

"If he flies the way he eats, you'll be in the sky all day. My Lord, that man can eat like none I've never seen." She shook her head and looked into his eyes. She knew there was no arguing. "Go on then. Ride in that fool contraption, but tell him if he gets you killed he can go somewhere else to take his meals. He won't be welcome in my place."

Samuel grinned at her, then raced through the door, mounted his horse, and rode toward the edge of town.

His dream was about to come true.

Sparks Hamilton, short and wiry, had orange-colored skin sprinkled with red freckles, giving him the look of a per-

simmon. He was forty-two years old, a widower, and a veteran of the Great War, where he served with the 92nd Division in France. During the battle of the Meuse-Argonne, German shrapnel tore through his calf, nearly severing his leg. He walked with an awkward limp, and wore baggy flying breeches, a worn leather coat, a white scarf around his neck, and a weathered leather flying helmet and goggles.

Samuel thought he looked like something out of a Howard Hawks war movie.

Hamilton had learned to fly after the war in his native Oklahoma City, working for free at the aerodrome in exchange for flight training.

"The only instrument we had back then was an oil gauge," he told Samuel as they walked around the Stearman. "We flew by the seat of our pants."

"How does an airplane this big get off the ground and fly, Mr. Hamilton?" Samuel wondered aloud.

The pilot chuckled. "Thrust over weight . . . lift over drag. You see, son, the engine, which provides the power, gives you forward thrust—overcoming the weight to give you forward speed. As thrust drives the machine forward, the shape of the wings then use the air resistance—the drag—created by the forward speed to provide lift. Take an eagle. The bird flaps its wings to build up speed, then rises into the air and holds its wings steady to float in the sky. When the eagle needs more thrust, it flaps its wings again. The difference is, with an airplane, the engine gives you constant thrust; the wings give you lift."

Samuel could figure out the obvious. "If the engine quits, you're not flying anymore."

"That's about the size of it."

"How does it climb and turn?"

"Altitude is controlled by power from the engine; airspeed is controlled by the pitch, or the attitude of the nose in relation to the horizon. Nose up, you lose airspeed, and gain altitude. You lose too much airspeed, you stall, the wings lose your lift, and the airplane quits flying. Too

*much pitch down, you gain airspeed, lose altitude, and fly
into the ground."*

"Sounds complicated."

*Hamilton shook his head. "Not really. Just a matter of
learning what to do . . . and what not to do."*

*Samuel reached into his pocket and took out the five
dollars. "I want to learn to fly, Mr. Hamilton."*

*Hamilton took the money and pointed to the front seat
of the cockpit. "Let's go punch some holes in the sky."*

*Minutes later the Stearman rolled along the dry, hard
ground, then began to pick up speed, the ride becoming
more bumpy as the front tires bounced unevenly. When
Samuel felt the tail wheel break ground, the cockpit sec-
tion of the fuselage suddenly lowered, bringing the Stearman parallel to the ground, giving him a clearer view.*

*Samuel felt the airplane break ground and skim along
the surface a few feet in the air.*

*In a matter of seconds the Stearman was climbing lazily
through the air, the roar from the pulsating engine near
deafening. The first real fear Samuel felt was when Hamilton banked sharply to the left, giving him a panoramic
view of the earth west of Bonita. To the left rear, he could
see Sabre Ranch, the Sharps family home; then it was obscured from view by the lower wing as the airplane
banked again and returned to level flight.*

*Upward they climbed, on wings of cloth and wood. It
was an exhilarating thing, this fragile machine with its
heavy load, defeating gravity, soaring, swooping, climbing, banking, diving—eagle-like—on wings that held
strong and steady.*

*The flight lasted half an hour, too short for Samuel, but
he was satisfied. Hamilton landed perfectly and taxied to
the small operations building and cut the engine.*

*They sat beneath the wing. Samuel said, "I want to be
a pilot, Mr. Hamilton."*

*The veteran poked at the ground with a stick and was
obviously in deep thought. "Have you ever thought about
becoming an army aviator?"*

"*I didn't know there was Colored aviators in the army.*"

Hamilton grinned. "There will be soon. The army is going to need pilots when we get into this war. They've already started a program that trains Colored men to fly. It's at a college down South."

"*Where down South?*"

"*In a little town called Tuskegee, in Alabama. The college is called Tuskegee Institute. In a few months the army will start building an airfield near the campus.*"

Samuel shuddered at the thought of going South. He knew how Coloreds were treated in Alabama, and knew his parents would object. "What would I have to do?"

Hamilton stood by the airplane, running his hand over the leading edge of the left wing. His face reflected a sadness, as though he had been deprived something in his life. "Apply to the college and sign up for the Reserve Officers Training Corps. That'll give you a chance to learn the military way while you're getting your education and flight training. It's a fine school, and the man who runs the Civilian Pilot Training Program is an old friend of mine. I'd be happy to write you a letter of introduction."

Samuel nodded gratefully. The two shook hands. "I'll write to the college tonight."

"*I'll have your letter tomorrow," Hamilton said.*

Samuel walked away thinking about the coming fury of the war; but mostly, he thought of the fury that would come from his parents.

It was Argonne's favorite story, and he did go to war from the air, where she was now flying toward during her country's newest uncertainty.

PART 2

OPERATION DESERT STORM

14

By the second week in Kuwait City, Major Jerome Moody and his small Special Forces team had established a radio linkup with SOCCENT through the satellite Keyhole 12, positioned above the Persian Gulf. They were surrounded by the devastation of the Republican Guard; the stench of decomposing bodies that filled the streets rose in the heat. But now, the "game" was on. Moody had been trained with the principle that destruction of the enemy from within its superstructure was the short road to victory. That lesson had been learned in Vietnam, refortified in Panama. The overall strategy was to destroy the Iraqi military machine; the tactics would be a gradual erosion of that mechanism on many fronts, starting at the core and ultimately working viciously to the outer perimeter.

His job was to establish a resistance movement, much like his predecessors in the Office of Strategic Services, who went behind the lines in Europe during World War II building small, autonomous networks that would disrupt the enemy at every stop on the road. The concept had been perfected by the Vietcong in Vietnam, and the

Green Berets had learned well from the lessons of the past.

His team had spread to different parts of the city, attached to "cells" that would coordinate their operations to give the enemy the impression that the force of fighters was much larger than in actuality. This concept of the Green Berets in their role as "force multipliers" would keep the Iraqis off balance, listening for footsteps in the night and being taken by surprise.

Like the other men in his team, he was dressed in civilian clothes, and carried papers that identified him as a Swiss working for the oil cartel. It was known by the Iraqis that many foreign nationals had been trapped within the city during the invasion. If they were captured, their cover story would withstand the most severe scrutiny. In case it didn't, each team member carried a pill that would end his life in a matter of seconds.

Moody's job was to conduct guerrilla operations and prepare the resistance to strike when the full assault began, and to waste precious time and effort in a futile attempt to gain momentary retribution. He had met with the arms dealer and regarded him as a warrior who could bring the resistance fighters together, who could make the angered Kuwaitis listen to reason. But he knew it would take more than resolve and weapons.

He had met with many members of the burgeoning resistance, but saw the most fatal flaw: coordination of assets. The brave Kuwaitis were sporadically hitting the Iraqis, but were ineffective in their efforts. A few killed by a grenade, or an assault by automatic weapons, merely angered the enemy, who, as a means of reprisal, were torturing and murdering men, women, and children by the score for every attack on them.

Moody, standing on a balcony overlooking the turquoise water of the Persian Gulf, could clearly see the Iraqi emplacements lining the beach for as far as the eye could see. *That is where they think we'll come from,* he thought. *The sea.* The Americans, they were certain, would never come through such a deadly obstacle as the desert and have to face a well-entrenched enemy.

That night, Moody slipped out to the balcony and began filming the Iraqis' seashore defenses. The positions were mostly sandbag bunkers manned by four to five soldiers. Interspersed were mortar and artillery. Barbed-wire barriers sat buried in the water fifty meters offshore. What surprised him was the lack of vigilant patrolling; rather, he heard music playing on captured transistor radios. There were no flares illuminating the night.

It was as though the Iraqis were on vacation.

Then the quiet was pierced by the scream of a woman.

Moody went to the front door of the apartment and listened. He could hear the pleading voice of a young girl; the sound of a slap, flesh against flesh.

The girl was begging the man in Arabic, but from the sounds coming through the cracks, he could tell her pleas were in vain.

He turned the knob on the door, and wearing his night goggles, could see a large man hovering over the girl, who appeared to be nothing more than a child. There was the sound of clothing being torn, grunting from the man.

Moody felt helpless. To interfere could jeopardize his mission. There was the sound of other voices: moaning, begging for the man to leave the child alone. He could see two figures appear; they were close enough for him to reach out and touch.

Another slap from the Iraqi soldier; more screams and pleas from the Kuwaitis. Moody's hand slipped to the inside of his shirt. He pulled out an automatic pistol, deftly threaded on a silencer, and eased the door open farther.

He took aim, pulled the trigger. The pistol coughed, the soldier fell. Moody stepped through the door into the hallway, flipped up his goggles and switched on a flashlight.

"Do you speak English?" he whispered to the people gathered near the soldier's body.

Their fright-filled faces nodded.

"Come in here."

An old man, a young woman, and the child hurried into the room. Moody closed the door and led the three into the defunct bathroom. The three Arabs were terrified, and when he started to leave the girl pulled at his arm, trying to hold him.

He touched her lips, saying, "Shhhh. I'll be right back." He dashed to the door, checked the hall, then dragged the body into the apartment and to the tub, where he placed the corpse facedown and then covered the body with pieces of the fallen ceiling.

Moody grabbed his radio and TACSAT phone and punched in the number of one of his teammates in a building two blocks away. Recognizing his fellow American's voice, he whispered, "Red flag," terminated the connection, and policed up his gear, which always sat packed and ready for a hasty departure. He hurried to the door, and as he started down the hall he paused, looked back at the Kuwaitis. They were smiling.

15

At seventy-two, Major General Samuel Augustus Sharps still had the physique of a wide receiver. His shaved head was shiny as a cue ball; he wore jeans, T-shirt, and Western boots as he sat at his desk in his library at his home in Falls Church, Virginia. Beyond the French doors, golf carts could be seen parked on the fairway of the exclusive golf community where he lived. He recognized two of the players, both prominent senators, who, the day before, had questioned each other's integrity on national television.

He looked at the letter that lay on the desk, the return name familiar to his family history, reread the request from a stranger whom he had heard from only three weeks ago at his office. The name was O'Kelly. A link in a long chain that bound two families by history, service, and sacrifice.

Dear General Sharps,
   My great-grandfather, Lieutenant Colonel Jonathan Bernard O'Kelly, and your grandfather, Sergeant Major Augustus Sharps, served together in the Tenth

Cavalry on the western plains and in the southwest
during the Indian campaigns. I recently read one of
his journals, and after diligent research, discovered the
incredible historical contribution made by your family
in the military service of the United States. I was able
to locate you through a friend at the Pentagon. I am a
reporter for the Army Times, and would love the
opportunity to interview you about your family
history. I believe your family represents a great page
of missing history of our nation. At your convenience,
I will meet you and will agree to whatever terms you
require. I hope to hear from you soon on this matter.
Respectfully . . . William S. O'Kelly.

There was something exciting, even unsettling in this request. Samuel walked to a Frederick Remington painting depicting a cavalry charge, and pulled the frame away from the wall, revealing a safe, which he opened to remove three thick, leather-bound books. Two were old and held together by a strap. On the spine of one, in gold letters, were his father's initials: A.A.S. His father had begun the journal as a young boy, piecing together the family history from an old notebook owned by his grandfather, and scraps of paper scribbled by his grandmother, which were more recipes than history, but served both purposes. Her recipe for a good family was simple: a good man and woman, strong children. Through the years his father added his own thoughts, adventures, and activities throughout his military career.

The second journal appeared in excellent condition, as though never touched, but he knew it was nearly filled with his mother's personal observations. On the spine were the initials HS—for Hannah Sharps.

He thumbed through his mother's journal, finding scores of pages dog-eared, marking a particular point of reference special only in the minds of family members.

"A piece of land . . . lots of love . . . and patience."

It was a recipe that had been used by the Sharps family from the end of slavery to the present.

He checked his watch and, seeing he was running behind schedule, returned the journals to the safe and rehung the painting.

William O'Kelly would arrive soon, bringing his questions, searching for truths. Most of which would be good; some uncomfortable.

There was a part of his life that was bothersome, even troubling to the point of being shameful. He had preached honor, duty, loyalty, and had not always adhered to that code.

He had tried to adhere to it, but in a turbulent world fraught with the ebb and flow of political uncertainty, that had not been possible. The death of his wife was the most painful moment of his life—including the death of Adrian. His son knew the risk involved when he chose to become a soldier.

Samuel Sharps had learned how to live with the possibility of death, and had nearly met that fate on many occasions.

But his wife—that was different. Cancer became the assassin that hunted his family when it was most vulnerable.

In reflection, he was pleased that he had taken O'Kelly up on his request. Actually, he thought it might be interesting to see how far the two families had come since their great-grandfathers first met.

16

William O'Kelly wasn't certain what he would find when he arrived at the Sharps home that afternoon. He rang the doorbell and a voice answered over the intercom, telling him, "Come around back. The side gate's open."

O'Kelly followed a rock path lined with elm trees to a wrought-iron gate, and continued until he found the man in the backyard.

General Sharps stood in the short Bermuda grass near the patio, gripping his nine-iron golf club. He eyed a yellow flag on the driving range a hundred yards in the distance which paralleled the nearby fairway. When all was clear, he swung, slapping the ball crisply over the fairway and onto the range. He was nearly down to the last of the range balls he kept for moments like this of quiet and solitude.

"Nice shot, General."

O'Kelly strode toward Sharps, his right hand extended in greeting; slung from his left shoulder was a nylon laptop-computer bag.

"Thank you." Sharps studied him as he approached,

having always evaluated a man's walk as quick insight to his character. The way he was trained to observe an enemy patrol approach, looking for signs of weakness in discipline and preparedness. O'Kelly walked straight, not swerving; fluid and smooth. Sharps liked that in a man. His handshake was firm, not overpowering in strength, as though holding something in reserve. He liked that, too.

O'Kelly was tall, with collar-length blond hair; a streak of gray in a swath over his ears gave the general a sense of time and age about the man. He wore Levi's and Western boots, and his sun-browned face suggested a man of the outdoors.

Right off, General Sharps liked the man.

"I don't practice as much as I'd like." He found himself searching for the right words, as though conversation was suddenly important, necessary, even, but for what reason he wasn't sure. Maybe it was the moment. After all, he had told himself, how often do the descendants of frontier soldiers who served together more than a century before meet for the first time?

General Sharps motioned toward a chair on the patio.

O'Kelly sat down, took out a notepad, flipped through the pages, reading aloud certain key points in the life of the man. "You went to Tuskegee Institute, became a Tuskegee Airman, fought in Europe during World War Two. Then, Korea, flying Sabre F-85s, then Vietnam as an advisor to Military Advisory Command–Vietnam. After retirement, you and a few friends formed a consulting firm, offering your expertise to major manufacturers of military hardware. Very impressive, General."

Sharps obviously felt uncomfortable talking about himself. "Can I get you something to drink?"

"How about a beer?"

Sharps disappeared through the French doors and returned with two bottles of San Miguel. He removed the tops, then raised his bottle and toasted, "To the buffalo soldiers."

The two men talked for a while about the current situation in the Middle East and its grave ramifications. When the conversation grew awkward, as Sharps always would feel when talking about the military, he said, "Mr. O'Kelly, you didn't come all this way to talk about the situation in the Middle East. What can I do for you?"

O'Kelly drained the last of the beer and sat the bottle on the concrete. "I'll shoot straight with you, sir: I want to write a book about the African-American military contribution to the United States. A book that would be seen through the eyes of one family. Your family."

"A war story?"

"Not just war. I want to focus on the development of the military family. There's an entire body of history that's missing from the classrooms and I want to fill in those empty spaces. I know your family is a four-generation representation of that history."

"Five generations," Sharps said with a smile. "My granddaughter graduated from West Point. She's now assigned to the Screaming Eagles. Although she is airborne-qualified, the division is now air assault." He added proudly, "She flies helicopters."

O'Kelly took a pen from his bag and wrote quickly, the sudden revelation reflected in his expression. "Five generations. Absolutely incredible."

Sharps nodded. "A project such as this would require a great deal of research. A lot of time." Sharps stared at the Remington painting, thought of the journals in the safe.

"I have the time. I love to research, finding the small keys that open large doors."

As the general looked at the Remington, a thought came to mind. He agreed with O'Kelly that the historical contribution of the African-American had been given little attention by historians. A few books had been written on the early frontier cavalry, most notably William Leckie's *Buffalo Soldiers,* a true account of the four "Colored" regiments that served in the Indian campaigns of the nineteenth century, and there were a handful of books on both the World Wars, Korea, and even Vietnam. But nothing that focused on the generational contribution of a single family. The project was exciting, and unsettling.

"You're talking about a military version of *Roots*."

"Precisely," said O'Kelly. "There's been dozens—hundreds—of books written about white families with a long tradition of military service to the United States. Not a single book has been written about the African-American military family. I intend to see that changed."

Sharps liked his confidence, but saw one glaring problem. "A white man writing about African-Americans? Don't you think that might be a difficult sell to a publishing house?"

"I don't suffer from delusions, General Sharps. I know that *might* be a slight problem."

Sharps's laughter boomed. "That *could* be a major problem."

O'Kelly appeared unshakable. "If Alexandre Dumas—a black Frenchman—could write about French aristocracy in nineteenth-century France, I can write about African-American history in the twentieth century. Besides," he said, with a touch of arrogance that tickled Sharps, "I thought of it first. I'm on the move with the idea. I'm not exactly riding a crowded bus."

He has a point, thought Sharps. "Where would you start?"

"From the top: beginning with the buffalo soldiers, and marching through time, right up to the present. I would use each generation's unique contribution to their particular period. The story would span nearly one hundred and twenty-five years."

"A novel?"

"No. A family biography. The Sharps family is more exciting and eventful than any novel. A story that's never been written. A story that lies covered with dust, waiting for what I feel is a great chapter of our nation's history."

Sharps studied the man. He could sense the commitment, and found the idea exciting, and educational. He

had long become disgusted with the Hollywood portrayal
of the African-American in society: welfare freeloaders,
criminals, drug addicts, pimps and prostitutes, the only
rare successes coming through professional athletics. He
knew there was a greater contribution made by African-
Americans since the end of the Civil War. After all, he
reminded people, General Colin Powell, the current chairman of the Joint Chiefs of Staff, didn't simply materialize
out of the clear blue sky. He was a product of more than
a hundred and twenty years of service, sacrifice, and dedication to country by millions of African-Americans. From
slavery to soldiering; from segregation to integration.
From the saddle of a charging horse to the head military
chair at the Pentagon. And his family had made every
grueling, painful step on that long march.

For African-Americans, the military had historically
been prime ground for upward motivation, individual success, family security, education, even social change. His
family had played a major role in that change; still played
a major role. He recalled his grandfather talking about the
old buffalo soldier—the Sergeant Major, as he was fondly
referred to—and how he was always recounting the history of the African-American contribution to the United
States military. Maybe it was time to give the old Sergeant
Major a place in history. He had earned it, along with
millions of other African-Americans. Their families included; especially the families.

"I might be able to help with some of the research.
When my father joined the army during World War One,
he began keeping a journal. It's quite extensive, and in-
sightful. He was encouraged to do this by his father. He,
too, maintained a journal."

"That could be invaluable," O'Kelly said excitedly.

"I can't allow you to take the journals from the prem-
ises, but you can make copies. There are incredible recollections in those papers. My father was one of the first
black officers to graduate from the Officers Training Center at Fort Des Moines, Iowa, in 1918. More than four

hundred thousand black soldiers fought in France. That is a part of history that has never been given its proper respect."

There was a gleam in O'Kelly's eyes. "I'll guarantee that it's given that respect in my book." He paused. "You said there is a written account of your family from the frontier days."

"Yes. I read them when I was young. They were fascinating. Especially my grandfather's account. After he retired he performed with the Buffalo Bill Cody Wild West show, along with my father and uncle. My grandmother even joined the show, and traveled with them until my grandfather was injured."

O'Kelly recalled a brief comment to that fact from his own great-grandfather's journal. "My great-grandfather wrote about the shooting match between your grandfather and Buffalo Bill. That must have been a memorable day."

Sharps looked curiously at the writer. "Were there other accounts of my family in his journal?"

Bill nodded. "Numerous accounts. He certainly had an affection for your grandfather."

Sharps said, "They were together when Colonel O'Kelly died. The Sergeant Major had gone to North Dakota to visit him when he had fallen ill. I always found that to be quite touching, considering the racial attitudes of the time." He chuckled, adding, "White folks and Colored folks didn't mix too well back in those days."

The reporter knew that to be true. "I suppose those years of soldiering together transcended racial differences."

"His second wife was a dear friend to my grandmother. She always spoke of her in such high regard." Sharps whistled. "Man, those two could cause more trouble on an army post than a wagon train of prostitutes."

O'Kelly grew silent for a moment. "I understand your grandmother was not very friendly with his first wife."

Samuel's eyes narrowed; his mouth grew taut. "No. She was something of a house servant to that woman." He said "that woman" with a particular acidity. "She didn't make life easy for Colonel O'Kelly, either. Made him quite miserable."

His grandmother had been a laundress, and to earn extra money took on the house chores of Lieutenant Jonathan O'Kelly, at Fort Wallace, Kansas, in 1866, his first duty station after graduating from West Point.

Camille O'Kelly came from a wealthy family in Illinois, fell in love with the dashing young cavalry officer, and followed him to the frontier. What she found was hardship, loneliness, long separation from her husband, and a total absence of social life. Shortly after Selona began working for her, Camille took to drinking and began abusing the young laundress on a daily basis. This was no secret around the fort, and, when the reports reached her grandmother, the old woman showed up with a knife and threatened to kill her if she ever touched her granddaughter.

He looked at the writer. "Do you know how she died?"

The journalist nodded. "Yes. She committed suicide. Hanged herself in the front room of their quarters." He paused, then added, "That must have been a shocking homecoming."

Sharps wanted no more of discussing Camille, and said, "Perhaps we could share information? I'd be interested to read the colonel's memoirs." There was a definite sound of hope in his voice.

O'Kelly appeared delighted. "I think that would be fitting." He patted the nylon bag, adding, "We can make two copies."

O'Kelly watched as General Sharps walked to the Remington and opened the safe.

17

The copying process took more than two hours, giving the men a chance to talk further about General Sharps's family and career. "My family was in the restaurant business in Bonita for over a half century. My grandmother started the business from the back of an old army artillery caisson at Fort Davis, Texas. She was a remarkable woman. The business became quite successful, with restaurants in several major cities throughout the southwest. Perhaps you've heard of the chain, it's called the Black Sabre."

O'Kelly recognized the name.

The more Sharps talked, the more O'Kelly began to visualize the book he planned to write. "General, I know you're a busy man. But I need to fill in a lot of empty spaces we talked about. Will you sit for an interview?"

"How about a tape recording? I could start at the beginning, bring it up to date. I think my granddaughter would be helpful. She even wrote a paper for a history class at West Point. She's quite knowledgeable about our family history."

"That would be a great help."

"Difficult though. As you know, the Screaming Eagles are on alert for deployment to Saudi Arabia. But, the wonders of modern technology can overcome many obstacles." Sharps wrote her telephone number on a slip of paper. "Give me a few days to brief her on the project. I know she would find your idea extremely interesting, and give her something to think about besides the fear of an impending war."

He looked at the name: Lieutenant Argonne Cameron Sharps, U.S.A.

Late that night, O'Kelly had finished his interview and was preparing to leave when Sharps offered a bit of advice. "If you have the time, I suggest you visit Bonita. My son and his wife live there. There's a cemetery there and I think you'll find it quite interesting." He handed O'Kelly a slip of paper with the directions.

"I had intended to go to Fort Grant as a part of my research. My grandfather's second wife is buried at the fort cemetery. Maybe I can pay my respects to both families."

"I think the spirits of my family would be proud to meet another O'Kelly." Samuel thrust his hand to William. "If I can be of further help, you can reach me at my office, or here at home."

They shook hands and O'Kelly left, his nylon bag bulging from the copied journals.

18

The maple grove trembled as the thunder of huge transport aircraft began lifting off the runway in a steady stream. The division was beginning its rotation to Saudi Arabia in traditional fashion: detail preparation, maximum efficiency, and with family members and veterans of previous actions standing in the shadows, stalwarts to the brave soldiers moving out.

The first force to depart was already in Saudi Arabia, the Aviation Task Force led by Lieutenant Colonel Richard Cody. His squadron of AH-64 Apache attack helicopters were on the ground—rather, the sand—August 18th, part of the minuscule defense force waiting for the Iraqi army should Hussein strike against the Saudis.

Now, the 2nd Brigade was en route, the 502nd Infantry of Normandy, Bastogne, and Vietnam fame, hurtling forth in fifty C-5As and sixty C-141 Starlifters, carrying nearly 2,800 Screaming Eagles, 117 aircraft, 487 vehicles—many TOW anti-tank wire-guided weapons systems equipped— and 123 pallets of vital equipment.

It was not a party atmosphere, but the families were there with banners that screamed encouragement and support, and with copious tears that openly voiced a love that can only be understood in that kind of a heart-wrenching moment that affected the lives of everyone gathered for the farewell.

The Screaming Eagles are on the way . . . wait!

The media set up mobile camera units, filming throughout the days and nights as the huge jets tore men and women from their families to be an interdiction force, then a saving force, in the lives of families decimated on the other side of the world. That was the essence of courage, of heroism, thought Argonne Sharps, as she stood on the tarmac watching the troopers board, walking in column file, never looking back once they had said their farewell to family and friends. Some troopers dropped and kissed the black tarmac. None looked back. They continued forward until swallowed up by the huge aircraft that would take them on a journey that would change their lives forever.

Argonne stood at attention on the tarmac with mixed emotions. On the one hand she swelled with pride; on the other, she felt left out. She would not go in this rotation.

The facilities for a full division in Saudi Arabia were not yet in place, nor had the division's equipment arrived. Helicopters were en route to Saudi ports but would not arrive for some time and have to take their place in the order of off-loading. The Screaming Eagles were not the only troops deployed. Armor from the United States and American bases in Europe were en route; Marine and Air Force fighting men and aircraft as well. And there was only so much port space in the Arab country.

Logistics would be one of the vital keys to the war. Troops and matériel would be arriving 24/7 until the Coalition Forces were standing ready on Saddam Hussein's front porch with the largest fighting contingency on an international level since World War II.

When the last of the airborne armada had lifted off,

Argonne signed out and went to her apartment. There was packing to complete for her flight home the next morning. She found herself excited, almost giddy at the thought of seeing her parents.

Troopers from the division were pouring out on leave and pouring back in on returning from leave. It was interesting. The troops leaving were excited, happy, and ebullient upon signing out. Those returning said little, as though saying good-bye had been the last of their reality checks that this was going to be a different world to which they would return.

19

Dr. Franklin Sharps sat in the living room of his home at Sabre Ranch, his eyes moving from the fading sunset beyond the windows to the mantel above the fireplace. He stared intently at the sabre fixed on wooden pegs, and thought about how many times that steel sword had been brought from its resting place to be offered over as a symbolic gesture to the fighting men of the Sharps family. He took a sip of brandy and settled back into his leather recliner, a slight smile on his face, recalling his father telling him about the day he was handed the sword.

His father, and mother, Shania, had come to Sabre Ranch to spend time with the family before Samuel reported for deployment to the European Theatre with the Tuskegee Airmen.

The ranch had been the Sharpses' home since the 1880s, when his great-grandparents, Augustus and Selona, established their roots on the rugged desert of Arizona.

Despite his great-grandmother's hatred for war, the passing of the sabre was a tradition she never violated with her anger toward her children being sent to fight for America.

*   *   *

On the morning of August 10, 1943, Selona Sharps, now age eighty-six, was pulled from a deep sleep by the sound of footsteps on the hardwood floor of her home at Sabre Ranch. She rose from the thick feather bed and, through squinting eyes, could see the outline of a tall man framed in the door.

She reached to her nightstand for her spectacles, then smiled as the image came into sharp focus.

"Good morning, Grandmother," said Samuel.

She slid over slightly, then patted the bed, saying, "Good morning, baby. Now you come and sit with your Grams."

At twenty-three, Second Lieutenant Samuel Sharps wore the uniform of the United States Army Air Corps, on his left breast the wings of an army aviator.

Selona's eyes brightened as two more people came into the room. Samuel's wife, Shania, and the baby she carried in her arms, their son, Adrian Augustus Sharps, Jr.

Samuel stood as Selona reached up and Shania gently placed the baby in her arms. Her ancient eyes joined those of the baby for a long moment; then she kissed him softly on the forehead before returning the baby to his mother.

"I'm going to give him a bottle, honey," Shania said; then she left the room.

Selona looked quickly at Samuel. "Are you hungry?"

Samuel patted his stomach. "Momma fed us. If I eat another bite my uniform will start popping buttons."

She laughed and her mind tumbled back over more than seven decades to another young soldier she had once fed.

"You look just like your granddaddy."

He sat on the edge of the bed and took her hands. "The Sergeant Major? Why, Grandmother, you know I'm better-looking than he was."

She slapped playfully at his hands. "You hush now. He was the handsomest man God ever put on this earth." She paused for effect. "Well, one of the best. You've done right well for yourself in the looks department."

"*I come from good stock.*"

Her eyes drifted toward the light bending through the window. "*I expect you'll be leaving this morning.*"

He gathered her frail hand in his long fingers. "*Yes. Pop is going to drive me to Willcox. I'll catch the train this afternoon.*"

"*I'm so glad Shania and the baby are staying here at the ranch while you're away.*"

"*It seems to be a family tradition. Momma and Aunt Theresa stayed here while Pop and Uncle David were in France.*"

She looked at him suspiciously. "*You're sure her daddy don't mind?*"

Samuel shook his head. "*He doesn't mind.*"

"*Seems the men in my life are always catching a train to go off to war.*" *Her voice cracked.* "*Your daddy went off to war from that same train station. That old platform's seen a lot of Sharps men go off to war. Even the same platform where they brought Darcy Gibbs's body when he was killed by old Geronimo's warriors.*"

Samuel nodded. "*At least Shania and the baby will be here to keep you all busy.*"

"*There's some comfort in that. I expect you'll be going over there and fighting them Germans.*"

"*Yes, ma'am. I've been assigned to the Ninety-Ninth Fighter Pursuit Squadron.*"

"*The whole world has gone and got itself into another ruckus.*"

"*That it has.*"

"*You got to promise me one thing*"

"*Anything for you.*"

"*You come back safe and sound. Don't go getting crazy and try to be a hero. Do you understand?*"

"*I understand.*"

She took a deep breath. "*Now, you go on and get on over there and help stop this war.*"

He leaned and kissed her gently on the forehead, then

*held her in his arms, knowing it might be the last time he
would see her alive.*

All morning, Samuel's mother, Hannah, had found things
to do to keep her mind off the coming sadness. Now fifty-
one, she had nothing but gratitude to God for the good
life He had given her.

Samuel's father, Adrian, had come home from his war
twenty-four years ago and she could remember few occasions since when she did not wake up looking forward
to the day. Adrian, still the dashing Adrian she had married before the Great War, had made a success in the real-
estate business and was still Bonita's great war hero, and
long ago she had taken over responsibility for Selona's
restaurant business and had her own success and satisfaction. Yes, the passing years had been good—even during
what people had called the Great Depression, when she
had become a sort of local legend for giving away more
food than she sold.

But now she had to face the heart-tearing moment she
had hoped never to experience again after she had said
good-bye to Adrian back in 1917. Selona had to do it
countless times when the Sergeant Major saddled up when
duty called; now it was Shania's turn and Hannah's heart
ached for her daughter-in-law.

So now she puttered in her kitchen as if keeping busy
would delay the moment. But through the window she
could see Adrian and Samuel walking toward the cemetery, and she knew what that meant: It was Sharps family
tradition to say farewell to the gallant men, and the gallant woman Vina Gibbs, who lay at rest there.

She watched them talk awhile, then start back toward
the house.

She knew what would come next.

Hannah put away the last of the washed breakfast
dishes, wiped her hands on her apron, and went into the

sitting room. Shania was sitting on a divan, feeding the
baby, when Samuel and Adrian entered.

Samuel's heavy military suitcase was packed and sitting
by the front door.

Adrian said nothing as he walked to the mantel, where
he reached up and removed the dented, battered sabre
from the two wooden pegs.

"Samuel, your grandfather carried this for nearly forty
years in the defense of this country. It was given to me
when I went to war in France. Now it belongs to you. I
know you will carry it with honor."

Samuel turned his palms upward and received the sabre,
and as the metal touched his skin, he thought he could
feel the presence of the Sergeant Major.

"I will, Pop."

The ringing of the telephone snapped Franklin back to the
present. He smiled at the sound of his father's voice. Most
of the conversation focused on Argonne and the current
world situation. "Funny that you called," Franklin said.
"I was looking at the sabre, remembering Momma telling
me about the day you were given it by Grams before you
left for Europe."

"That's a coincidence," Samuel said. "I had an interesting visit today."

Franklin listened while his father explained the letter,
then the visit from William O'Kelly. He found himself in-
trigued by the notion. "I think it's a great idea. But hold
off on calling Argonne. She'll be arriving tomorrow from
Fort Campbell. I'll fill her in."

There was sadness in Samuel's voice. "She understood
this could happen the day she accepted her appointment
to West Point."

"I know." He suddenly felt uncomfortable about the
interviews. "Have you considered how Kevin might feel
about someone snooping into our lives. After all, there are
some sensitive moments where he is concerned."

"I think our family can withstand just about anything, son. From the Indian Wars to Vietnam, hell—we've seen it all. We've earned the right to tell our story. It might inspire other young black families to step up to the plate and be counted."

"I suppose you're right. Eunice will probably object," Franklin replied.

"I'll worry about Eunice. You know how protective she is about Kevin."

Samuel's daughter-in-law was an attorney for the NAACP, and was sensitive to anything regarding Kevin and Vietnam.

"The truth can't hurt us," Samuel said staunchly. "We're survivors."

"That we are, Pop. That we are."

20

Upon arriving at the Phoenix airport, Argonne Sharps searched the faces in the crowd until she saw two familiar smiles. Her father hurried toward her and Dolores beamed as the three joined for the first time in months.

Franklin collected Argonne's luggage, then the three walked to the fixed base operation at the airport where his Cessna 310 was waiting. The flight to Bonita went quickly, and soon they arrived at Sabre Ranch. Her father had built a small dirt airstrip which allowed him easy access to the property; a Quonset hangar provided storage for the aircraft. In barely no time she was in her bedroom, unpacking her suitcases.

There had never been any secret of the fact that her father despised the military. He saw the service as a destructive force in his family's recent history and had been totally opposed to her appointment to West Point, hoping she would attend college in Arizona and study medicine. He had lost a brother in Vietnam; another brother had nearly taken flight to Canada; and his mother and father had separated in the last years of her life owing to an affair Samuel had had with another woman. Now, with war on the horizon, it had become increasingly difficult to hide his emotions.

He was sitting in the living room smoking his pipe when Argonne finished unpacking. He had been quiet during the flight from Phoenix, but she had learned to read the man's face as though it were a printed page.

"How are things looking for the shipment to Saudi Arabia?" Franklin asked.

"Going smoothly, I suppose. Thousands of little problems, but nothing major. The unit is quite excited, actually."

His thoughts drifted back to 1965, when his unit was readying for Southeast Asia. "Yes, it all seems so exciting at the beginning. But, when the shooting starts, that's when the reality sets in and it's no longer a game. One minute you're laughing and joking with your buddy . . . the next he steps on a land mine. It can turn ugly very fast."

Argonne stared at him for a moment. "We don't consider it a game, Daddy. There's no doubt in anyone's mind about what we're up against."

He shook his head; there was a tinge of sadness in his voice. "All the lives of those young men and women—the families—being disrupted over the ambitions of one insane man. And yet, it could all be avoided with one bullet through his brain."

She smiled at this familiar line. "America doesn't assassinate heads of state. Not even if they're the enemy."

"Get a clear shot and take it, that's what I say. I think with our technology we could eliminate one man. Which makes me suspicious." He sighed heavily, adding, "It seems we have to unlimber the guns from time to time to show the world who's the boss. Look at Grenada. There was no need for that invasion. Or Panama. Nothing but military muscle flexing."

This conversation was bothering to Argonne. "You're starting to sound like one of those protesters." There was a tinge of sarcasm in her voice. "And I disagree on Pan-

ama. It was necessary in order to remove a narco dictator."

"Perhaps. But I've been to war on the other side of the
world." He recalled the Vietcong, and North Vietnamese,
adept at jungle fighting, defending what they considered
their land from an invading army. "I don't think Saddam
Hussein is going to pull out of Kuwait. Despite what your
mother might hope. He's trying to be the number-one
honcho in the Arab world."

She walked to the mantel and ran her finger along the
stock of the Sharps rifle, the symbol of their family name.
The Sergeant Major had changed his name to Sharps—
from the slave name of "Talbot"—after joining the 10th
Cavalry in 1866. "I think you're right. He has too much
at stake. And, he actually thinks he can defeat the Coalition. At least, drag it out until we quit."

"What are your thoughts?" he asked.

"All the briefings indicate the opposite. Look at the war
with Iran. More than a million casualties. I don't think he
is a man who uses good judgment. We just hope he
doesn't make his move until we're ready."

"The Allies better pray he doesn't. You might control
the air . . . but the Iraqi ground forces could roll up Saudi
Arabia with the same ease they took Kuwait. I still can't
believe he didn't attack after Kuwait. He'd own the whole
area. And, I wonder where Israel fits into his plans."

"But he didn't," she said. "That's all that matters. Now
he has to be punished." She paused. "Israel is the weak
link in our chain. If they get into it, the Arab members of
the Coalition will pull out, and that could mean the Saudis. That would be disastrous."

"Punished!" Franklin said incredulously. "The only
people who will be punished are the Iraqi people. Especially the civilians. Baghdad will look like Beirut by the
time it's over."

"What is the world supposed to do, Daddy? Sit back
and let another dictator rule a major part of the world?

The Germans had Hitler—now there's Saddam. No, sir. He has to be stopped."

He could see there was no talking to his daughter. She had always had a streak of stubbornness. Much like her grandfather, and to some extent, like himself. "Argonne, let's not argue about this any more. It'll only upset your mother. Lord knows, she's upset enough. I know you feel strongly about this mission. I want you to know that I'm behind you. I might not like it, but I'm not going to let you think for a moment that I'm not in full support. I know what that feels like. Remember: It's the children of the guys who went to Vietnam that will be fighting this war. We're behind you . . . one hundred percent."

She walked over and kissed him on the forehead.

"We're the finest-trained army in the world, Daddy. We're going to win this war. I promise you that, sir. And I'm not going to get hurt. Besides, you know the military's policy on women in combat. I'll probably be a REMF."

He laughed. "Rear-echelon mother—"

She interrupted. "That's changed too. It now means 'rear-echelon males and females.' "

They ate dinner that evening by the cottonwoods, where so many family gatherings had been held over the more than one hundred years since the Sharps family first built Sabre Ranch. Dolores had been troubled by something and went directly to the heart of the matter only minutes after they sat down to eat.

"Argonne," she said, "is there a man in your life? Someone special you've been dating?"

Franklin shook his head. "Don't start on that, dear. She'll find a man someday."

The daughter wiped her mouth with a napkin. "Not yet, Mother. But don't worry. I'll give you grandchildren sooner or later. I really don't want a relationship at this moment. Frankly, I'm glad I don't have anyone special with all that is going on. I've seen what this is doing to other couples, both married and single."

Dolores wouldn't let it go without her final word. "Well, I think you're probably right. When this 'thing,' as you call it, is over, I hope you'll consider finding someone special."

21

Before going to war, there was a ritual all Sharpses knew had to be fulfilled. The next morning Argonne rose early, saddled her father's most powerful horse, and rode east to a deep canyon. It was dark before she arrived and as the sun came up the roan stallion, named Santee, showed a momentary restlessness, throwing his great head forward, then tried to rear up until he was settled by the tightening of the reins.

"It's almost time," Argonne whispered.

She was watching the eastern sky as the sun began to filter through the crackback ridges of the mountains northeast of Bonita. She wore a short-sleeved riding jacket, exposing arms the color of honey, and crisply starched pants that blossomed above her knees before disappearing into tall, highly polished riding boots. The dark blue cavalry hat she wore over her hair was pulled down slightly at the brim, just above her dark eyes, which shone from within the brim's shadow.

The saddle on Santee was a McClellan, more than a century old, but well cared for through the generations. Her great-great-grandfather's Sharps rifle rested in the car-

bine boot on the right side of the saddletree; on the left
was his three-foot-long sabre.

Moments later, the sun broke over the horizon; a red
flood of sunlight swept the land and flooded into the canyon, running like fast water across hard ground. A narrow
trail could be seen in front of Santee, a path that disappeared over the rim.

Suddenly, her arm flashed up; her fingers touched the
edge of the brim in a sharp salute. Argonne spurred the
horse, stood in the iron stirrups, and leaned back as
the stallion bolted over the edge into the redness of the
canyon.

Down the stallion plunged, the speed building as Argonne's right hand held firm to the reins, checking the
power of the animal, while the fingers of her free hand
drew the steel sabre rattling against the saddle. With a
smooth movement she extended the blade toward the
imaginary enemy that lay waiting at the bottom. At that
moment the sun flashed off the steel blade and she felt the
tightness of fear when she realized she was leaning dan-
gerously over the neck of the charging stallion.

She pulled the reins taut, leaned back as far as possible,
and distributed her body weight evenly, winning for the
moment against the forward pull of horse and gravity.

Down they drove, leaving a spray of dust too heavy to
rise in the hot air. The deeper rider and horse descended,
the thicker both collected a sheen of red dust, until the
two appeared as flaming apparitions. It was only in the
final moments of the descent, when the horse dove over
the last ledge, and she heard Santee's hooves crack against
the hard floor of the canyon, that she commanded . . .

"Attack!"

The canyon came alive with the sound of pounding
hooves, the rattle of the empty sabre scabbard, and the
snort of the stallion in full charge.

Argonne stood in the stirrups, leaned forward while extending the sabre beyond the stallion's rising and plunging
head, preparing to receive the enemy charge. At the precise

moment she and the imagined enemy would have been joined in battle, the sword flashed forward, narrowly clearing the head of the stallion; then she pulled on the reins, wheeling the horse into the opposite direction.

A scream burst from her lungs as she spurred the stallion to full gallop and again stood in the stirrups with the sabre extended. She slashed and cut, parried and thrust the blade at the enemy as though she were fighting a legion of demons, unaware that she was not alone.

Finally, it was over, as Argonne drew the horse to a halt and, sitting at attention, saluted smartly with the sabre, then returned the blade to the scabbard with one crisp move.

On the canyon floor there was only silence, except for the heavy breathing of the stallion.

On the ledge above the canyon, her father sat on his horse, watching the mock battle. She knew that he came here to the edge of the ranch and made this ride whenever he needed to feel young again. She rode up to where he waited; her face was covered with a layer of dust. He took a canteen, poured water onto a handkerchief, and handed it to her.

"That was a fair piece of riding, young lady. You certainly haven't lost your touch with a horse."

She patted Santee's neck; dust flew into the air. "Having a good horse under me made it look easy."

They rode slow, talking about family. "Adrian and Kevin and I used to ride out here every day when we were kids," he said. "Riding fast, hollering like a bunch of Comanches. Scared your grandmother to death."

"Do you think he'd be proud of me?"

Her stepfather never had a problem discussing Adrian with Argonne.

When he returned from Vietnam, Franklin was torn to pieces emotionally; his widowed sister-in-law was the only respite he found in a life that had been filled with turmoil.

The two spent many hours walking about the ranch, riding in the desert as she helped put his life back together. During the course of the relationship the two fell in love and were married. Neither ever had a problem with the union, though others raised a leering eyebrow at a man marrying his dead brother's wife.

Both had decided that once they married, the subject would never be taboo.

When she was told the truth—as a little girl—it seemed troubling for her at first. But, as the years passed it never seemed to matter. "He'd be very proud. You favor him more than you do your mother."

"That's what Mom says. I've thought a lot about him lately."

Franklin reined up his horse. He gave her a stern look. "Don't go listening for footsteps, Argonne. This is not a 'like father, like daughter' situation."

"I know. The thought just occurs from time to time."

"Then get rid of the thought."

"OK," she said, then spurred the horse forward, bolting ahead of him. "Come on, race you to the house."

Moments later they were charging toward the ranch, Argonne in the lead, with Franklin holding back slightly on the reins, allowing her to lead.

22

Late that afternoon Franklin received a telephone call that excited him. He had taken several days off from his practice to spend time with Argonne, but now told Dolores, "I've got to go into Phoenix for a few hours. An emergency has come up. I'm needed at the hospital."

He hurried to the Quonset, fired up his Cessna, and taxied onto the airstrip. In minutes he was off the ground, banking toward the west. There was nothing unusual about this sudden departure to Dolores. It had happened numerous times, and came as no surprise.

Argonne and her mother decided to drive into Bonita, the quiet western town where the Sharps first arrived in 1885 during the Geronimo campaign. Fort Grant was now an industrial correctional facility for troubled youth, but the flavor of the Old West was still present.

As was the first restaurant started by her great-great-grandmother, Selona Sharps, back in 1885. As in the past, only one daily meal was served. Unlike the restaurant chain Dolores managed as the family business, the tiny Bonita café was the social and often political focal point of the tiny hamlet.

The smell of the house favorite—rabbit stew—met their nostrils at the front door. The customers, mostly ranchers and local business owners, nodded and smiled at Argonne, who wore Western boots, cowboy hat, and Levi's. There wasn't a person there who wasn't aware that she was going to war. Word always traveled fast in a small town.

She sat at a table traditionally reserved for the family, but it soon filled with friends wishing her luck on her journey to Saudi Arabia. One cowboy, Tug Gebhart, a rustic wrangler in his sixties who still punched cattle and was something of the local historian, couldn't resist the urge to talk about Selona and the early days of the Sharpses' arrival in Bonita.

"That woman was some piece of work," he began, as though telling the story for the first time to a room filled with strangers. "She started this restaurant with an old Chinaman, who owned the laundry next door. But it weren't too popular at first. Folks didn't take quick to newcomers, especially Blacks and Asians. But Selona's goodness won them over."

"That and some damn good shooting!" another cowboy added.

Tug eyed the man and continued, "Yessir. Damn good shootin'. The bank had been robbed and there was Selona, right in the midst of the whole fracas. Instead of running for cover like everybody else, she whipped a rifle from a scabbard on a nearby horse, took aim, and shot him from the saddle. Then shot two more. Saved the townfolks' money."

"There weren't but two," the man said.

Tug looked at him hard. "Who's telling this, me or you?"

The man quieted and let Tug continue uninterrupted.

"Well sir, after that, folks couldn't get here fast enough to eat her food and yarn about the event." His gaze swept to Argonne. "I remember Selona from when I was a tyke. Always there to help people in need. She was the finest lady I'd ever met. A good, decent, God-loving woman that went out of her way to help others."

Argonne beamed. "I wish I could have met her, but at least she stays alive in memory." She glanced around the restaurant. The walls held several pictures of Selona: her cooking kiosk when she traveled with the Buffalo Bill Cody Wild West show; a photograph of her with wounded World War I soldiers she volunteered to help while they recovered from their wounds in Tucson; and one of her and the Sergeant Major, him dressed in full uniform.

"And your granddaddy," Tug went on. "I doubt anybody'll ever forget ole Samuel riding that mule in his race against that tank! Lord, what a Fourth of July to remember."

The place exploded in laughter, many had been there that day and recalled how foolish he had looked astride a big mule, a roaring tank his opponent in a cross-country race.

"He won that race, by golly. But only by a hair. His winnings was enough to get him off to college down there in Alabam'. Lordy, was Selona mad about his a-goin' down South.

"And he did all right for hisself. Come out of the war a real hero." His eyes twinkled as he looked at Argonne. "Now, you're going off to the fightin'. Guess that's a family tradition, what with your daddy being killed in Vietnam, and your stepdaddy fightin' over there too."

Dolores arrived as the other cowboy tried to add to the storytelling, rescuing Argonne in the nick of time.

She shook hands and exchanged hugs with the patrons and the two left the restaurant. On the drive back to Sabre her mother said, "How folks love to talk about Selona."

"She must have been quite a lady."

"She was by what I've heard. Of course, I never met her. She had passed on before my time. But I feel her presence everywhere. Especially in the restaurant."

"Do you think she would have approved of my being in the military?"

Dolores shook her head. "No, dear, she would have been vehement about you being a soldier."

"Why do you say that, Momma?"

"She had been a slave, and never lived long enough to see African-Americans given proper treatment by the armed services. She felt Blacks should fight first for our rights here in America before fighting for other people's rights on foreign soil."

"Sounds like someone I know," Argonne said.

"Don't begrudge your father for how he feels. He just doesn't want you to be hurt the way he was in the Vietnam era."

A long silence followed until they reached the ranch. There, she saw the Cessna taxi toward the Quonset. "Looks like Daddy is home early."

"That's odd. I wasn't expecting him until later tonight."

Dolores parked and they walked toward the hangar. Rounding the front, both stopped suddenly. Argonne yelped and ran toward a tall man getting out of the aircraft.

"Paw-Paw!"

Major General Samuel Sharps alighted, his face beaming. They embraced, holding each other as though clinging to the edge of a precipice. "How's my baby?"

She smiled. "I'm great, Granddaddy. How's my favorite pilot?"

He tapped his midsection. "Trim, lean, and bad to the bone."

Before she could say another word, another familiar voice called from the backseat of the Cessna. "You guys want to help me out of this contraption?"

Argonne flung the door open, a huge grin brightening her face. "Jacob!"

Jacob LeBaron Sharps, her younger brother, sat in the rear seat. His smile stretched from one ear to the other. "Didn't think I'd miss this shindig, did you, big sister?"

He climbed out and stepped into her embrace. They hugged for a long time; then she stood back and gave him a close scrutiny. He was tall, lanky, like his father. His hair was braided in long Rastafarian coils. "You look thin. You haven't been eating proper. And you need a haircut," she said.

Like his grandfather, he slapped his stomach, replying, "You sound like Momma. I'm Sharps-lean. A family tradition." He eyed her figure. "Except for some, of course. Looks like you've put on a few pounds. And my hair is perfect. Not like your airborne boy cut."

She raised a teasing fist and replied, "At least I don't look like a refugee from Haiti."

Their father interrupted, saying, "Come on you two . . . don't get started. You'll have plenty of time for sibling rivalry."

Argonne laced her arms with her brother's and grandfather's; the three walked toward the house, followed by a glowing Franklin and Dolores.

23

The next morning, Argonne was awakened by a knock at her door. "Come in," she said, in a yawn. Jacob entered, carrying a tray; the smell of coffee reached her before he did. He sat on the edge of her bed, poured, then passed her a cup.

He was her brother and she could not look at him without thinking of him as a baby. A boy, soft, struggling, crying.

"How is school?" she asked. "We didn't get to talk much last night. Mostly, we just listened to family stories . . . again."

"Again."

Her eyes twinkled. "You love every minute of it, Jake."

He nodded. "It is something I miss." A long sigh followed. She sensed something was wrong.

"You have a problem?"

"I'm thinking about joining the regular army."

This took her by surprise and it wasn't what she wanted to hear. "You're in medical school, Jake. That's a privilege few enjoy in this country. Especially African-Americans. You know how hard Dad worked to get you accepted."

"I know. I want to be a medic. Like Pop. I know there's a war coming. I don't want to sit on the sidelines and watch from the bleachers. It's not the thing a Sharps ought to do."

"Bull," Argonne snapped. "You can serve better by finishing your education. There's a greater need for doctors than there will be for medics."

"Not from what I've heard on the news. Jesus, Argonne, that crazy sonofabitch has the fourth-largest army in the world. That means a lot of body bags. And a shit-load of wounded."

"That might be so, but you don't just sign your name and suddenly wind up on the battlefield. You have to go through basic training, then ten weeks of combat-medic school. The likelihood of your going to a combat unit in the Gulf is a long shot at best. Besides, the war—if there's to be a war—won't last long. You'll miss out and wind up losing three years you could have dedicated to medical school."

That wasn't good enough for Jacob. "The Sharps family has always been dealt the long-shot hand, sis. And what makes you think there won't be a war? And that it won't last long? All the talk on television is that it'll be the next Vietnam."

"That's nothing but media hype," she said. "Those bastards hope there will be a long war. It'll make good copy. Or so they think. If there is a shooting war, it'll be swift and decisive."

"What am I supposed to do? Be the only Sharps that wanted to serve . . . but stayed home?"

"Grams Selona would have said 'Yes!' Check that. She'd have said 'Hell yes!' " She patted his hand. "Don't you understand, you'll be too late. It'll be over before you're ready to go."

"You sound awfully confident. Look at Vietnam. Rag-tag soldiers held the great United States up for nearly a decade. When it was over, all we had was dead soldiers and bad memories."

"That was different. Vietnam taught us lessons we won't repeat. Besides, we have the United Nations Coalition, which includes Arab nations. Policy and world opinion will be on our side. Not opposed to us. The Russians are broken as a threat. The Chinese won't get involved. Saddam's surrounded by people who hate him, including his own people."

Jacob didn't agree. "I saw a CNN interview with a Middle East arms dealer who does business with Iraq. He claims at least fifty thousand Coalition soldiers will die, and maybe tens of thousands of civilians in Saudi Arabia. Not to mention thousands of Israelis."

"That's a bunch of hot air." She paused for a moment, then spoke of the facts known to her. "The Iraqi army is nothing but a big paper tiger. Sure, they have thousands of tanks, but that means nothing if they're not maintained properly, and—more importantly—operated by professional soldiers. They don't have a professional army."

"I think the Kuwaitis would disagree," he said.

"The Kuwaitis didn't have an army, Jake. Besides, the Iraqis hit them with such overwhelming numbers, there wasn't really a fight to begin with. Intelligence reports are quite clear that considering the numbers and logistical superiority, the Kuwaitis did rather well in the beginning."

"What about the Iraqi air force? They blew the Kuwaitis out of the sky in short order."

She grinned. "Most of those pilots are Russian mercenaries. Saddam Hussein hired them after the Soviet Union folded. Our pilots are a helluva lot better. If there's an air campaign, our forces will blow them out of the sky."

Jacob looked at her incredulously. "It sounds like you've been fed a huge bowl of propaganda."

"It's not propaganda."

He shook his head in disbelief. "I hope not. But, I feel like I should do something. I don't want to just sit on my butt."

"You are doing something. You're going to be a doctor. That's more important than being a soldier."

He started for the door. "You sound like Pop."

"He's right. I hope you haven't mentioned this to him."

"I haven't."

There was a look of relief on her face. "I don't think he'll take it as calmly as me."

"All hell will break loose," Jacob said.

She threw her pillow at him, and said, "Get out of here, baby brother. I need to get dressed."

He left and she sat for several minutes, thinking of her words. She prayed it wasn't propaganda.

24

A cool breeze drifted in from the desert; a carpet of stars filled a black, moonless sky. Samuel was sitting on the front porch, looking up at the heavens, when Franklin sat beside him.

"Beautiful night. One of my favorite moments in life has always been to just sit here and enjoy the night."

"Mine too," Franklin said. "When I was a boy, I used to think that God created the night just for my pleasure."

"I thought that same thing. I even named certain stars. Like they were a pet that nobody else owned." Samuel watched his son light his pipe. The flickering light revealed the face of a father in turmoil. "She's going to be all right, son."

"I'm having a lot of trouble handling this, Pop."

"That would be obvious to the blind and deaf," Samuel said. "Which is to be expected. I remember when you arrived at Cam Ranh Bay in 1965. I saw you standing there, looking strong and squared away. I could tell you were scared, but I think I was more terrified than you."

"That was quite a memorable day." Franklin took a long puff on his pipe. He exhaled slowly, studied the smoke as it wafted into the darkness. "I just can't imagine her flying onto a hot landing zone. Or, behind enemy lines on a recon."

His father tried to be reassuring. "The military's policy on women in combat is clear, son. She'll be in a rear-echelon sector."

"She flies a Kiowa, Pop. That's a recon chopper. You know as well as I that recon is conducted beyond enemy lines."

Samuel shifted uncomfortably. He was trying to find words of assurance, but not having much luck. "She'll be with one of the finest units in the world. And the nice thing about her job is she's an aviator. It's easier to get out of trouble in an aircraft than in a jeep."

"What if she doesn't? What if she's captured? It doesn't take much imagination to know what the Iraqis will do to her. Christ! Look how they treat their own people. And we both know rape is a common tool used against prisoners of war. Hell, if they'll rape a man, what do you think they'll do to a young woman?"

There it was, thought General Sharps. The strongest opposing argument facing the deployment of women in combat. One with which he did not find the slightest disagreement. "First she would have to be captured. I always worried that might happen to you when you were in the bush. It would have been a prize to capture a general's son."

Franklin understood. "Yes. Remember Tom Taylor?"

"How could I forget?"

Captain Thomas H. Taylor, a West Point graduate, was the son of former 101st Airborne Division Commanding General Maxwell Taylor. When the Screaming Eagles arrived in Vietnam, General Taylor was the ambassador to South Vietnam. His son, a graduate of West Point, was a rifle company commander with the 1st Brigade's 502nd Infantry.

"A hard charger," Franklin mused. "A real soldier."

"I heard about him in Saigon. Scared his father to

death. He refused to go on staff, wanting to lead a rifle company." Samuel looked at him questioningly. "Did he really run around the area wearing black silk pajamas at night? And slept in a hammock."

"Yes, he did. And he refused to carry an M-sixteen. Just a forty-five pistol."

"Why that?"

"He said his men carried an M-sixteen. If he needed one, it would mean all was lost, that it wouldn't make any difference, and that he hadn't done a good job of training his soldiers."

Samuel still needed to know one thing: "Why the silk pajamas?"

Franklin laughed. "He told everyone he was raised to retire at night wearing the proper sleeping attire."

Both laughed, and Samuel said, "Yes. Like Argonne, he could have used family influence to get a cush job in the rear. But he chose to lead his troops."

"I suggested that to her," Franklin revealed to his father.

He laughed. "What did she do, threaten you with a sharp bayonet in the eye?"

"Damn near. She just flat told me to keep my nose out of her business." He chuckled, adding, "She said, 'I'm a soldier. When the bugle blows . . . you stand to the watch.' "

Samuel thought of the Sergeant Major. "Reminds me of someone else I know."

Both men laughed. "I'm so proud of her, Pop. I don't tell her often enough, but I believe she knows how I feel."

Samuel understood. He had made the same mistakes with his children. "She does, son. Believe me . . . she knows."

Franklin looked at his watch, then the stars, and told his father, "Big day tomorrow. I better get some sack time. You coming in?"

His father stood and stretched. "Not just yet. I better

report to your mother and brother and say good night to them."

"Good night." They shook hands and Samuel stepped off the porch and walked to the cemetery at the back of the house. He looked up at the archway leading to the family plots and stared at the sabres joined at the fulcrum and whispered, "I suppose we'll be adding another one soon."

He walked to Shania's grave, where he knelt and said a silent prayer. "Well, sweetheart, it looks like we've gone and gotten ourselves into another ruckus. Seems like every time the world goes insane there's a Sharps caught in the craziness. But, don't you worry about that little grand-daughter of ours. She's tough and well trained. I know she'll do just fine."

He leaned down and kissed the grass covering his wife, rose, and stepped a few feet away to the grave of his oldest son. He stood silent, as he always had in the past. He never could quite find the words to express himself. Perhaps, he thought, it was because he never really knew him while growing up. Samuel had missed out on so much of Adrian's youthful years.

At least, he reminded himself, he had Franklin and Kevin and the grandchildren. With them, he had formed a wonderful relationship, keeping his promise to his dying wife.

25

The last day of Argonne's leave was highlighted by a family gathering at the ranch, including friends from the surrounding area. Dozens of tables had been erected at the picnic area in the tall cottonwoods that stood like sentinels for a family that had endured the best—and worst—of times.

Her cousins were there, along with others from her great-granduncle's side of the family.

A steer had been donated and was turning over on a large spit, and as expected, the food was lavish and plentiful. A Western band played on a small stage; children ran about, their laughter echoing through the warm air. As she watched from the porch, Argonne felt a deep sense of pride and gratitude.

She watched her mother and was tickled at her floppy hat, reminding her of pictures she had seen of Selona. A yellow ribbon was tied above the brim.

"It's good the weather is tolerable. No rain, and not too hot," said Dolores.

Argonne noticed the sadness in her mother's voice.

"Come on, Momma. Let's go dance!" She grabbed her

mother by the hand and dragged her toward the music, yelling to the bandleader, "Play some mariachi music!"

The music began.

Mother and daughter reeled and twirled in the Mexican-style fandango, raising a storm cloud of dust; the others joined in, the music reached a feverish pitch, and by the time the dance was over, all were coated with red dust mixed with perspiration.

"I feel wonderful," shouted Dolores.

"Me too. I haven't done that in years," Argonne shouted back.

"I thought I'd forgotten how," said her mother.

The crowd applauded wildly, and the two women walked off together, arms linked, toward the house and a cool shower.

As the hour drew late, the guests began to trickle away. Tears of farewell fell, hugs were exchanged, and then the family was alone. They all gathered beneath the cottonwoods by a roaring fire that crackled brightly. The air was cool, as it was in the evenings on the desert.

Invariably, this led to the traditional storytelling the family always enjoyed and awaited with eager expectation. This led Samuel to discuss his meeting with William O'Kelly and his idea of writing a book based on the family history.

"I think it's a wonderful idea," said Argonne. "And he's right. The Sharpses may not be the only African-American family with so many generations of military service, but I think we rank with the best of them."

Franklin had sat quietly, musing over the idea before he spoke. "Interesting concept, I must admit. Has he given you an outline of his project?"

Samuel nodded. "He has. I'll give you a copy. It lays out the whole story, from the Sergeant Major to the present." He looked at Argonne. "I told him you might be a perfect source of information."

It was true. Of all the family, she was the one most interested in the Sharpses' history. "I had thought that one day I might do the same thing. Looks like he's beat me to the punch. I'm sure he'll do a better job than I. After all, he is a professional writer."

Jacob chimed in, "Sounds like a white man making money off our family."

Samuel held out his hand as though fending off an attacker. "Not at all. As a matter of fact, just the opposite. He plans on giving all his royalties to the United Negro College Fund. And I have that in a written agreement."

Samuel looked at Franklin. "He wants to come here and spend a few days. Get the feel of the family. You mind letting him bunk here for a few days? You two already have something in common: He's a Vietnam veteran. Served in the one-oh-first."

"Then he can't be all bad," Argonne put in.

With that the family trickled back to the house, except Argonne, who went to the fire, threw on a log, and sat close to the flames. As a little girl she had often come to the cottonwoods, built a fire, roasted marshmallows, and spent hours reflecting on her family past, considering the present, and wondering about the future.

She glanced up as the branches rustled, and for a moment it was as though the branches were talking to her, as she imagined when younger. She then lay on her side and curled up and fell to sleep.

When she woke up, almost an hour later, she realized someone had covered her with a blanket.

26

The next morning the family gathered in the living room after breakfast. Argonne's luggage sat waiting by the door. No one appeared anxious to speak, muted by the weight of the moment. Franklin stared at his daughter as though memorizing every minute detail of his child who was going to war. Samuel was by the fireplace, where he gazed solemnly through the window. Jacob sat by his mother on the couch, fidgeting.

"My God," said Argonne, "this is more like a requiem than a family gathering."

This seemed to snap Samuel out of his trance. He walked over to Franklin and whispered in his ear. His son nodded and went to the mantel. He reached up and removed the cavalry sabre from the pegs. The scabbard was dented, the shine faded by time, but the sword inside was sharp, the blade glinting brightly as the sunlight touched the metal when Franklin slipped it out and in again.

Argonne knew what was coming. She stood, as did the others, and watched her father approach.

"Young lady, you are the fifth generation of the Sharps family to go to war. We have all carried this sabre—or a replica of it—as a symbol to remind ourselves of the honor, service, and dedication we have given for this nation. It was always the prayer of Grams Selona that this sword would never be taken down and passed on to her children. But fate has dictated differently. Carry this with pride, and with respect for those who came before you."

He extended the sabre, holding it with upturned palms. She accepted the weapon lovingly. "Thank you, Daddy. I'll bring it back one day."

Dolores choked momentarily; then, with the world once again gearing up for a terrible war beyond the walls of the house, the Sharps family embraced, and sent another of its children off to war.

PART 3

OPERATION DESERT DRAGON

27

The blast of heat that greeted Argonne at the airport at Dhahran, Saudi Arabia, was more than anything she had ever experienced either in Arizona or in the Mojave Desert of California. The moment the nose of the giant C5-A opened, brilliant sunlight spilled into the cargo aircraft, blinding the soldiers as they sat strapped in the hundreds of seats in the aircraft's belly.

Slowly—mechanically—the troopers unsnapped their seat belts, rose, stretched weary muscles, and endured the traditional army procedure of "hurry up and wait" to begin debarkation. Huge "Alice packs"—the combat soldier's rucksack—filled to the brim with essential equipment lined the decks. Helmets, weapons, and duffel bags sat like giant turtles, waiting to be hoisted onto the bodies of young men and women primed for war.

Finally, the troops began unloading, walking herky-jerky down the ramps, their bodies straining beneath the weight of their gear. First impression gave one the thought of ants marching from the apex of an anthill. Each man, each company, flowed from the bowels of the giant transport until the individual trooper stepped into the full force and brilliance of the desert sun.

"Welcome to Hell," one trooper muttered as he stepped into the furnace.

Immediately, camouflage fatigues wilted with sweat in the sauna temperature and wrapped their bodies with the hot breath of the desert. "Heat snakes" wiggled across the scorching tarmac, appearing like a lake that gradually obliterated the shapes of the troopers walking in a long line from the C5-A. By the time they had marched ten yards, their bodies were soaked, and canteens were emptied as the soldiers poured water over their heads and chests.

"Man," Desmond Baker groaned from behind Argonne. "I thought Chicago could get hot in September. This place makes Chitown look like frozen tundra."

She wiped at her eyes; sweat stung like sharp needles and her clothes were already starting to stick to her skin. "I'm ready to go back to Torrejón."

The flight from Fort Campbell had stopped at the giant U.S. Air Force base at Torrejón, Spain, where they were allowed to deplane to a waiting crowd of volunteers passing out towels, razors, shaving cream, soda pop, cookies, doughnuts, and bottles of fresh water.

"I hear that," the specialist moaned. "I guess those hair dryers were good training."

Argonne forced a smile. Brigadier General Hugh Shelton, Assistant Division Commander for Operations, and one of the first to deploy to Saudi Arabia with the Advance Team, had suggested that the troops prepare for the incredible heat by breathing the hot air flow from hair dryers. The whir of the electric blowers filled every area of the fort; some even carried them into the field during training sessions.

"What I wouldn't give for a frozen Popsicle, right now," Argonne muttered.

"Wouldn't last long enough to get it out of the wrapper," Baker countered.

The troops route-stepped for a half-mile in one long,

undulating column, helmets bobbing like corks on rough water during the painful procession toward large tents where they would await transportation to what had been deemed Camp Eagle II. In Vietnam, the major camp for the Screaming Eagles had been dubbed Camp Eagle, in the jungles near Phan Rang. Like its predecessor, this camp was not ready for the division's arrival. Unlike Camp Eagle, there were no green army tents waiting—that would have been torturous in the murderous heat. The Saudi government had provided 2,500 Arabic-style tents, more suited for the climate. The structures were set up in military fashion by battalions, dressed right and covered down. One trooper noted that the tents looked like giant sand tortoises, similar to the ones the division had encountered in the Mojave Desert.

They sat in their own sweat, feeling nothing but the incredible dragon breath cocooning around their bodies. Muscles had already begun to cramp, heads and eyes ached, and they had been in Saudi Arabia less than an hour. Empty plastic water bottles littered the huge army field tent where they waited for the buses that would transport them to Camp Eagle II, already nicknamed "Camp Camel."

Argonne leaned back on her rucksack, too exhausted to think about what lay ahead, or what had been left behind.

What in the world are we doing here? she wondered.

As though reading her mind, Baker piped in with a pained voice. "Man, Lieutenant . . . they expect us to fight in this shit?"

"Fight and win, Baker. That's what we are expected to do. And will do. Let's just hope Saddam's troops don't cross the line before we're acclimated and ready to fight."

Baker knew that could only mean one thing. "More training?" he asked.

"Lots more. And you will have to keep the birds in tip-top shape."

"Sweet Mother of God," he moaned. "I feel like I'm inside a Westinghouse clothes dryer."

She picked up a handful of sand that had drifted around her feet. "I don't envy your job, Baker. This stuff is going to cause our turbines a lot of problems."

The crew chief chuckled, and said, "All I got to do is work in it. You got to fly in it. But it's going to be rough when we get the *shamals*."

The word had filtered back through the pipeline about the desert sandstorms, called *shamal* by the Arabs. The Americans had another name for the tornadic clouds of sand: "brownouts." Paint would be sandblasted from vehicles; aircraft could be buried within minutes. Human beings could be stripped of their clothes and skin, and blinded, if not protected.

"I can't wait," Argonne replied.

Finally, the buses arrived, and the soldiers, aviators, and crews began boarding, to sit in cramped seats, bodies aching, no room to move, air-conditioning barely able to cool their faces.

The caravan of buses gradually began moving. Open windows offered little refreshing breeze; the blast of hot air reminded Argonne of breathing the hair dryers at Fort Campbell.

"Damn," Baker mused. "I could use a cold beer right now."

Argonne chuckled. "If you find one, get one for me."

The soldiers knew there would be no cold beer, nor a beer ration as in past wars. Saudi Arabia was a Muslim nation, and its government had made it clear that the laws of Islam—which banned alcohol, prostitutes, and other known "soldier characteristics"—would not be tolerated with the American presence.

Finally, the journey to Camp Eagle II—located at King Fahd Airport—drew to an end. Argonne had no idea what awaited once they arrived, but all knew it had to be better than what they had endured since their combat boots touched Arabian soil.

28

Camp Camel lay forty miles northwest of Dhahran, off the highway leading to Riyadh, at King Fahd Airport, which, when construction was completed, would be the world's largest aviation facility. It was initially designed to handle the flow of millions of Muslims on their pilgrimage to Mecca, and almost immediately the American presence could be seen.

The tent city was set up on the outskirts of the airport, and was growing to accommodate the division. The newly built latrines were the first place the troops visited upon arrival, since each soldier was required to consume eight gallons of water on a daily basis, which kept the taps flowing on the human plumbing.

Argonne recalled Baker saying, "Eight gallons! I couldn't drink one gallon of water. Cold beer, maybe, but not water. No human being can drink eight gallons of water." He paused, then calculated aloud, "Water weighs eight pounds per gallon, times eight . . . that's sixty-four pounds of water a day, Lieutenant. How's a body suppose to hold sixty-four pounds of water? Damn. Sixty-four pounds! How are we going to carry that much water?

We're already carrying a hundred pounds in our rucks!"

Argonne had to laugh. "With air-assault spirit, Baker." She pointed to the lines at the latrines. "Besides, it'll go through you from one end faster than you can pump it in from the other end."

He shook his head. "I sure wish Saddam had invaded Jamaica. Their climate is more to my liking."

Again she laughed as they moved closer to the portable toilets. "At least you've retained your sense of humor, Baker. That's good. I think you're going to need it before this tour is over."

"Yeah, ma'am. I can just see myself laughing all the way through this mother—" He paused. ". . . This mother of all wars."

Bodily necessities and functions weren't the only quickly discovered realities of the troopers' new environment. Soon to be discovered by all, Camp Camel was not inhabited only by Americans; there were other residents.

Scorpions. Huge black beetles as big as a fist. And vipers, whose venomous bite could kill in a matter of minutes if not treated. And, of course, the ubiquitous camel, the mule of the desert, often found in herds roaming the sandy terrain.

Welcome to Saudi Arabia!

Argonne plopped onto her bunk in the female officers' tent, removed her boots, poured water on her feet, and began rubbing her toes. Having grown up in the desert, she was no stranger to desert reptiles and insects. She had killed, skinned, and eaten more than her share of rattlesnakes just to prove to the guys she grew up with that she could cut the hard path. Gila monsters didn't cause her to blink.

However, others were not so familiar with the domestic creatures.

A bloodcurdling scream exploded from the end of her tent, and she saw a lieutenant from the battalion administration company go racing between the rows of bunks.

There were six women in the tent, and all stood pointing at the frightened woman's bed.

Argonne smiled, took her M-16, and walked to where the intruder sat on a white pillow. With a swift stroke, she knocked the scorpion to the floor, butt-stroked it, and calmly wiped the remains off with a towel. "Don't get into bed without checking for these little devils. That includes snakes and anything else that might be trying to become our roommates," she told the others.

At the chow hall she took a tray and stood in line, moving toward the odor of her first hot meal in two days. *At least,* she thought, *it's not MREs,* the new army's answer to C rations.

She sat at a table with other soldiers and could see the fatigue etched on their faces. They ate automatically but not with purpose. Food at this point was necessary—like the water—not because they were hungry; rather, because it was required by their bodies. There was none of the standard mess hall chitchat; silence ruled. When finished, the soldiers cleaned their trays, donned their helmets, slung their rifles, and walked out into the burning sun.

Later that night she took a long cold shower, allowing the air to dry her body, wanting the coolness of the water against her skin as long as possible. On the walk back to her quarters she could hear the low rumble of barracks chatter coming from the rows of tents; a few shouts of laughter, but not the energetic bustle of a battalion of fighting soldiers.

Nearing her tent she suddenly looked up, and stood stunned; mesmerized. The sky held her attention as though she had discovered a new universe.

In a way, she had. The stars of Arizona and the Mojave offered nothing in comparison to the vastness of the lights twinkling in the heavens. She stood there for several minutes, unable to tear her eyes away.

Finally, she went into her tent, lay on the bunk, and fell instantly to sleep.

29

Specialist Michelle Martinson spent her first night in the Saudi desert parked behind her M-16 automatic rifle. The perimeter was manned by a small security force, and while there wasn't a great fear of being attacked by a large element, there was the lingering concern of infiltrators testing their positions. An infantry rifle company had been deployed to add to the security, but the Guard unit was ready with their own reception if the Iraqis "crossed the line."

The 144th was positioned in the desert region east of the Tapline highway. "Tapline" was short for the Trans-Arabian Pipeline, which ran north and south. There was no doubt that should the Iraqis invade Saudi Arabia, the road would be one of the primary targets, and since water was the most essential human need to the United Nations troops pouring into the country, the North Dakota Guard unit would be a primary target. This put everyone on edge; that and the fact that much of the work was done at night in order to function more effectively in the heat. Nearly the entire Coalition force had become nocturnal, causing change in every way imaginable, especially sleeping habits.

Sleep by day, work by night became the operational procedure. On the highway, vehicles groaned through the night in a constant flow running both north and south; the sound of engines added to the eeriness of a terrain that seemed to create its own macabre world.

Beside her, Specialist Four Jack Taylor, from Minot, North Dakota, peered across the vast expanse of sand and removed his helmet, wiping at the sweat streaming down his face. A farm boy, he had never imagined the world could have a place so hot.

"Almost looks like North Dakota in the winter, doesn't it, Mickey? It's flat. Quiet. Except for the trucks on Tapline."

She understood what he was getting at. "Looks like snowdrifts after a blizzard. In a way, I wish it was snow."

Taylor chuckled at the thought. He looked at the bag containing his chemical-warfare equipment. The soldiers kept the lifesaving masks, suits, and gloves within easy reach. Should an attack come, the Iraqis might use their Scuds to bombard the forces with chemical agents in a preemptive strike.

"I hope to hell we don't have to put on the chem gear. I can barely move as it is." The dreaded chemical-protection suits were the worst nightmare of every soldier in Saudi Arabia. "Hell, that's like wearing your own personal hair dryer." He paused, then added, "Christ! I think that would be worse than the gas. At least you'd die quicker with gas."

"I heard that," she said.

His comment made her shiver, and for the first time since joining the Guard, she questioned her decision. While Mickey had fully understood there was a possibility of deployment to a hostile area, the idea of chemical or biological warfare had never entered her thoughts. War was supposed to be about the "Three B's": bombs, bullets, and bayonets. Not "bugs."

The 144th had practiced daily donning the suits until each soldier could become fully protected in less than a minute. In a place as primitive as time itself, modern warfare had reduced survival to a matter of seconds. And the training did not end at Camp Ripley, in the cool forests of Wisconsin. Now, planted in the sweltering sand, the troops conducted daily exercises in "suiting up" for a biological attack.

"You think he'll go for it if he has to?" asked Taylor.

"I wouldn't be surprised at anything that crazy sucker might do if he gets boxed in."

Taylor shifted his weapon to port and leaned on his side. "My great-grandfather was in France during World War One. He was gassed. That mustard crap. Ate up his throat and lungs like slow acid. He died screaming for my father to take a rifle and shoot him."

Martinson wiggled nervously. "You are certainly a great person to stand guard with, Taylor. A real conversationalist. You know how to make a girl feel comfortable."

"Sorry. It's just, well, you know, all this silence gives you a chance to think about things you wouldn't ordinarily think about. You know?"

"Yeah. I know. I know something else . . . I'm hungry."

Mickey reached into her pack and removed a plastic pouch of MREs (meals, ready to eat). A high-protein field dinner, each unit consisted of a main course, a portable heating element that cooked the dehydrated course in less than a minute, and other condiments, including hot sauce.

She poured water into the "stove," slipped the food pouch inside, and laid it at an angle, allowing the water to begin boiling. When ready, she ate, slow and deliberate, trying not to think of her mom's home cooking as she chewed on the sliced ham. "Any idea when the mess hall will be up and running?"

Taylor shook his head, peered through night-vision binoculars at the open ground to his front. "Not for a while, I'm afraid."

Mickey took another spoonful and swallowed. "God . . . even mess-hall food will be a treat compared to this stuff."

Taylor laughed, his eyes trained to the front. He continued to search while she ate; in the sky overhead the sound of helicopter rotor blades cut through the night.

She looked up, wondering for a moment about who was flying the chopper. Her dream was to become an army aviator, and a prayer slipped from her lips for the crew as she heard the engine's noise gradually fade.

30

In July, 1990, prior to the Iraqi invasion of Kuwait, army planners at Central Command, headquartered at McDill Air Force Base, Florida, conducted a two-week map exercise of the Mideast situation. The scenario called for an assumption that a large Iraqi force would invade Saudi Arabia. Not Kuwait.

The 101st played significantly into this OPLAN—operational plan—with a covering force mission. Anticipated was a massive armor assault by the Iraqis through the Saudi border. To stop the invaders, the 101st's aviation "tank killers" task force would charge forward to engage the tanks, accompanied by the "Hell on Wheels" 3rd Armor Division, which would attack approximately twenty miles inside the Saudi border.

At that point, both forces would fall back approximately eighty miles and hook up with the 24th Mechanized Infantry, led by Major General Barry McCaffrey. There, the two armor elements would engage the attacking Iraqis with a frontal counterattack while the 101st aviation and other tactical air strike forces from the Air Force, Navy, and Marines struck on the flanks, literally enveloping the invaders on three sides. The only recourse for the Iraqis would be to retreat back to their border with what one Army officer called "the hounds of hell biting at their ass."

Ironically—or clairvoyantly—this very scenario was now being put into place under the name of Desert Dragon. Major General Binsford Peay II, Division Commander, 101st Airborne, later stated, "Desert Dragon was a highly complicated operation, requiring close coordination of many combat assets. Besides a tremendous amount of liaison, it featured delaying actions, withdrawals, spoiling attacks, phase lines, and passing units through one another at night—the most difficult maneuvers an army can undertake, and the hardest to control."

It was a sophisticated plan, and its execution would require three fundamental actions by the troops: move, shoot, communicate. The Screaming Eagles arrived ready, fully trained in these requirements, drilled in the fundamentals of desert warfare, and equipped with special applications designed specifically for that environment, and were considered the role model in a shooting war in Saudi Arabia.

Four of the nine battalions had cut their teeth in the Mojave Desert with "laser warfare" with the OPFOR—opposing force—as had all helicopter units. Two battalions had served in the Sinai. Once in-country, the division merely fired up the engine, popped the clutch, and moved forward . . . toward the action.

Like their Vietnam brethren—who moved immediately from the troop ship at Cam Ranh Bay in 1965—the troopers hit the ground ready to go to fight.

The 101st was ready for Operation Desert Shield by having prepared for this very contingency becoming operational through an internal plan designated Operation Desert Destiny. This division plan was an ongoing, daily revised and updated plan that continually changed as battalion after battalion of the Screaming Eagles arrived in-country.

This required the constant acquisition of forward area intelligence, both satellite and airborne.

From the right seat of the OH-54D Kiowa Warrior, co-pilot Warrant Officer One Monty Ohlhauser peered through the helmet-mounted display of his aviation night-vision system (ANVIS), a symbology system that provided situation information and communications control. He glanced to his right, where Argonne appeared greenish in the glow of his night-vision system.

The desert had a near-turquoise appearance as the reconnaissance chopper raced three hundred feet above the desert. Lights from military outposts sprinkled along the defensive line glowed incandescently, appearing like huge fireflies embedded in the sand. Other signatures appeared as well, requiring closer observation to determine identity. Heat reflections from humans that had to be determined as friendly or foe.

Refugees had continued to flow from Kuwait, though not in as large numbers as the early days of the Iraqi invasion. Where once there had been long lines, now there was small groups that had managed to avoid Saddam's troops in their perilous trek across the sand to Saudi Arabia. This caused problems for the Coalition soldiers, not knowing until the last moment if the arriving Arabs were fleeing or attacking.

Argonne spoke into her microphone, her voice tinged with sadness at a small caravan of Kuwaitis. "Those poor people."

Ohlhauser sighed heavily. "They still have a long way to go to make it to our lines. I wish there was something we could do."

"Maybe there is, Buckaroo." She changed frequencies and reported the position of the refugees to headquarters, hoping there might be a patrol in the area that could offer assistance. Switching back to her primary frequency, she knew she had done little to help, but it was the best she could offer. That and a silent prayer.

In the days since the arrival of her helicopter, she had gradually acclimatized and had hardened to the task at hand—which was night surveillance. One weapons pylon of her Kiowa was equipped with seven Hydra 70 rockets; a .50-caliber forward-fixed machine gun was mounted on the second. Designed to fly in different combat modes, the chopper could carry Hellfire missiles to attack hardened targets, or air-to-air Stinger heat-seeking missiles for air combat.

The distinctive mast-mounted sight (MMS) situated above the rotor blades enabled the Kiowa to operate by day and night and engage the enemy at the maximum range of the weapons systems and with minimum exposure of the helicopter. The mast contained a suite of mounted sensors which included a high-resolution television camera for long-range target detection; a thermal imaging sensor for navigation, target acquisition, and designation; a laser rangefinder/designator for target location and guidance of the Hellfire missiles and designation for Copperhead artillery rounds; and a boresight assembly that provided in-flight sensor alignment. An integrated global positioning system and inertial navigation system provided navigational reference, while communications was based on the "have-quick UHF and SINCGARS FM anti-jam radio."

The Kiowa was known as a deadly bad boy that could fight air battles or ground elements with speed and ferocity. It could, with its speed and agility, get out of trouble as quickly as it could get into it.

What made her first flight in Saudi Arabia more difficult than any Argonne had known since flight school was the lack of ground reference. It was like flying over an ice-covered lake: difficult to tell where the sky ended and the earth began. This affected her "situational awareness," and made her stomach tighten, knowing she had to rely totally on the helicopter's instrumentation.

Her concentration, therefore, had to remain riveted to the task of flying; normal chat between her and Ohlhauser was limited to essential conversation. She fixated on the horizon, where the NVG image gave her a point of reference, but mostly it was the altimeter.

Argonne thought of the flight as comparable to flying at night through a cloud of dirt, which kept her eyes constantly shifting to the temperature gauge. She knew how to make an emergency landing; she had done hundreds of such simulated exercises in flight school and at division. But never in a combat area of operation.

By the time her mission was concluded and she had landed at Camp Eagle II, her flight suit was soaked—not from the heat, but from the rawness of nervous tension.

After debriefing, she returned to her tent and collapsed onto the bunk, still dressed in her flying uniform.

31

Jerome Moody was awakened in Kuwait City by the haunting shrillness of a mullah saying morning prayers over a loudspeaker from atop a nearby mosque. Odd, he thought, as he listened to the words recited from the Koran, that the thought of God could remain in a country ravaged by such brutality. But, since both sides were predominantly Islamic, the war had not changed either faction's need for its spiritual diet.

His first task each morning was to give a "sit rep," a situation report, to 5th Group Headquarters SOCCENT—Special Operations Command of Central Command.

The satellite linkup took only seconds, and he gave his report. "We have five teams equipped and ready to begin operations. The underground leader is competent and more than capable. Targets are being located and status is being determined."

"What is the situation with the civilian population?" asked the voice from Saudi Arabia.

Moody thought about the grisly sights around the city. "Executions are almost continuous. The Iraqis continue to sack the city and have literally stripped the businesses and

facilities bare. About the only thing that hasn't been up-
rooted is the concrete on the streets. Hell, they'll probably
get around to that in the future."

There was a pause, and then the voice said, "It's become necessary for you to return to our location for a
detailed debriefing. An extract has been arranged for
twenty-three hundred hours tonight."

Moody didn't know what to say. He started to object,
then decided to remain silent. This was part of the original
plan. "What about the other members of my team?"

"They're to remain in place. You'll be briefed on your
next mission tomorrow morning."

"Yes, sir," Moody replied halfheartedly. "What are the
coordinates for the extract?"

He took his map and listened to the officer's directions.
He didn't write anything down; his memory burned the
coordinates into his brain as his eyes locked on to the
location on the map. "We won't move until after dark.
My Kuwaiti contact will get me there on time."

The voice signed off from Saudi Arabia and the Green
Beret shut down the linkup. He crawled to the balcony
and peered along the beach. The Iraqis were fortifying
their positions with a wall of sandbags. Thousands of
troops had moved along the sandy stretch of the city in
anticipation of the Coalition invasion that might one day
come should Iraq remain in Kuwait as a hostile force.

For Moody, there was little doubt the invaders would
leave, but not of their own accord. They were now too
confident that nothing could prevent them from having
their way both physically and politically.

Arrogant bastards, he thought. The Iraqis had put
themselves into the perfectly created killing zone, refusing
to believe the stage was being set for the largest Allied
amphibious invasion since D-Day at Normandy.

32

In the early-morning light, Franklin Sharps knelt by his mother's grave, said a silent prayer, then walked back to the house. In the utility room in the back of the house he sat at a workbench, and from a drawer took a dozen empty brass cartridges and began reloading the .50-caliber shell. First, he put in a new primer; powder followed, and finally he inserted and crimped the projectile. After slipping the bullets into a cartridge belt he took down the Sharps rifle from above the fireplace, walked to the stable, saddled his horse Maximus, slid the rifle into the scabbard, and rode east toward the hills as he had done hundreds of times in his lifetime. What shining times those had been. Especially with his brother Adrian, before he left for Vietnam. Now he felt a deep sense of loss as he urged the animal into a gait, his thoughts becoming so entwined his head began to ache.

After thirty minutes he reached a spot that stood as something of a monument in the rites of passage of the Sharps family since his great-great-grandparents had first settled the land in the late nineteenth century. He sat in the saddle beside a stand of saguaro cactus. Each stood nearly ten feet tall, and bore the marks of dozens of bullet holes, all of which had filled in over the past century, now blackened scars against the green of the cacti.

He wheeled Maximus and rode to a rock outcropping, where he dismounted and tethered the horse. He drew the Sharps .50-caliber buffalo gun from the scabbard, knelt behind a rock, and loaded a round into the breech. Adjusting the sights, he figured the distance of one tall cactus at six hundred yards. Taking careful aim, he slowed his breathing, then squeezed the trigger. The loud *boom* and the kick of the butt against his shoulder sounded and felt wonderful.

He snapped the breech open smartly, flipping the empty cartridge into the air, and caught the casing before it hit the ground, as his father had taught him to do. He reloaded, aimed again, and fired the second round. He repeated the process until the cartridge belt was empty of live ammunition.

"Feel better?" he softly whispered to himself.

He rested against a rock, the rifle cradled across his lap.

His mind now seemed clear, as though this sojourn with the past had reconnected him to the present. The past. The present. All were joined by a common denominator of five generations of his family history: War! From the Sergeant Major and Selona through his grandfather and Hannah to his father and mother, him and Dolores; now, Argonne.

The family thoughts put it all into perspective for him, making everything so clear and simple. Since the first moment of learning that his daughter might go to war he had felt impotent, unable to control the events around him.

Suddenly, it all made sense and he knew what he had to do.

He kicked the horse's flanks with a sharp stroke of his boots and rode toward the ranch.

Dolores was in the kitchen when she heard the sound of hooves slapping the hard ground in the driveway. She walked to the living room and stared through the window where she saw Franklin disappear into the stable. What had compelled him to take the Sharps and go for a morning ride? He had not done that in years.

Ten minutes passed and he came through the front door and returned the rifle to the mounts above the fireplace. He started for his office but was stopped by her words.

"Aren't you going to clean that rifle?" She knew it was considered a family sin not to immediately clean the buffalo gun after firing.

"I will in a few minutes, honey. I've got something to take care of first."

She watched dumbfounded as he went into his office and closed the door.

Franklin sat at his desk and thumbed through his address book with trembling fingers. When he found the name he was searching for he punched in the telephone number and waited. The ringing seemed interminable when the voice of an old friend answered.

"Edward . . . this is Franklin Sharps."

Outside his office, Dolores's ear was pinned to the door, but all she could hear was a low murmur, nothing intelligible. She had been standing there for several minutes when the door opened. Franklin wore a huge grin; his eyes danced with an excitement she had not seen in a long time.

"What are you up to?" she asked warily.

"Is breakfast ready? I could eat a horse."

"You'll have to eat your horse if you don't tell me what's going on."

He took her by the elbow and gently guided her to the kitchen, where he poured a cup of coffee and sat at the table.

"Who were you talking to on the phone?"

Franklin shrugged innocently. "Just an old friend."

"What old friend?" Her suspicion could not be contained.

He sipped from the cup, then told her, "You remember Edward Delaney? My buddy from medical school?"

She thought a moment. "Yes." Then she stiffened, re-membering more about the man. "Isn't he the one who is the director for some world health organization?"

"That's right. Doctors for the World."

"What does that have to do with you, Franklin?"

His voice grew low but deliberate; his words were care-fully chosen. "I asked him if his organization had any plans to become involved in the situation in the Middle East."

Her right eyebrow rose. "You mean in Saudi Arabia?"

He squirmed in his chair. "Yes, in Saudi Arabia."

"What does that have to do with you?" From the sound of her voice and the look on her face, it was obvious she already knew the answer but didn't want to hear the words.

"There's a need for surgical people, what with all the refugees pouring in from Kuwait. I told him I'd like to volunteer to go with his outfit to Saudi Arabia." He drained the last of the coffee. "Besides . . . if this turns into the bloodbath that Saddam Hussein and other world lead-ers are predicting . . . the United Nations Coalition will need all the doctors on the face of this earth."

"Franklin, have you taken leave of your sense?"

"Of course not. I'm quite aware of my psychological situation."

So angry she couldn't speak, Dolores merely stood and seethed. He said nothing. He had made a decision and there was no dissuading him from what he thought was the right course.

She stormed away; Franklin sat calm. He knew she would ultimately accept his decision.

33

☆ ☆ ☆

Argonne was awakened by the company clerk with orders to report to squadron operations. She was tired, but dressed quickly and reported to the tent, where she recognized several Blackhawk pilots studying a map perched on an easel.

"Come in, Lieutenant." Argonne's squadron operations officer, Major Terry Whitpan, a tall, rangy cowboy from Wyoming, motioned her to his side. Standing with him was Captain Walter Jennings, a Blackhawk pilot, and his copilot, Lieutenant Ross Daniels. There was an aura of excitement she immediately sensed. At the same time, she was studying Ohlhauser. He looked terrible. He had suffered for several days with dysentery and had forced himself from his bed to take part in the mission.

"Are you OK, Buckaroo?"

He nodded weakly. "Still a little green around the gills, but I'll make it."

"I think you better scratch on this mission."

He shook his head. "I said I can handle it."

Whitpan pointed at the map. "SOCCENT has requested we extract a Special Forces officer at this loca-

tion." He tapped a circled area on the map. "He'll be
guided to the pickup point by a Kuwaiti friendly. Once
aboard, he'll be flown to King Fahd. The Blackhawk will
conduct the extract, the Kiowa will be a scout observer
and provide additional security."

"Sir, why not use a Cobra instead of the Kiowa. More
firepower," Argonne said.

The major pointed to another area near the extract
point. "The Cobra is an attack helicopter, not a reconnaissance machine. This will be an opportunity to conduct
a deep recon of the area." He gazed steadily at Argonne.
"Are you up to this, Lieutenant?"

She snapped to attention. "Yes, sir. Air Assault!" What
she really wanted to do was scream with joy. For the first
time she would be going deep into enemy territory.

"Good." He gave a thumbs-up to the Blackhawk pilots.
"Y'all work out a plan with the Kiowa crew. Assemble at
twenty-one hundred hours. Liftoff is scheduled for twenty-
two hundred."

The ops officer left and the pilots gathered by the map.
Ohlhauser weaved as the pilots determined their altitude,
headings, and flight of departure. Later, when finished,
they started for the flight line.

In the dimly lit night on the tarmac, Argonne heard a
sudden gurgling, then a retching sound. She walked
quickly to her copilot, who was bent over, vomit streaming onto the ground. "You can't go, Monty. Go to the
dispensary and check in."

"I can do it," he gasped.

The Blackhawk pilots approached. "What's going on,
Lieutenant?" one of them asked.

"My right seat is sick, sir."

"Damn. Can he fly?"

"Yes—" Ohlhauser started to speak.

"No!" Argonne snapped. "I can't take the chance he
might get worse during the flight."

"I agree," said the Blackhawk pilot. "Get to the dispensary, Mr. Ohlhauser. That's an order."

Ohlhauser walked away and disappeared in the darkness.

"Are you up to continuing this mission, Lieutenant?" asked the pilot.

"Yes, sir. We're trained to fly alone, if necessary."

He checked his watch, took his radio, and walked away from her. He returned a few minutes later, telling her, "Ops has approved. There's no time to find you a copilot. Let's get rolling."

Minutes later the two choppers lifted off the tarmac and roared toward Iraq.

34

Argonne Sharps reveled in the stories told of her ancestors, especially Selona, the family matriarch. Born a slave, her father had escaped bondage, fought with the 54th Massachusetts, and after the Civil War, the 10th Cavalry. As a girl, her mother, Della, and her grandmother Marie followed the 10th from post to post, where her father soldiered and the women served as laundresses. As a teenager, Selona had been brutally beaten, raped, then scalped by a band of renegade Texas Rangers while at Fort Sill, Oklahoma Territory.

That was when Argonne's great-great-grandfather, Sergeant Major Augustus Sharps, courted her, married her, and came up with the idea of using a piece of fur cut from a buffalo robe to fashion her a hairpiece. The wig became a badge of honor for the young woman, who became a legend in her own right as she followed her husband from one fort to another, raising two boys while dreaming of one day owning her own home and land.

Tonight, Argonne would be going into a hostile environment, and for the first time in her life she felt nausea rising from her stomach. The sudden rise of the helicopter made her dizzy, and she heard a voice calling to her from the past; one she had heard as a child when frightened by lightning storms.

The voice was her father's, telling the story of how Selona Sharps had once faced danger on the Western frontier.

On April 1, 1885, H troop of the 10th Cavalry had left Fort Davis, Texas, and arrived at Fort Grant, Arizona, at the end of the month. Once known as the worst fort in the Army, the post sat on a grass-covered plain in the shadow of Mount Graham, the tallest of the Pinaleno Mountains. Although it had gradually improved over the years, the garrison still lacked proper accommodations for the families of the noncommissioned officers.

Augustus spoke with Major Van Vliet, the commander of the squadron that included the men of D, E, H, K, and L troops of the regiment.

"Sir, me and the men with families would appreciate it if I could ride into Bonita and get them settled for the night."

Van Vliet nodded. "I regret there are not adequate quarters here for your families, First Sergeant."

"They'll make do, sir. We will be back by daylight."

Augustus saluted and he and four troopers rode off while the 10th set about establishing their presence at Fort Grant.

Augustus rode at the head of the caravan of wagons, which by now had been reduced to only a few.

"Beautiful country," said Augustus, waving his arm toward the mountain. "And smell that air. It's as fresh as flowers."

Selona was driving the lead wagon. She was tired, dirty, and wanted a bath, a luxury no one had enjoyed in several weeks.

"Mean-looking country, if you ask me. People in town probably going to be mean, too. They ain't going to be used to seeing Colored folks around here. Probably going to hate Coloreds as much as they hate Injuns."

Augustus spurred his horse, yelling to her as he rode out on point, "You said the same thing about Fort Davis."

Selona stood and yelled back, "Fort Davis had Coloreds before we got there."

"So did Fort Grant. The Ninth Cavalry was stationed there for years," he yelled back and then rode harder, as though her tongue were an Apache arrow.

She sat down heavily, gripping the reins angrily. She stared at the rumps of her two mules and turned to Adrian, who sat behind her with David. "I been staring at them rumps for weeks. Soon as I get me a house I'm going to make mule rump roast."

The wind picked up, whipping the sand off the desert as the tiny caravan moved away from the mountains on a supply trail. She started to get uneasy, fearing she and the others might become separated in what she realized was now a sandstorm.

"Adrian," she shouted into the back. "You and David get under cover. Get a bandanna over your mouth and cover over with a blanket."

She stopped the wagon and worked her way to the rear, where she could see Vina Gibbs sitting in her wagon, a Spencer rifle cradled across her lap.

"Vina . . . I can't see. Augustus rode ahead and there's no telling where he's at."

"What we going to do?" Two more wagons pulled alongside, joined by the troopers from the flanks.

Corporal Darcy Gibbs dismounted, took his rope and tied it to the rear of Selona's wagon, then connected the end to the mule behind him, which was pulling the Gibbs wagon.

"Tie off the wagons to the lead mules behind the front wagon. This'll keep them all joined together. The mules can't run nowheres," Gibbs shouted to the troopers. "Get *back inside the wagons. This'll blow through soon, then we'll move on."*

"What about Augustus?" Selona said. He was alone in the sandstorm in hostile country.

Gibbs shook his head. "Get in the wagon. Don't worry about the sarge. He knows what to do . . . he knows what we're doing. We've done this before."

Gibbs climbed into the wagon and pulled out a blanket. "Cover the eyes of your mules, else the blowing sand'll cut their eyes to pieces and they'll bolt."

Selona climbed through the rear and grabbed a blanket. When she was sure Adrian and David were secure, she jumped down and covered the eyes of the mules, constantly fighting to keep her balance and her wits.

When she started back for the wagon, she felt the presence of something close. Staring through the haze, she saw something faint and ghostlike; then there were more.

Eight men sat on horses; eight men with long hair and faces covered with bandannas. They carried rifles and were draped with bandoliers of ammunition.

Apaches!

The very name of the tribe of Indians frightened her. On the first days of the trip from Fort Davis, there was a fear the caravan would be attacked by Mescaleros. She had walked with Augustus while he checked the picket guards, heard noises that frightened her to the bone, and remembered wetting herself from fear. Now, alone, she had her children only a few feet away. She raced for the wagon, climbed to the seat and pulled out the Colt pistol. She snapped back the hammer and pointed it but saw nothing but the blowing sand and heard only the howl of the wind.

Minutes passed and still there was nothing; then she saw a horseman and took aim.

"Selona!" Augustus shouted. He was riding toward her, his head bent, his face covered. When he reined in beside the wagon she saw the eight riders following. She started to raise the pistol, but his hand pushed the barrel down.

"They're White Mountain Apache scouts. They won't harm us. I ran into them just after the storm hit." He motioned to the scouts. They dismounted, forced their horses to the ground, then covered the animals' eyes. The eight took blankets and lay between their horses' legs, covering themselves. Gradually the scouts and horses disappeared under a layer of sand.

Augustus was in the wagon, tying the front flap; using his large body to protect Selona and the children, he used a blanket to make a tent around the four of them inside the wagon, which was now filling with sand.

An hour later the storm had passed and the sky was clear. All the Negroes came out of their wagons and began to shovel the sand. Selona watched the scouts rise and shake themselves. She couldn't help but notice how much darker they were than the plains Indians. And fierce-looking. Their eyes seemed to shine like black diamonds.

"Why are them Apaches scouts for the army? I thought we was out here to fight the Apaches. They'll probably kill us in our sleep."

"They're reservation Indians," Augustus said. "They'll push on to Fort Grant from here."

"They don't look like reservation Injuns to me."

About that time one of the scouts approached Augustus, then stopped suddenly. He was tall and sinewy, and carried his rifle with ease. He stood staring at Selona until she grew uncomfortable.

"What's he looking at?" she asked Augustus.

The sergeant followed the Apache's line of sight, then burst out laughing. "He's looking at your wig!"

Selona reached up and grabbed the wig and tore it from her head. She shook the buffalo fur at the Apache, whose eyes were as round as her dinner plates.

"Here. Take it. You're probably going to get it one day anyhow."

The Apache pulled back into the group of other scouts, all of them jabbering and pointing at her scarred head.

Selona clamped the wig onto her head, tied it down

with her calico scarf, and, with pistol in hand, climbed into the wagon and snapped the reins.

"Hiyah, mules."

The caravan pulled away one wagon at a time, leaving the mystified scouts staring at Selona as she passed into the golden sunlight of Arizona, now unafraid, for she had met the Apache, and scared the living hell out of them with her buffalo wig.

When her father's voice subsided, Argonne couldn't help but laugh, and looking at her hands, saw that the shaking had stopped. She would be all right; steeled by the past, hardened for the future.

35

The steady purr of the engine had a soothing effect, allowing her to focus on the mission at hand. The desert below, spreading like a sea of green, gave off no indication of light through her night-vision goggles. The Blackhawk cruised to her right front, appearing like a giant dragonfly, rising and falling gently from the occasional thermals drifting up from the earth.

At first, there was an eeriness to flying alone. The tight fit of the cockpit seemed more acute, though there was one less pilot. The "tunnel vision" feeling from the night-vision goggles narrowed to a smaller visual corridor. Even the absence of the copilot's movement made her feel more alone. Knowing there was a comrade in the next seat is a comfort to a helicopter pilot. Unlike fighter pilots, accustomed to lone flight, helicopter pilots rarely fly solo. Having a second pilot lessened the chance of CFIT, controlled flight into terrain, a major problem of night flying, where the pilot becomes complacent, fatigued, or careless. More choppers have crashed from CFIT since the Vietnam War than from enemy ground fire. But she finally relaxed and began to enjoy the exhilaration of her first real mission.

The flight had gone smoothly until the two choppers passed into Iraqi airspace. That was when everything that could go wrong turned toward that direction. It began when the Blackhawk copilot, talking on a closed communication circuit, reported, "Six Gun, this is Dagger. Over."

"Six Gun to Dagger. What's up?"

There was a pause. "Be advised. We have a problem."

"What's the problem?"

"One of our engines is overheating."

"Damn," Argonne said aloud. The sand of the desert had thus far been a greater enemy than the heat or the Iraqis. And it couldn't have come at a worse time. "What's your intentions?"

The voice replied, "To continue on the mission. I'll keep giving you a sit rep."

"Have you contacted ops?"

"No. We won't do that unless it's necessary to abort. Stay on our six. We'll keep you informed. Out."

She began to worry. There could be no more a disastrous place for the Blackhawk to go down than their current location. She couldn't squeeze the entire Blackhawk crew into her tiny cockpit.

The radio went active. "Six Gun, this is Dagger. We're heating up on number two. We've been ordered to abort."

"What about the extract?" she said.

"No can do. You'll be on your own," Dagger replied.

She glanced at her watch. "I'm twenty minutes from the extract point. I've got the coordinates locked in. I can do it. I'll pick him up, get moving, and race you home."

There was a nervous pause. "Let me check with ops. We're gyroing back."

She watched the Blackhawk bank and execute a 180-degree turn. She was flying on her own now, no longer aided and comforted by the presence of the AH-60 and the soldiers aboard.

Seconds passed like hours until the pilot of the Black-hawk reported. "Cleared to complete mission, Six Gun. Good luck. Out."

Argonne didn't feel the apprehension that had hammered her nerves moments ago. She was a professional and waiting in the darkness was an American soldier who had risked his life more times than she. He was what mattered.

She checked her watch. Eight minutes to extract. Her senses and instincts were now running at full alert, her ears keen to the frequency the SF soldier would use to contact her at the extract point. Listening. Eyes alert. Watching. Heart pounding.

36

Major Jerome Moody and Muhammad Mustafa moved silently, quickly, through the desert, both wearing night-vision goggles. They would pause from time to time, check the map, shoot a compass azimuth, change direction when necessary, and encounter another of the seemingly endless sand dunes. Both men sweated profusely, and their eyes were irritated, since the eye pouches of their night-vision goggles flushed their orbits with each step.

The two had exfiltrated deftly through the streets of Kuwait City, avoiding Iraqi patrols, gun emplacements, and searchlights, finally reaching the open country north of the city. Now in the open desert, they stopped and gulped water feverishly. Moody checked his map again, noting his position, and said, "We should be about two kilometers from the rendezvous point." He looked at his watch. "We're ahead of the schedule."

Sweat streamed down the Arab's face, but there was no other sign of fatigue. *A tough sucker,* thought Muhammad. "You travel through the desert like a camel. No wonder we are ahead of the schedule."

Moody grinned, his teeth glowing green as seen through Mustafa's night-vision goggles. Then he thought about something that had bothered him since being ordered out of Kuwait City. "I hate leaving you and the team behind."

Mustafa shrugged. "You have your orders. You must obey." He patted the Green Beret soldier on the knee. "You will return. And the next time you'll come with more men."

Moody wasn't so certain. There was little more the Iraqis could steal from the Kuwaitis. All that was left were the oil fields, and they could be easily destroyed by tactical air strikes, leaving the monster with nothing but the loot from Kuwait City. "You don't think Saddam will pull his troops back to Iraq? Despite the sanctions?"

Muhammad shook his head. "That is impossible. Look at the losses he was willing to suffer with the war against Iran. He *owns* Kuwait . . . it is a pearl he will never relinquish."

"He won't own it long, my friend. The world has grown tired of his treachery."

Then both men stiffened. The sound of voices speaking Arabic drifted to them through the night. Then the sound of a dog barking. The voices suddenly grew louder.

Moody pointed to the northeast, and said, "Move. Very quietly." He started to ease forward when his instincts caused him to turn around. Mustafa was not following; the Kuwaiti was stooped, moving low across the desert in the direction of the Iraqi patrol. Then, he paused in his stride, raised two fingers in the sign of the "V" and whispered loudly, "Good luck, my friend. *Inshallah!*"

Moody watched helplessly as the freedom fighter disappeared over a dune. Moments later the staccato sound of automatic rifle fire, and the barking of a dog, tore through the night. An explosion—probably a grenade—shook the air; then another. Moody was torn between mission and friendship: go forward to the helicopter rendezvous, or go back to fight beside a friend.

He turned and raced southwest, toward the rendezvous,

knowing that the Kuwaiti was willing to give his life for the Special Forces soldier to reach the pickup point. After several minutes, the gunfire stopped. There was no sound of the dog, only the silence of the desert.

The Green Beret ran with all his strength, pausing only to check the map and look for references that guided his course: a series of oil wells.

When he reached the point of extraction, centered between three oil wells, he burrowed deep into the sand near the base of a dune, took his radio communicator, and spoke softly. "Green Arrow One, on the concourse."

He was amazed to hear a woman's voice reply, "Green Arrow One, this is Eagle Three Six. Inbound, ETA in five minutes. Sit tight."

Moody relaxed, staring at the flames rising into the night, licking at the darkness as though dragons spewing forth the fires of hell. There was no movement of workers or soldiers, which surprised him. The Army had picked one of the most unlikely spots the Iraqis would suspect for a helicopter extract: right in the middle of their front yard.

When the distinctive sound of rotor slap could be heard, he stood, waving his arms in the direction of the incoming chopper.

Through her night-vision goggles, Argonne detected the whitish signature of a human body. She was flying low, less than twenty feet above the ground, when she throttled down, eased the collective back, and lowered to a hover a few feet from the desert.

The cockpit door opened and the Green Beret slid into the seat beside Argonne. She instantly throttled up, kicked hard right rudder, and raced across the sea of sand.

Moody sat quiet for several minutes, then slipped on a communication headset. "Thanks. You got to my ass just in time."

"Quite all right. Are you OK?"

"Getting better by the moment. I didn't know women aviators flew this far beyond the border."

"Things change when necessary. Things change."

He sat back in the seat of the Kiowa and began to relax. His thoughts went first to his friend Mustafa. Then to the pilot. Her face was cowled in her helmet and he wondered if she was pretty.

37

The sun was rising behind the Kiowa as it approached
King Fahd Airport. The helicopter's shadowy image
stretched like a long finger across the tarmac as Argonne
eased onto the landing site. Moody felt the aircraft settle
gently, watched her hands deftly shut down the engines
and flight systems. When she removed her helmet, he
looked at her with a wide grin.

"My God . . . you're beautiful."

She was tired, but managed a slight smile. She studied
his face in the light. "You're not too bad yourself. By the
way . . . who are you?"

"Moody. Jerome. Special Ops. Major. You?"

She gave him her name and they shook hands.

He said, "Come on . . . but don't get too close. I can't
remember the last time I had a shower."

This made them both laugh.

An hour later, Moody had showered, dressed in his desert
camouflage fatigues, donned his green beret, and hurried

to the mess hall. Argonne was sitting off to herself; she still wore her flight suit and looked tired.

Moody went through the chow line, carried his tray to where she sat. "Mind if I join you?"

She motioned to a seat. He noticed she had not touched any of the food on her plate.

"Not hungry?"

She shook her head. "I'm afraid my stomach is still somewhere in the sky over Iraq."

Moody ate voraciously. "I never thought I'd actually relish army chow. But, this is better than what I've been eating recently."

She studied his features for a moment, then asked, "Can you tell me about it?"

"No," he said flatly. He checked his watch. "I have a debriefing in twenty minutes. Should take about an hour. Are you going to be here?"

"I have to return to base."

He couldn't mask his disappointment. "Just my luck. I get rescued by the most beautiful woman in Saudi Arabia, and I can't take her to dinner to show my appreciation."

She thought for a moment. "Do you have a way I can reach you?"

"SOCCENT. Here at Fahd."

She took a pen and wrote her unit phone number on a napkin. "I'll give you mine in case I can't reach you, but conversation has to be short and brief. I'm sure you understand."

"I understand. If you're not there, I'll leave a message." He took the napkin, and studied the number for a moment, and wrote down his number. "I don't know how long I'll be here. If they send me out, I'll contact you." He paused. "I know I'm moving a little fast . . . but, think you could get a few days' leave? I'd love to show you Riyadh."

She smiled. "You haven't asked if I'm married, engaged, or seeing someone."

Moody blushed. "I was afraid to ask." Then, he asked,

"Are you married? Engaged? Seeing someone special?"

"None of the above."

The Green Beret's face broadened into a grin. "That's the second-best news I've had since midnight."

"What was the best?"

"Your beautiful voice over the radio when you were picking me up in the desert."

She reached across and touched his hand. "I'm so glad I was able to get you out of there. I almost had to abort."

He looked at her quizzically. She explained about her copilot, then the Blackhawk.

Moody released a long sigh. His hand closed over hers. "I guess that means we were destined to meet."

"You're crazy."

"Certifiable. I'm Special Forces. Being crazy is one of the prerequisites."

Their eyes locked, hands gripped, but time was now the enemy. They left the mess hall and walked toward the flight line. He stayed with her until they reached the Kiowa, which sat waiting, fueled and ready. She preflighted the aircraft, slipped on her helmet, then turned to Moody.

"You have a good flight." He held up his wallet with the napkin inside. "I'll be in touch."

She saluted. "Yes, sir."

The whine of the engine, and rotation of the rotors made the air shudder; sand flew, but he stood his ground, watching the elegant craft lift off, bank, and race toward the north.

At cruise altitude Argonne set a course for base camp. She flew over the Tapline, but paid no attention to the hundreds of vehicles threading through the desert on the long highway. Her thoughts were on the next time she would hear the voice of Major Jerome Moody.

38

Lieutenant, if you ever pull a stunt like this again, you'll clean latrines until we deploy back to Fort Campbell! Do I make myself clear?" Major Whitpan's nose nearly touched Argonne's forehead; she could smell his breath. Raw. Hot. Angry.

She was braced at attention; the heat in the tent was nothing compared to the fiery wrath spewing from the chief of operations. "I can explain, sir."

"You damn well better give the Holy Grail of explanations, Lieutenant. You flew without copilot support, then you continued on the mission once the Blackhawk aborted. You were alone, without any air cover!" He was still in her face; his eyes burned until the blue looked like ice.

"I flew without my copilot because he was ill. I'm trained to fly the bird solo. You know that, sir. As far as not aborting, the Blackhawk pilot said headquarters approved me to continue. I did nothing wrong, sir."

"Why didn't you turn back? What if the 'Hawk had gone down? Those men were relying on your support."

"We had a Special Forces soldier waiting, sir. That was our mission. We were so close. I figured I could pick him up then catch up to the Blackhawk. If it had gone down, I would have been there in a matter of minutes to give air cover until Search and Rescue arrived."

Whitpan walked in circles around her, pulling at his chin. "That still doesn't excuse your actions. You got lucky. And luck is not what this fighting force works by, Lieutenant. Professionalism. Teamwork. That's the difference between winning and losing. Not flat-hatting all over the desert at night, by yourself, with no support."

"Yes, sir." She was not going to give ground. No matter the consequences. Considering the situation, she felt as though she had made the right decision and would stand by it.

Whitpan turned toward the tent opening. A stocky colonel appeared. Whitpan walked over to him and they spoke out of range of her hearing. Finally, the senior officer nodded and left.

Whitpan's voice lightened up. "There must be a God in heaven, Lieutenant. Or, at least one angel."

She didn't understand. "Sir?"

"The commander of SOCCENT just got off the horn with Colonel Cody. It seems that 'Sneaky Pete' major you rescued has recommended you for the Bronze Star."

Argonne's eyes lit up. "I don't care anything about medals, sir."

"Be that as it may, you've been recommended." He then added wryly, "You two must have had one helluva conversation on the ride back to King Fahd."

She couldn't contain the smile that spilled across her face. "It was most interesting, sir."

He lightened up further, but still in a steely voice said, "You pull something like this again, Lieutenant, and I'll eat you blood raw. Do you get my meaning?"

"Sir. Yes, sir. Air Assault!"

"Good. Now get some rest. I checked on your copilot. Massive dehydration. He would have been a liability on the flight. But no more shenanigans. I'm getting too old for this kind of shit. Dismissed."

Argonne saluted and left.

PART 4

TACTICAL ASSEMBLY AREA (TAA)

39

In December the division had deployed to several different sites along the Saudi-Iraqi border, in the event of an attack from Saddam's Hussein's vast army. 18th Corps was prepared to counterattack as more Allied troops were spilling into the country, taking up key positions to give the Iraqis a hot welcome should they cross the line.

Mock Iraqi positions were replicated; the troopers trained for day or night assault. Most of the training was at night, the reason twofold: the night temperature was more bearable, and, more important, there was no doubt that the ground war—if it came—would be fought at night whenever possible. The night-vision capability of the Allies was enormous in comparison with the Iraqis', which, for all practical purposes, was nonexistent.

Home was not forgotten. The camcorder, the satellite phone, and E-mail became priceless tools of the "technological soldier." Prior to approval from the Saudi government for the introduction of Western forces into the Islamic nation, certain ground rules were formulated. There would not be bars and brothels as seen in Vietnam; alcohol was prohibited completely. That, however, was

overcome by good old American ingenuity. It was said
that the highest stock on Wall Street was that of the com-
panies that produced mouthwash. A bottle of Listerine
looked innocent enough in a "care" package from home.
But, either unbeknownst to the mail operators, or inten-
tionally overlooked, more bourbon, scotch, and other libations reached the troops than mouthwash.

Further indicative of the necessity to satisfy certain
needs, sex was not out of reach. What was thought as
rumor was in fact truth, as a number of young women,
operating from the back of Humvees and other isolated
"boudoirs," literally made small fortunes practicing the
oldest profession known to Man.

Troops coming back from the FOBs (forward operating
bases) would find showers, hot meals, cots, and recrea-
tional facilities waiting. The soldiers acted like children
visiting Disney World for the first time.

Tempers often boiled over the tolerance level, and fights
were not uncommon, especially once the units deployed
to the rear area. Scores were settled out of sight, but not
on the line. Entrenched behind sandbags and knowing the
enemy was not too far away, the soldiers coalesced, shar-
ing food, drink, thoughts, and news from home.

Women stood the line along with men; guard duty,
grueling perimeter patrols—gender had no special treatment on the line, even in the latrines.

But the training continued for the day all knew was
inevitable: when the Allies took the fight to the Iraqis!

Mickey Martinson and the North Dakota National Guard
unit were always close to the line. Her unit was working
24/7, providing the most essential lifesaving commodity in
the desert. This made the unit a particularly important
target, but each man and woman accepted the risk as any
other soldier would.

Huge water bags, called "blisters," lay throughout the
inside of the perimeter near the Tapline highway. They

gave the impression of being monstrous slugs, beige in color, gleaming in the sun. From the air, they looked like boils on the desert sand.

One advantage the water-treatment detachment enjoyed over the other units was a swimming pool. A large bag had been formed into a makeshift swimming pool and sunk into the hard ground. Although the weather was no longer as hot as on their arrival, the pool was a focal point for the men and women of the 144th Quartermaster Detachment. It had essentially become an oasis in the desert.

Mickey was sitting by the "pool" wearing cut-off desert camouflage BDUs (battle dress uniform), listening to a tape from home. Above, helicopters raced through the sky; in the distance, on the ground, the steady drone of trucks ran northwest and southeast on the highway. She wore her hat down over her eyes, dozing in the sun. Her sunburned face highlighted her light hair.

Captain Crager approached. "Specialist, you guys have worked hard and haven't complained. I'm going to approve rolling R&R, send a group of four on two-day passes into Dhahran. You're on the list." She smiled. "Are you up for a break? Like to take a hot bath and enjoy some air-conditioning?"

Mickey snapped to attention. "Yes, ma'am." This was the best news she could have heard outside of a letter from home.

Crager envied the soldier. How she longed for a hot bath, clean sheets, and water with ice. Not to mention the air-conditioning. "Group up in front of the command post at sixteen hundred. You'll be requisitioned transportation, orders, and be certain you bring your weapons."

Mickey snapped off a sharp salute. At her tent she began stuffing personal items into a small nylon bag, including T-shirts, Levi's, tennis shoes, and makeup kit. There would be no dresses, since she didn't have one. The only thought she had was that she didn't have to sit in the sand for the next forty-eight hours.

An hour later she was in front of the CP, ready for her

first break from the conflict since arriving in Saudi Arabia. Three others soon arrived, and they piled into a Humvee, carrying their civilian clothes, M-16s, and duffel bags filled with combat gear and the always-required chemical gear. The vehicle roared out of the encampment and turned onto the Tapline. Music from Armed Forces Radio played from a transistor dangling from the rearview mirror.

"Here, Mick, take a bite of this." PFC John Olson handed her a plastic Listerine bottle. She took a long drink and passed it back to Ted Wolpers, a maintenance sergeant. He took a long pull and handed it to the soldier beside him, SP4 Nick Ruhland.

The scotch burned her throat, but it tasted wonderful. She wasn't a drinker, but she was too thrilled to give it another thought.

The ride to Dhahran would take several hours, and an hour into the trip the sun was starting to set, and the booze was taking effect. The four started singing with the music as the light began to fade and a silky dusk eased toward them from the east.

The revelry within the canvas walls of the "Hummer" increased as more plastic bottles surfaced. It wasn't until Olson suddenly hit the brakes that the group's full attention flew to the outside of the vehicle.

"Jesus," yelped Wolpers. He pointed to the left and the joyous laughter suddenly fell silent. All eyes were fixed on a brown, moving tidal wave of sand. None had ever seen such a spectacle.

Ruhland's voice was barely audible over the roar now filling the air. "It's a brownout!"

That was the nickname for the deadliest natural force on the desert—a *shamal*.

For the first time since arriving in Saudi Arabia, they felt fear. They were on a highway where the traffic was

practically bumper-to-bumper, moving fast in both directions, and they could barely make out the road.

And all knew there were no rest stops along the Tapline.

40

"Holy shit!" Olson yelled. "This is worse than a North Dakota blizzard!" The world outside had folded a dark, brownish cloud of sand around the Hummer. Inside, the four soldiers had put on their goggles and were using T-shirts and underwear to stuff the leaking spots in the canvas top where sand was flying through like piercing needles.

"Let's go to a blizzard drill," barked Wolpers, a potato farmer from Cavalier, North Dakota. He had been caught in dozens of wintry storms; this was similar, except the heat replaced the cold. "Pull off to the side. Get the flares."

Olson eased off the road, and feeling soft ground brought the vehicle to a stop.

"Light the candles, Mickey," Wolpers ordered. "I'll get on the horn to the command post." He took the radio microphone and reported the situation to the CP.

Martinson took two flares, and hugging the Hummer, she eased to the rear, struck the igniter, and stuck a flare into the sand. Then she went to the front and did the same. Olson was placing one in the sand beside the driver's door. The vehicle was now lit on three sides, giving some warning of their presence to approaching traffic.

The four sat and, as though caught in a blizzard, followed the number-one rule of survival: never leave the vehicle.

The steady groan of trucks gearing down came in steady bursts as the flow on the Tapline was gradually coming to a crawl.

"Damn fools," mumbled Ruhland. "Don't they know better than to keep going. The road will be gone in a few minutes. They could wind up driving for hours and not even be on the damned highway."

Wolpers sighed aloud. "All we can do is ride it out and hope they send out the snowplows. I've heard the drifts can get to be eight feet high."

The thought scared Mickey. "You mean we could get covered over?"

Olson shined his flashlight through the driver's-side window. Below, he could see a wall of sand that was building. "It's already over the tires."

They sat listening to the howling wind. As long as they could hear the noise, feel the buffeting, they would not be covered over by the sand. Soon they were sweating profusely. The men took off their T-shirts; Mickey soon followed, sitting there in her bra, perspiration spilling down her face.

"It's like a sauna," Olson groaned.

Ruhland reached to the rear and pulled out an emergency kit. Captain Craven had every vehicle loaded with MREs, a medical aid kit, flares, salt tablets, and water to last twenty-four hours. Ruhland removed a water bottle, took a swig, then passed it around.

"Nurse it slowly, children," Wolpers cautioned. "We don't know how long this is going to last."

Mickey laughed. "What a kick that would be . . . I can see the headlines: 'Water-transportation personnel die from thirst in desert storm!' "

The point had them laughing. "Yeah," chimed in Olson. "One Canuck cooked in Saudi sand furnace." He was Canadian, one of thousands of "neighbors to the north" who joined the American military. As in the Vietnam era, Canadians were given American citizenship upon completion of their first hitch.

Hours passed; the smell of MREs replaced the miasma of fear that had begun to swell inside the Hummer. An eerie quiet now prevailed beyond the confines of the vehicle. Then Wolpers said, "People, we've got trouble." He reached to the floor, lifted a handful of sand. Then he pushed at the roof, which appeared concave.

He shined the flashlight around the interior. "The sand is still sifting in through the cracks."

Ruhland poked gently at the roof. "I'd say we're buried over. Must be a ton of sand on top of us."

"Hit the headlights," Wolpers snapped.

Olson snapped on the beams, and there was nothing but blackness beyond the front windshield.

There was no hiding the concern. "We can't just sit here." Wolpers was breathing heavily. "We'll run out of air."

Mickey said the obvious. "We can't roll down the windows, either. The sand will fill in like water. We'll all drown in it."

"Helluva choice," said Ruhland. "Drown or suffocate!"

Their minds were churning. Finally, a thought from Wolpers. "Did you guys ever see that Chuck Norris movie, *Wolf* something? Or something *Wolf*? Norris was a Texas Ranger. David Carradine was the bad guy. He buried Norris alive inside his four-wheel-drive."

"Yeah." Ruhland said. "He fired up the four-by and drove right up and out of that grave. But, man, that was Hollywood. This is for real."

"And this is the baddest four-wheel on the planet," Wolpers countered. "If this baby can't push a few tons of dirt, we'll tell the Army to get our taxpayers' dollars back."

Again, silence.

"We don't have any choice, guys and gal. Unless you want to try and swim up through God knows how many tons of sand that might be on top of this vehicle."

"Give it a shot. If that fails . . . we swim," Ruhland said.

They all nodded. Wolpers patted Olson on the shoulder. "Turn over the engine." He looked at the others, saying, "If you ever believed in prayer, now's the time to shoot up your best."

There was a long pause; then Olson turned over the engine. They could not hear the sound, but felt the vibration coming through the firewall.

Nothing.

Olson tried again. More trembling, and then the RPM indicator jumped to idle.

"She's lit!" Olson said.

"Drop her in full four-wheel low and give it gas," Wolpers ordered.

Olson shifted into four-wheel drive, shoved the stick into Low, and hit the throttle.

"Just like in snow," Wolpers told him. "Get it rocking forward, then backward."

Olson began the process, first forward, then back. Forward. Back. Rocking along the longitudinal axis. The interior was filled with cheering voices, and without a visual point of reference there was no immediate way of knowing if they were moving or spinning their wheels.

Groaning, straining sounds came through the firewall and from the rear drive shaft.

"We're moving," Mickey shouted. "I can feel it!"

"Yes," Wolpers shouted. "Yes!"

The Hummer, the toughest four-wheel-drive vehicle on the planet, pushed forward, moving tons of sand, inching toward what no one knew.

"It's getting thinner!" Olson shouted. "I can feel it."

Before anyone could respond, the Hummer suddenly lurched forward. The headlights beamed through the black Arabian night.

The soldiers piled out, standing in air that now seemed chilly. They could not see the highway. In the distance, tanks, huge trucks, all equipped with Caterpillar blades on the front, were steadily plowing the road.

Mickey took a deep breath, then looked up and saw the most beautiful sight in her life: stars twinkling in the black heaven.

41

William O'Kelly sat at his desk at the *Army Times* in Springfield, Virginia, scanning the stories coming in from company reporters covering the situation in Saudi Arabia. He had to laugh at the constraints placed on the writers covering the "war." The pool was being force-fed with what the Central Command commanders wanted the people of the world to know. It did make sense, depriving the Iraqis of using a free press as an intelligence source the way it had been done in Vietnam. Now it was a whole different kind of reporting. Not everyone liked the new regimen, but there was no choice for the reporters. They were to be treated the same as the civilian press.

The commanders of the Allied troops were former junior officers during Vietnam, and saw the absurdity of allowing too much information to flow into the hands of the enemy. O'Kelly had personally been on patrols with camera crews from the various national and international broadcasting networks. While he did not doubt their courage, he often felt the journalists were more concerned with garnering a story than the risk their presence placed on the soldiers.

A civilian was a liability, not an asset. And the only thing they shot were their cameras. Not M-16s.

The greatest frustration facing reporters in Operation Desert Shield was the pool system. Essentially, the military had established a system of censorship that began during the Reagan Administration. In the Grenada invasion, President Reagan had banned reporters from accompanying American combat troops to the tiny Caribbean island during the initial assault phases. Later, President Bush refined the new policy during Operation Just Cause in Panama, by allowing a select number of reporters to cover the operations. However, they were limited to only those aspects of the overthrow of the Noriega regime that painted a positive image of American involvement.

Now, during Desert Shield, the military had refined the theory further: it was one of the finest media manipulations in the history of the United States military. Nearly two thousand reporters from scores of countries were covering the Gulf, but most had not even seen Allied forces except in the streets of Dhahran or Riyadh, or, if lucky, at one of the daily briefings allowed by General Schwarzkopf. What information was made available was disseminated by little more than a hundred handpicked reporters, most of those chosen because their publishers had long experience in Saudi Arabia before the invasion of Kuwait.

The PIOs—literally—became the censors of the war. Reporters able to conduct interviews did so under the tight-mouthed, steely gaze of the unit's public information officer. Usually captains or majors, their ubiquitous tape recorders in hand, they recorded every word spoken by the soldier, including name and rank. Reporters conducted their job with the hot breath of the PIO burning on their necks.

O'Kelly's thoughts were interrupted when Jack Daldrin stuck his head in his cubicle. "You got a minute?"

"Sure," O'Kelly said. He switched off the computer and twirled around his chair, facing his assignment editor.

Daldrin was a plump, rotund man, but one of the best reporters during the final year of the war in Vietnam. He was one of the last Americans to lift off the roof of the U.S. embassy as Saigon fell to the Communists. Tough. Articulate. Fair.

"What's up?" O'Kelly asked.

Daldrin flashed a big grin. "Your name has come up on the rotation to the Gulf. You're going to Dhahran."

"Good Christ!" O'Kelly groaned. "For what? There's no reporting going on in that part of the world. There's nothing but 'pooled' information coming directly out of Central Command. All we're going to get is what the PIOs want us to have. Might as well stay here and watch the whole war unfold on CNN."

"Sorry, Bill, you're next on the list. You leave in two weeks. Get your shots, passport, and your credentials in order." The editor left without another word.

O'Kelly's eyes roamed to the nylon bag sitting in the corner of his office. He hurried from the cubicle and caught Daldrin. "Reporters are assigned to specific units, right?"

There was a curious look on the editor's face. "That's right. You have something in mind?"

"Yes." He thought of Lieutenant Argonne Sharps. Here was his chance to kill two birds with one stone. Or, at least, not have the assignment result in a total waste of time. "I want to be assigned to the One-oh-first Airborne, you know, my old outfit. That might get me a chance to get closer to the troops. Hell. I'll even wear one of my old Nam jungle jackets with the combat patch."

Daldrin had to admit it might not be a bad idea. "I can't promise that, Bill."

"Come on, Jack, we're the *Army Times*, for chrissakes! Surely we've got a little pull within our own organization."

"Can't make any promises, but I'll see what I can do," the editor said.

"I've got some vacation time coming. I want to take ten days before I head across the pond. There's a personal matter I need to attend to."

"That shouldn't be too hard to arrange," Daldrin said. "Put in your request, I'll approve it. But be sure you get the shots and other things in order."

"No problem," O'Kelly said.

The reporter looked at the nylon bag and smiled. *Perhaps,* he thought, *I might get something out of this I can really use.*

42

The October heat was as unrelenting and brutal as the day the division arrived. But the nights offered some respite for the troopers of the Screaming Eagles, who were now deploying from Camp Eagle II into the desert at forward operating bases. The 101st's FOBs and other assault bases were arrayed on the western flank of the defensive line, preparing for a possible Iraqi counteroffensive.

The intelligence gurus had predicted that if the Iraqis did attack Saudi Arabia, the attack would come in a two-pronged offensive. The initial objective would most likely be spearheaded toward An Nu'ayriyah, a major location on the Tapline highway. This would cut off traffic moving west from Dhahran, and create a smaller pocket of fighting. It would also put the Saudi Arabian coastal docks in serious jeopardy.

The second prong, estimated to jump off following the day the offensive began, would be a flanking movement from the west, opening up the floodgates for possibly a half-million or more Iraqis to come streaming through. To blunt this plan, the Screaming Eagles were deployed into the desert, operating out of two FOBs: Forwarding Operating Base Bastogne, south of An Nu'ayriyah, and Forward Operating Base Oasis, west of Bastogne, and south of Qaryat al 'Ulya. The FOB received its name due to the presence of a nearby oasis visited by Bedouins. Division Commander Major General Binsford Peay II chose the name Bastogne for that FOB from the division's World War II heritage, and like the one in Belgium, the base sat at a crossroads that was vital to the defense of Riyadh and Dhahran.

Oasis was the most extended, and the most vulnerable, since it would essentially be trapped between the two prongs should a counteroffensive begin. The two initial objectives were to put in an airstrip, and begin training for what all believed would ultimately become a shooting war between the Allies and the Iraqis.

FOB Oasis, a ghost town with an interesting history, was an abandoned cinder-block and adobe village inhabited by abandoned camels, plus scorpions, snakes, and huge beetles. However, it was isolated, and the structures provided perfect replications of what was believed to be the very type of structures the Iraqis were building in their desert positions across the border. Should the U.S. cross the line, the troops would be familiar with the type of structures they would have to fight the Iraqis in.

The intense heat, rigorous training, and deprivation forced the three rifle brigades to rotate from the desert bases to Camp Eagle II, at King Fahd Airport, but neither was ever without constant military vigilance.

Hundreds of miles from King Fahd, the base at Oasis required an airstrip so that troops could be ferried to the location in hours, by air rather than days over what might only be a desert route if the offensive began and the Tapline fell into Iraqi control. Engineers discovered an airstrip abandoned decades before by oil explorers and quickly brought in the equipment to build a small airport that could accommodate the Hercules C-130, the all-purpose workhorse of the United States military and other Allied nations.

*   *   *

Flying into Oasis, Lieutenant Argonne Sharps thought she was approaching a makeshift runway on the dark side of the moon. Through her night-vision goggles, the earth was pockmarked with infantry positions; there was no light, not even a strobe at the airstrip. She could see movement on the ground; flashes from weapons etched the greenish night, and had she not known there were training ops under way she might have thought she was flying into a raging battle.

"Oasis, this is Six Gun. Permission to land."

The controller, operating from a cinder-block hut, cleared her for landing. As she worked the throttle, collective, and rudder, the Kiowa touched down lightly. She and Ohlhauser took their gear bags and walked into the flight operations center.

Neither could believe what they saw.

"Dodge City, Saudi Arabia," Ohlhauser said, flabbergasted. He could see huge beetles race across the sandy floor. "Camp Camel looks like the Marriott compared to this shithole."

"Home is where you find it, Monty." She had to struggle to try and sound optimistic.

The controller, a specialist, wore nothing but T-shirt, boots, and gym shorts. "Welcome to hell. Sir. Ma'am," he said dryly. He pointed out the door. "The officers' suites are on the other side of the airstrip. I hope you brought plenty of towels."

Both understood. The bugs were so thick the troopers slept with their faces wrapped to protect their eyes, mouths, and skin.

The controller checked a clipboard. "There's an ops meeting at zero-six-hundred. I'll wake you at zero-five-thirty. Welcome to forward base Oasis."

The two pilots picked up their gear and made the short trek across the runway to the small building designated for the pilots. The night was filled with the sounds of

M-16, M-60 gunfire, and the sporadic thunder of an exploding artillery simulator.

The place made Argonne shiver, the weirdness of the base was what she would have expected to find on the set of a macabre Hollywood movie production. Cots lined the wall, and she cared little about the privacy. She was tired and hot, and longed for a cold shower.

But that would not come until she returned to Camp Eagle II after the next rotation.

43

The training regimen was as brutal as anyone had imagined in their worse nightmare; however, the troops of the 101st were in top physical condition. The training at Fort Campbell and Panama was paying off where heat exhaustion was concerned. On her third day at Oasis, Argonne had fallen into the daily drill of training, more training, and sleep.

She had become accustomed to the black beetles, scorpions, and gargantuan flies that appeared as small black clouds throughout the camp. The heat index ran over one hundred degrees in the shade. Were it not for the water the war would have been over before the first shot could be fired.

Argonne was at the water supply point when one of the huge tankers arrived at Oasis that afternoon. She filled her canteens and water bottles and was starting to walk away when a voice called to her from the cab of the truck. She turned to face a young enlisted woman.

"Excuse me, ma'am." Mickey Martinson stepped down from the passenger side and saluted.

"Yes, Specialist. What can I do for you?"

Mickey nodded at the aviator wings on Argonne's flight suit. "You're a pilot?"

Argonne forced a thin smile. It was unusual to see women pilots in the desert, especially beyond the rear area. "Yes. I'm with the One-oh-one Aviation Battalion."

"May I ask what you fly?"

"A Kiowa."

"Wow." Martinson said. "I hear that's a bad bird."

"It is." Now there was curiosity in Argonne's voice. "Are you interested in aviation?"

"Yes, ma'am. I had my papers in for flight training through the North Dakota National Guard. I'd hoped to go to flight school after graduation this summer, but, along came this situation."

"What's your major?" Argonne asked.

"Nursing."

"Well, that's a great field for women aviators. Flying 'dust-off' missions, that sort of thing." The "dust-off" was the extraction of wounded soldiers from the battlefield. Her father had often said that the "Dusties" were the bravest soldiers in the Vietnam War.

"I know, ma'am. That's my goal."

"Have you had any flying experience?"

Martinson nodded. "I have a private pilot's license. Fixed-wing. But no rotor time. I've only been in a chopper a few times. Huey 1-Bs. Never even seen a Kiowa."

Argonne looked at her watch. "How long are you going to be here, Specialist?"

"A few hours."

"Do you know where the airstrip is located?"

"Yes, ma'am."

"Report to me in an hour. I'm not hard to find."

Mickey grinned broadly. She saluted. "Yes, ma'am. I'll be there in an hour. Thank you, ma'am."

Argonne walked away, suddenly noticing she was walking with a swagger. What the hell, she thought. It was rare that she received respect from soldiers she didn't fly with.

*   *   *

In what seemed like the longest hour of her life, Mickey hurried to the airstrip, where she searched the makeshift tarmac and the parked helicopters. She saw Argonne standing by the cockpit of a helicopter and assumed it was a Kiowa. Martinson hurried to her and saluted.

Argonne began with a general walk-around of the exterior of the aircraft, pointing out the features of the compact recon chopper. Then both climbed into the cockpit. Martinson was all eyes and ears, hanging on every word spoken by the lieutenant. The heat was grueling; Argonne wiped at the sweat streaming down her face while patiently explaining the functions of the various systems of the unique fighting machine.

"What will be important for our mission—should we get into a shooting war—is the night capability. That's where we have a definite edge."

Before another question could be asked by Martinson, the air suddenly shook with the heavy sound of rotor slap. Mickey sat frozen, her mouth agape as eight AH-64 Apache gunships suddenly appeared over the airstrip. Flying low, their sleek design gave her the vision of some prehistoric bird of prey.

"Oh, wow," exclaimed Mickey. "That is the most incredible sight I have ever seen."

Argonne agreed. "That's our version of the Navy's 'Top Guns.' Magnificent, aren't they?"

One by one the attack helicopters settled onto the tarmac. The tandem cockpits of the lead Apache opened and two men alighted. Both carried their helmets and nylon flight bags.

"That's Lieutenant Colonel Richard Cody," Argonne said to Mickey. "He's our aviation battalion commander." Both snapped to attention and saluted.

Cody, a legendary pilot of the 101st, smiled and returned the salute. "Good afternoon, Lieutenant." He nodded at Martinson. "Specialist. Are you ladies out here working on your tans?"

Argonne said, "The specialist is in the North Dakota National Guard. She wants to fly helicopters after she finishes college."

The smile on Cody's tough face reflected his pleasure at hearing of the enlisted woman's ambitions. "I wish you luck, Specialist. Who knows, maybe one day we'll get to fly together." He walked away, followed by the other flight officers, quickly disappearing into flight operations, where two armed sentries suddenly appeared at the main entrance.

Rumors are the lifeblood of the military, and the 101st was no exception. While no one except the high command knew for certain, Cody and his AH-64s had become the focal point of what many believed was to be a "top secret" mission.

Argonne had heard the whispers. She even knew of the hard training going on at FOB Bastogne—known as "Camp Hell"—where Cody had eight Apaches preparing for something the aviators knew would be very significant should the Allies lock horns with the Iraqis.

Finally, it was time for Martinson to return to her detachment's location. She and Argonne saluted, shook hands.

"Drop in again if you get back to Oasis, Specialist. Maybe I can arrange an observation ride for you."

"Yes, ma'am, and thank you, ma'am." She hurried toward the water point, not noticing that she was soaked with sweat.

That night, Argonne heard the engines of the Apaches begin their windup; then there was nothing but the noise of the attack helicopters reaching takeoff revolutions. She stepped out of her quarters and watched as each one lifted off and started north.

She knew initially that something was happening, and that whatever it was, the 101st Aviation Battalion would play a major role in it.

44

William O'Kelly arrived in Tucson, rented a car and drove east on the interstate until he reached Willcox, then continued north to Fort Grant, where he stopped long enough to lay flowers on the grave of a relative joined by marriage, not blood. Marcia O'Kelly had been his great-grandfather's second wife, who had been killed in a rock avalanche at nearby Mount Graham in 1885. Fort Grant was no longer a military installation, its grounds now used by the state as an industrial school for juvenile delinquents.

The main house sparkled from new paint, and a note on the front door said, "Mr. O'Kelly. I had to go to town. Make yourself at home. Dolores Sharps."

He had spoken with Dr. Franklin Sharps and Dolores the night before. General Sharps had kept his word and arranged for the writer to spend a few days at the ranch to further his research.

Rather than go inside, he walked around the grounds, through the stable, then noticed a small house near a thicket of cottonwoods. "Vina Gibbs's house," he said to himself, recalling something he had read in one of the journals. The cottage was neatly kept and fringed with desert flowers.

The most remarkable feature of the Sharps property was the cemetery. The moment he passed beneath the sabres, he looked up and saw the sun dance off the steel.

He wondered what they represented. Why four?

A white bench caught his eye. "Selona's Bench." He had read that in one of the journals. He sat down, facing the graves, all of which had potted flowers around the edge.

"Peaceful, isn't it?" a voice called from behind.

A handsome woman approached. She was wearing jeans, Western boots, Western shirt, and cowboy hat. "Quite peaceful." He stuck out his hand, walking toward her. "You must be Mrs. Sharps."

"Dolores," she said.

"I'm William O'Kelly. Bill. I believe General Sharps alerted you that I'd be arriving."

Dolores liked him right from the beginning. She and Franklin had not been reluctant to invite a stranger into their home simply because it had been suggested by her father-in-law. After meeting him, she realized how trustworthy were Samuel's instincts in other men.

"You must have a little bird dog in you, Bill," she said in a musical voice.

"Why's that?"

"You came to the most cherished part of the ranch." Her arm swept toward the graves. "Here lies the real legacy of the Sharps family. Heroes one and all."

He pointed to the sabres. She explained that each stood for a generation that had fought in a war for America.

Very impressive, he thought. And poignant, a focal point for his book.

They sat in the kitchen, where he drank iced tea while she had coffee. In no time he felt comfortable, as though he had been in the house before. In some ways, he reasoned, he had. He had devoured the journals and believed he knew as much about the Sharps family as anyone outside the family.

"A fascinating family history you have, Dolores. One of the most intriguing I have ever heard."

She beamed with pride. "Yes, it certainly is. I'm very proud to be a part of this family."

"I don't know if you're aware, but I'm going to Saudi Arabia soon. I hope to spend some time with your daughter. I think she's a fascinating part of your family history."

"Very much so. And like a mother, I'm opposed to any of my children going to war. Especially my daughter." She didn't explain, merely said, "You will meet a very special young woman."

"I'm sure I will." He recalled something. "You're from New York, I believe. I know how you and Franklin met, but I don't know about you and Adrian."

A sadness came over her face, but it faded quickly to an enchanting smile. "He was a handsome cadet at West Point. I was living in New York City, going to City College. I was working part-time at Macy's when he came in the store. His mother's birthday was coming and he wanted to buy her a scarf."

"And . . . ?"

"And . . . he was so polite and handsome. He was wearing his West Point coat and I found that quite impressive." She sipped coffee. "Everything sort of took off from that point. We were married the day after he graduated from the academy." A distant, vague look came upon her face.

He felt now that he was intruding upon the personal past of a love that was cut short.

She asked, "Which of the family members do you find the most interesting?"

"That's very difficult to answer. Each is so unique in their own special way. Of course, Selona is truly incredible. And the Sergeant Major is a man I'd like to have known. He served with my great-grandfather. I would like to have heard what he would have to say about the man."

He smiled, and added, "But, I think I know. They respected each other, and in my view, they were friends though it wasn't considered proper by military and social standards."

"What in particular did you find most interesting?"

He was quick to answer. "That is easy. When Samuel left for Tuskegee. He stopped at Fort Davis. I found that quite touching. It seemed to have filled a gap for him in his life."

She remembered.

45

*T*he first two days of Samuel's journey to Alabama had gone smoothly, the Arizona country seeming endless, as was New Mexico. He had spent the first night as he had the second, pulling off the highway, making a small camp, eating the food prepared by his mother, and sleeping beneath the stars on a buffalo robe given him by his father. The robe was old but in good condition, making him comfortable on the ground. Like the Sharps rifle, which he kept close at hand.

The third day he passed through El Paso, drove east a long distance, then turned south, off his original course, but a necessary detour nonetheless. He had made a promise to his grandmother, a promise as important to her as his trip was to him.

He reached Alpine, Texas, a small town in the Big Bend country east of the Rio Grande. There he stopped at a filling station and found an old man sitting in front. Samuel was quite amazed, for the man was of his race, old, with a weathered face. As the man began filling the gas tank he studied Samuel with a curious eye. He wore a red calico shirt with a green sash tied around his waist,

Apache style; Indian jewelry hung around his neck; and his hatband was of rattlesnake skin. He looked more Indian than Negro.

The man saw Samuel's curiosity. "You ain't from around here, are you, boy?"

Samuel shook his head. "No, sir. I'm from Arizona."

"Arizona, huh. I heard there was Coloreds living in Arizona." He thought for a moment, then asked, "Was any of your kinfolk a cavalry soldier?"

Samuel beamed proudly. "My grandfather spent thirty years in the Tenth Cavalry. He retired a Sergeant Major."

"Your grandpap, you say?" The old man hawked and spit, then said, "My pap was in the Tenth Cavalry. Course, I never got to know him. He was killed by Texas Rangers when I was just a papoose."

This caught Samuel's attention. "What was his name?"

"Private Winston Jackson. H troop. Tenth Cavalry. Killed right near Fort Davis, back in eighteen and eighty-two. Buried there at the fort, along with a whole lot of Coloreds. Mostly soldiers, but a few wives and children."

Samuel felt as though he had been swept back in time. He knew the man!

Not by acquaintance, but by the stories told around the fire in the cottonwoods. The stories told by Selona and Adrian, who had become the family historian, recounted the years the Sharps family served on the Western frontier. From Fort Wallace to Fort Sill, Fort Davis to Fort Grant; not a page in their family history left unaccounted. There was one he always especially enjoyed. The story involved murder, revenge, and flight to another country. But what made it most intriguing was a name so unique, the uniqueness itself caused the name to stick in his memory.

He took a deep breath and asked, "Might you be kinfolk to a man named Chihocopee? Chihocopee Jackson. The son of Juanita Calderon Jackson? I know he used to live in these parts. And your name is Jackson."

"There's lots of Jacksons in these parts. Especially over

in Brackettsville. There's a whole town of Coloreds over there."

Samuel had heard of Brackettsville, where descendants of the buffalo soldiers had chosen to build their own town. But he sensed something deeper; perhaps the place, the name, or the way he dressed. "Are you related to Chihocopee Jackson?"

The old man stopped pumping, then stared at Samuel; a long, penetrating perusal that made Samuel uncomfortable. "How would you know my name, boy?"

Samuel felt a wave of exhilaration. "When I was a youngster, my grandmother use to tell about when she and my uncles were with my grandfather at Fort Davis. She had a friend named Juanita Calderon, who married a soldier named Jackson. They had a son named Chihocopee."

Jackson laughed. "That's a Seminole Indian name, given to me by one of my great-uncles. His name was John Horse. He was an escaped slave from Georgia who lived with the Seminoles in Florida, then moved to the Indian Territory in the eighteen-fifties when the federal government put them and four other tribes on reservations. The Seminoles and their Colored friends came to Mexico after slavers started capturing and selling them to plantations in Arkansas and Louisiana. They made a deal with the Mexican government to patrol the Rio Grande and protect settlers from Indians. In return, the government gave them sanctuary. After the Civil War, many of them crossed back into Texas and served as army scouts. They was called—"

"Seminole Negro Scouts," Samuel blurted.

Chihocopee laughed. "You know your history. I'll say that for you, boy." He pulled the pump from the gas tank. "What did you say your name was, boy?"

"Adrian Samuel Sharps, Jr. Folks call me Samuel, after my grandfather. He served with your father in the Tenth. My grandmother is Selona Sharps. She and your mother were friends."

Like the past meeting the present, their hands were drawn to each other by a mutual history.

"Lord, have mercy," Chihocopee said softly. "I'd have never thought it possible. My momma used to talk about your grandpap and grandmam like they was saints."

"Not saints. But good folks. My grandfather died just before I was born. While my father was fighting in France during the Great War." He paused, then asked, "Whatever became of your mother?"

He smiled proudly. "After the 'incident,' she took me to Piedras Negras, across the Rio Grande from Del Rio. I grew up there with the other Coloreds. When I was thirty-four I went into the Army. I fought in France, myself. With the Ninety-Second Division."

"My father fought with the Ninety-Third."

"It is a small world, Samuel Sharps. A small world, indeed."

Then Samuel remembered the "incident." "Your father was murdered by Texas Rangers. Then your mother killed the one she thought was responsible, scalped him, then stole an Army horse and rode off with you strapped to her back. Word was she took you back to Mexico to live with her family. I don't remember the Ranger's name, but I know he had once done harm to my family."

Chihocopee chuckled. "Captain John Armitage." He pointed to the northeast. "He's buried up yonder, along with the Coloreds." He cackled. "I'll bet he's still rolling in his grave. Sleeping alongside all them Coloreds."

Samuel chuckled at the irony. "I would imagine."

Then there was a sadness on Chihocopee's face as he softly said, "My momma is buried there with my pap."

"Alongside him?"

Chihocopee shook his head slowly, as though remembering something important. "There wasn't room to bury him alongside her. I dug her grave on top of his. She's buried in the same plot."

Samuel released a long exhale. The thought was very touching.

Chihocopee looked at him wryly. "You want to go there?"

"To the cemetery at Fort Davis?"

Chihocopee nodded.

Samuel said, "That's why I've come here. To keep a promise to my grandmother."

Chihocopee rubbed his hands tightly, then said, "Let me lock up. We can be there in a few minutes in your car."

Chihocopee locked the front door of his filling station and climbed into the DeSoto. Moments later Samuel was driving toward the cemetery . . . to keep a promise.

The fort had been abandoned for decades; the parade ground overgrown with tumbleweeds; in the distance Samuel could see the dilapidated barracks buildings appearing like gray skeletons against the alkaline terrain.

They stopped where the road ended, at what was once the sutler's. Samuel remembered the stories of his grandmother starting her first cooking venture with Frank Conniger, who ran the sutlery. Her dream was to own a piece of land.

He took his Kodak camera and opened the trunk, where he removed the bucket and asked, "Where's the cemetery?"

Chihocopee pointed and they walked through the scrub brush, past ghostly houses once called Officers' Row, then to Suds Row, where the laundresses lived with their enlisted husbands. The adobe huts were now nothing more than small mounds surrounded by weeds, silent markers of the past, eroded by time and wind.

When they reached the cemetery at the base of Sleeping Lion Mountain, Samuel stopped suddenly. "I don't believe this, Chihocopee."

Jackson smiled proudly. "I did it all myself."

The cemetery was well kept; flowers were on many of the graves. The markers were painted and the ground cleared of weeds. A white picket fence framed the interred.

Samuel spoke with near reverence. "You should be very proud."

The two began a slow procession along the rows of graves. Some bore names while others were nameless, their markers the only evidence they once existed. Chihocopee stopped at the grave Samuel figured was Jackson's and Juanita's. There were bones of various animals spread on the top; flowers framed the grave and there was a coyote skull nailed to the wooden marker.

"My mother promised me to mark her grave in Seminole tradition," said Chihocopee.

They stood for a long moment; then Samuel looked around, noting that one grave stood out from the others. It was grown over, in terrible need of attention. To Samuel, it was like a weed in a flower garden. "Whose grave is that?"

Chihocopee laughed. "Captain John Armitage. He don't get much respect around here. But I didn't dig him up. That would have been spiteful."

Samuel began strolling again until he found what he had been instructed to find. Two wagon wheels were embedded into the ground; painted white, they appeared to have weathered decently. Samuel knelt and took the bucket and poured the red dirt of Arizona onto the alkaline dirt of the two graves.

"Do you know them?" asked Chihocopee, noting the name on the two wheels. "All I know is their name is Talbot."

Samuel nodded slowly. "I didn't know them. I only knew of them. They are my grandfather's parents. Their slave name was Talbot. My grandmother asked me to sprinkle some of the dirt from my grandfather's grave onto their graves. She thought it might bring their spirits closer together. They spent so little time together while alive."

Chihocopee said nothing. He understood. His parents shared a similar fate.

Samuel handed the camera to Chihocopee. "Would you take our picture?"

Chihocopee took the camera and snapped several photographs of Samuel kneeling between the two tiny graves. Then he rose and started looking again until he found another grave. The name was barely discernible, what with age and weather wearing at the wooden plank that served as the marker. But he could still make out the name of Miss Marie.

"Did your family know her?" Chihocopee asked.

Samuel smiled. "She was my great-great-grandmother on my mother's side of the family. She died not long after my grandfather was posted to Fort Davis."

Samuel knelt by the grave while more photographs were taken; then he rose and started to walk away. He was stopped by Chihocopee, who said gently, "Sometimes I sleep here at night. It's peaceful and no harm will come from these folks."

Samuel understood. "I think I'd like that. I doubt there's ghosts here that we have to fear."

Chihocopee grinned and pointed at Armitage's grave. "Only him, and he ain't said a word or roamed this ground since he was planted."

They laughed and walked together toward the DeSoto to get his gear.

That night they slept beneath the West Texas stars where their kin had slept six decades before, not knowing if they would see the sun rise should Indians, bandits, or Mexican revolutionaries attack the soldiers and their families.

Samuel slept near his grandparents on the buffalo robe, while Chihocopee slept atop the grave of his parents. Coyotes barked in the hills and mountains, and the sound of sidewinders twisting through the brush etched the still night, but they slept soundly, knowing that should there be a threat, they would be guarded by the ghosts of the buffalo soldiers.

46

Franklin arrived around nine that evening. He showered O'Kelly with apologies for his late arrival, explaining that he had been called in for emergency surgery. Now the telephone rang, taking the physician to his library. He motioned for the reporter to follow.

"That's wonderful, Edward," Franklin said. "I'll start preparing on this end, and wait for your call. I'll need a couple of weeks to get everything squared away." He hung up and looked at the writer; he was obviously pleased.

"Good news?" asked O'Kelly.

"Yes. Very good news." He leaned back in his chair. "Have you ever heard of Doctors for the World? It's a world health organization."

"I certainly have heard of them. Matter of fact, I reported on their work in Bosnia and Kosovo. A great outfit. Are you going to team up with them?"

"Yes. That was Dr. Edward Delaney. He's the international director. I've been approved to help out in Saudi Arabia."

O'Kelly could see that Sharps was excited. "I met Dr.

Delaney in Kosovo. He's a good man. Very dedicated, and your father said your daughter is stationed in the Gulf."

Franklin beamed. "Yes. She's a pilot with the One-oh-first Air Assault."

The writer said, "You know if there's a shooting war the Screaming Eagles will not only be in the thick of the fight . . . they'll more than likely be the vanguard."

"I know," Franklin said. "It's constantly on my mind. I can't seem to think of anything else unless I'm in surgery. Then, and only then, am I able to fully concentrate on something."

"How do you feel about women in combat? It's an issue that keeps surfacing."

"I don't see how our forces will be able to avoid the fact that women will be exposed to grave dangers." He thought of the war in Vietnam. "Most people overlook the fact that women have been killed in combat. Mostly from the medical corps, but women were also ferry pilots in World War Two."

"I don't think America will be too supportive if we start to see body bags returning filled with our daughters. It could turn the whole situation around," O'Kelly observed.

This put Franklin in deep thought. "In a way this issue has created its own potential monster. But one thing is certain . . . you'll never convince my daughter that any man is better qualified to fly in combat than her. She's one helluva pilot. And afraid of nothing."

"Which worries you?"

"It terrifies me. I know she would never back down from a fight. Especially one that involves our country." He went to a huge world globe, rolled it open to expose a bar. "Care for a drink?"

"Scotch. Straight up."

Franklin poured both a glass of Aberlour. He raised his glass to O'Kelly. "To family."

O'Kelly said, "It's good that our families have been re-united."

Another thought came to the physician. "Have you been to the cemetery at Fort Grant?"

"Yes. It was my first stop once I left Tucson."

Sharps looked a little uneasy. "The Grant cemetery isn't very well kept."

"I noticed that. My great-grandfather's wife's grave was overrun with weeds."

Franklin knew that. "We've tried over the years to take care of her grave, but it's been difficult."

O'Kelly sensed there was something on the doctor's mind. "Maybe my family could hire a private firm."

"How would your family feel about exhumation? Her remains could be buried here at Sabre Ranch. With friends she loved and loved her dearly."

O'Kelly had already hoped for that option, and surmised, "It's a great and serious idea."

Franklin enjoyed his honesty, and openness. "It's just a legal formality. One that can be easily overcome. There was talk by my grandmother of doing it back in the thirties, but she didn't know how to reach your family."

O'Kelly conceded to the goodness of a man whose family had taken one of his family to be one of theirs. "I'll contact my family. I doubt there'll be any objections. Some of them might even attend."

They shook hands. "Thank you for allowing me to come, Franklin. I will show the utmost courtesy and respect to your family heritage."

"I couldn't hope for more."

In the guest room, O'Kelly opened a journal and began reading. The setting was Fort Davis, Texas.

47

*A*t Fort Davis, Texas, in 1880, Selona Sharps was twenty-three and already stooped like an older woman of fifty.

She had been scalped when she was younger and wore a piece of buffalo hide as a wig, now tied tightly with a scarf, which gradually worked loose from the wind, and the heat of the laundry fires. Sweat ran from her forehead, until the hairpiece came to rest just above her eyebrows. She would pull the scarf back, resettling the wig, then hitch up her skirt and throw another piece of wood onto the fire burning on the dry, sunbaked West Texas ground.

The morning wind blew hot and dusty, wrapping around her tired legs and back as she stirred at a layer of white, gurgling lye soap foaming above the dirty clothes in the large iron kettle. She would pause from time to time and wipe at her forehead, then throw on more wood and step back as the froth hissed, then bubbled and popped against the heat of the day, which was nearly as punishing as the heat from the fire. Her long stick fished around the bottom, raised up a pair of sky blue trousers as another blast of hot dust swirled around the fire.

Looking down the line of boiling kettles on Suds Row, Selona could see the other laundresses buzzing about their kettles. At each of the eight iron cauldrons, the women held children, except Selona.

Nearby her two sons Adrian and David were playing beneath a pinion tree by a swing fashioned from rope and an old McClellan saddle.

Adrian was tall, with deep ebony skin, like his father. He was a quiet lad, prone to sit for long spells on the back porch, his eyes scanning the desert, in search of the many types of animals that lived not far from their house.

David was short, with cinnamon-colored skin, a mixture of Negro and Mexican, like his mother and father. He had been brought to Selona the night of his birth for her to raise after his mother died. The mother had been a young prostitute in a local "hog ranch," the father unknown.

During the summer the boys lived in a small tent in the back of the house on Suds Row, near the rabbit pens, spending their days scampering about half-naked like a pair of Apaches. They knew no fear, which terrified Selona.

She looked up as Vina Gibbs approached, pregnant with her fourth child. She had an armful of wet clothes and was wringing out the water with her powerful arms. She was a big-boned woman, the wife of Darcy Gibbs, Augustus Sharps's best friend and comrade in the Tenth Cavalry.

That was when Selona, out of the corner of her eye, caught movement in a thick patch of sage twenty feet away. She eased to a wooden box stationed near one of the kettles, all the while talking, but not to Vina.

"David . . . jump up in that saddle with your brother."

David knew what that meant and was in the saddle as fast as her hand went beneath a white cloth lying on the box.

"Lord have mercy!" Vina moaned. She, too, had seen the movement.

Selona's hand whipped straight out, steady, and with a smooth move she cocked the Colt revolver and fired at the motion.

The boom *shook along the Row, raced through the air, and ricocheted with dramatic echo against the caverns and crags of nearby Sleeping Lion Mountain, bringing Suds Row to a sudden silence.*

The laundresses looked up and saw Selona step beyond the pinions, knew everything was all right, and went back to work.

The boys watched as she hiked up her dress, Colt horse pistol still in hand, and walked cautiously now from clear ground into the thick sage. She would bend, look, then step again, all the while watching. There was nothing but silence as she squatted, adjusting her eyes to the brown sage, then suddenly hurried a few feet forward and reached with her free hand into a thick patch of sage.

The rattlesnake was four feet long, and would have been longer had the bullet not blown the head clean away. She raised up the rattler, smiled, and stepped back, walking as though stepping on stones to cross a brook, careful should there be more rattlers.

"Good shot, Momma," David said.

Selona grinned as she handed the snake to Adrian, telling him, "Put this in the root cellar. Later on I'll skin it, clean it, then wrap it in a wet rag." Then she whispered as though conspiring, "We'll have it for breakfast in the morning."

David snatched the snake before Adrian's fingers could take it and ran off toward the house with Adrian in hot pursuit. Selona called to them, "Don't tear up that snake . . . I'm going to make your daddy a hatband from the hide."

That was when she realized it was the first time she had thought about Augustus since waking that morning in her empty bed.

*   *   *

The sun beat down mercilessly, relentlessly, and there wasn't the slightest sign of life west of Fort Davis, beyond the Alamita River, which was nothing more than a small stream that time of year.

Nothing could live out here except hard men used to hard times, thought Corporal Augustus Sharps, 1st Troop, H Company, Tenth Regiment of Cavalry, as he led his horse at a walk. Now thirty years old, he had filled into a tall man, his facial features looking fuller within a ten-day growth of beard, the number of days he and his men had been on patrol.

Following in close trail were Private Darcy Gibbs and Trooper David Bane, a short, muscular young man who had been in the Tenth for two months; a "young soldier," as new recruits were called until they finished their first year of service. A third trooper was out front, scouting for sign of ambush.

Augustus took his canteen and halted his horse, removed his kossuth hat, and poked the top inward, forming a depression. He poured water into the depression, then held the hat to the horse. The horse sloshed the water, which Augustus tried to catch with his fingers. He licked the wetness, forgetting the horse's saliva that mixed with the water. Water was more important than any thought of germs. A man might die from germs; the same man would surely die without water. The horse as well, and all soldiers knew it was better to be thirsty and riding than to be a little sated and walking through the desert of West Texas. Then he took some buckshot from his pocket, shoved the lead pellets in his mouth, a trick he had learned to stave off thirst, and took a small sip of water.

"Tighten up," he ordered. The troopers tightened the cinches on their horses.

"Mount up." They threw their legs over the McClellans and settled their weary bodies into the saddle. Augustus led them out at a canter; sitting tall in the saddle, he could see a rising cloud of dust to the front. Beyond that he could see the Davis Mountains.

The trail of dust grew closer and through the rising waves of heat he saw the familiar figure of Trooper Gabriel Jones approaching. Augustus pulled up as Jones drew to a halt.

Jones wiped the sweat from his forehead. He pointed toward the mountains. "Nuthin' ahead. Just a sweet stroll into the fort."

"We'll water the horses at the Alamita, then push hard for Fort Davis." Augustus started to say something else, but his mouth froze. To the east there rose such a storm of dust the very size of the cloud suggested a lot of riders.

"Patrol?" asked Bane. He was eighteen years old and had not yet developed the ability to mask his fear. That took more than two months; more than two years. Sometimes, it never came at all to some troopers.

"Don't rightly know," Augustus muttered.

"Could be Mexicans. Or Injuns," said Gibbs.

"We'll sit a spell," said Augustus. He motioned toward an outcropping of rocks some twenty yards away. To Bane he said, "Take the horses at a walk. Nice and slow. Don't throw up any dust."

Bane took the link attached to the left side of his horse and snapped it to the halter ring of the horse to his left; the others did the same, then removed their Springfield carbines from their saddle boots. This joined the horses and Bane walked them behind the rocks and waited while the others selected a position in the rocks.

The boiling heat of the desert chapped their dry lips further as the dust drew closer; soon, they were able to make out the shapes of twelve riders.

"Ain't nothin' from a cavalry troop," said Augustus matter-of-factly. "The horses are many-colored." All the horses in a troop were the same color; this gave their comrades a means of quick identification.

Augustus eared back the hammer on his Sharps. The others did the same and quietly removed their pistols and laid them at their sides. Augustus took fresh rounds from the cartridge case and laid them on a rock. He adjusted

*the rear sight. "We'll take them at fifty yards . . . if they
be Mexicans or Injuns."*

The riders approached in a group and Augustus immediately eliminated the possibility that the riders were Indians. Indians generally rode in single file to deceive trackers of their numbers. That still left Mexicans, or any number of gangs of horse thieves and outlaws in Texas.

"Jason Talbot." Augustus breathed heavily, wishing the riders had been a threat. A physical threat. Jason Talbot, a local rancher, was more of a mental threat than physical.

Jason Talbot was the brother of the man who once owned Augustus and his family.

The buffalo soldiers stood, their Springfields resting on their hips, fingers lightly on the trigger.

Talbot, a tall man, slowed his horse to a walk and approached warily. His face was covered with dust; his gray mustache hung to his chin. His black diamond eyes were like banked coals; fiery, gleaming, even in the heat.

Talbot reined in his horse; the others, all white men except for one Mexican, sat quietly in their saddles while Augustus and Talbot talked.

"You niggers seen any men running a string of horses through these parts?"

Augustus felt the chill streak along his spine as he had many times before. He spoke calmly. "I'm Corporal Augustus Sharps. My last name used to be Talbot. Do you remember me, Mr. Talbot?"

Talbot's voice was chilly. "I know who you are. I remember when you was a pickanniny over to my brother's ranch." Talbot spit. "I heard you was wearing Yankee blue."

The buffalo soldiers looked uneasily at each other; then to Talbot, who was undaunted as he spit again. "I asked you if you've seen any men with horses."

Augustus lofted the Sharps onto his shoulder. He shook his head. The hell with this man, he told himself. Then he laughed. "Lost the trail?"

Talbot's face hardened. "You Army boys are supposed

to protect us ranchers from horse thieves and Injuns. Not doin' much of a job, are you?"

"We do just fine, so long as you folks stay out of the way and let us do our job." Augustus spit, which took all the moisture left in his mouth. But it was worth the dryness to see the look on Talbot's face.

Talbot wasn't a man to leave without the last word, especially if he could hurt a Colored man wearing Yankee blue. "I'm buyin' my brother's place. The crazy old fool has been evicted by the bank. I want you to know I'm going to plow the whole place under and plant cotton."

Talbot wheeled his horse and rode off without another word.

Augustus stood stunned; he thought he heard Gibbs cursing, but wasn't sure if he could hear anything except the great anger resounding from his very soul. His legs weakened for a moment; then he righted, squared his shoulders, and wiped at the perspiration clouding his eyes.

Or was it perspiration?

He took several deep breaths, then slowly walked to his horse, feeling the heat of the anger from his men. And he knew they still had a long way to go and there was nothing that could stop him from reaching his destination.

"Mount up. We've got a lot of riding," Augustus ordered.

"Hadn't we best move slower, Sarge?" asked Bane.

Augustus grinned. "Talbot and his men will have scared off anything that might be waiting for us."

The sun was setting when the patrol reached the Talbot ranch, but Augustus didn't ride directly down. He sat on a hill studying the large adobe ranch house, which was in sad disrepair, watching with particular interest the various cross-shaped gunports cut into the closed windows and door.

One port at the door was open; the barrel of a rifle jutted through.

When Augustus rode down, he rode slow, making certain they were seen in clear sight. Stopping at the front door, he spoke to the man he knew was holding a rifle trained on his heart.

"Mr. Talbot. This is Augustus. Do you remember me?" He always said that when he rode to visit the graves of his mother and father, knowing old man Talbot's mind now worked on a moment-to-moment basis.

The door opened and Talbot stepped out, wearing a tattered Confederate uniform. His left arm was off at the shoulder but Augustus knew he could still shoot a rifle.

Talbot eyed him for a moment; then in a wild, crazy voice that sounded like the wind, he shouted, "The bank took my ranch. I ain't got nothing no more. Now you it! It! I tell you."

Augustus spoke slowly, saying with a steady voice, "It's me Mr. Talbot, Augustus."

Talbot merely stared long and hard, then turned for the house, but paused at the door. "You was one of my nigras, weren't you?"

"Yes," replied Augustus.

Talbot's cruel voice barked, "I used to have a lot of nigras. Now the bank owns them." He opened the door, then called as he stepped into the darkness of the house, "Take them and be gone."

Augustus stepped down from his horse and took the blanket from his saddle and walked to the rear of the house. A small cemetery sat in hard open ground where wagon wheels half buried in the ground marked the graves of his mother and father.

Gibbs spread a blanket on the ground while Augustus and the others took off their blouses.

Then, beneath the scalding sun, the buffalo soldiers took their sabres and dug into the hard, bitter ground, performing an act no human being should have to perform.

*   *   *

The following day the small patrol rode into Fort Davis and after reporting to the orderly room, Augustus dismissed his men and went to his quarters on Suds Row.

When she saw him approach, Selona dropped the stick she was using to stir one of the washing kettles and raced toward him. As she neared she suddenly stopped, and looked peculiarly at the blanket and blouse tied to his saddle in two bundles.

He dismounted and she slowly stepped into his open arms and kissed him on the cheek. There was something in his eyes that was different, not like the times before when he returned wearing a big grin and swept her off her feet.

"I thought you would be here yesterday."

Augustus replied solemnly, "I had to go over to the Talbot ranch. Old man Talbot lost his land to the bank. His brother bought the land and said he was going to plow up the ground and plant cotton."

It took a moment before the reality made her eyes widen and she could only stand there and feel the depths of human shame. And the anger.

Augustus picked up the bundles and walked into the house.

Selona stood stone solid for a moment, then slowly walked into the pinions and sat beneath a tall cactus and wept.

That afternoon the heat was almost unbearable, but Augustus dug the two graves, smaller than any he had ever dug before, like a grave for a child. He took Gibbs's hand and was pulled out and faced the group of buffalo soldiers, the wives from Suds Row, and several officers from the regiment.

Chaplain O'Donnell stepped forward and read a brief prayer; then the remains were interred alongside the remains of scores of Negroes, many of whom who had died fighting to protect the white settlers and former slave owners of the Texas frontier.

Colonel Grierson took his violin and began playing "The Old Rugged Cross," joined by a few troopers of the regimental band. The voices of the gathering joined the music and for a long moment, on the edge of the violent frontier, the remains were given the decency the bodies had not known in life.

Slowly the group broke up, leaving only Augustus, Selona, and the children to their private moments.

"I never knew them, Augustus. They never knew their grandchildren. Never knew they would even have grandchildren. But you know what's the most hurtful?"

"What?"

"They didn't even have a piece of ground where they could be buried and rest in peace."

Augustus walked off, stooped at the shoulders, followed by the boys.

Selona visited Marie's grave, as she did every day, and had brought along a gourd of water for the flowers she planted each spring. The grave was marked by a white board bearing Marie's name and the year of her death; there was no year of birth, since Marie hadn't known it.

"Well, Grams, you finally got your piece of land," she whispered.

Some piece of land! Six feet deep, two feet wide, and six feet long. A flood of memories rushed as she thought of the craggy little woman.

"You got me that husband, and we've got children, but there's no piece of land in sight. I don't think I'll ever own any more land than what you've got, Grams."

How in the world could Colored people save enough money on Army pay to buy land?

But it was her dream, one Selona felt gnawing at her with more intensity with each rising of the sun. As though Marie would never rest in peace until a part of the earth belonged to her.

"I'm going to own me a piece of land," she whispered.

"Someday me and my family's going to have our own land. I don't want to be buried in some lonesome place like Momma, you, and Daddy. The children never knew any of you. Won't know what you looked like. How you sounded."

She sprinkled each of the flowers lightly, then stood and started back to her kettles on Suds Row.

When O'Kelly switched off the light on the nightstand, his thoughts went to the graveyard, to the eternal piece of land owned by the Sharps family matriarch.

48

Argonne was awakened from a frustrated sleep at FOB Oasis. The orderly told her, "There's a telephone call for you, ma'am." She slipped on her sneakers and hurried to the orderly room. From the Special Forces compound at King Fahd Airport, Jerome Moody could tell she had been sleeping. "Did I wake you?"

"Yes. We had training ops until sunrise." She checked her watch. It was nearly nine in the morning.

"Any chance you can get a break?" Moody said.

"What do you have in mind?"

"Come to Dhahran and we'll go out to dinner."

"Let me see what I can do. I'll get back to you in a few hours." She hung up, and since the heat was already sweltering, she took a shower and went to the operations center. Major Whitpan was studying a group of maps as she approached.

"Good morning, sir." She stood at attention while his eyes slowly scanned the maps.

He nodded. "Couldn't sleep, Lieutenant?"

"No, sir. Too hot." There was a long pause. "Sir, I'd

like to request a few days' leave. I have a friend I'd like to see at King Fahd. He's in Special Forces and I think he's about to go on another mission."

The major wiped a handkerchief across his face, blotting the sweat from his forehead. "This is a forward observation base, Lieutenant. You know there's no leave until the rotation is complete."

There was no hiding her disappointment. She started to about-face when he said, "However, there is a favor you could do for me that would take a couple of days in Dhahran."

Her face brightened. "What do you need, sir?"

"There's a congressional delegation arriving tonight on a fact-finding tour. One thing they want to be briefed on is the 'female thing' in this theater. You'll be accompanied by a public-information officer and give them a tour of Camp Eagle. You know the drill. Laugh a lot and say very little." Whitpan smiled wryly, then added, "That ought to allow you the opportunity to spend some time with your gentleman friend."

Operation Desert Shield had thrown women into the limelight, since thousands were in the desert preparing for the possible shooting war all felt was inevitable. Congress was keeping a critical eye on the "female thing," fully aware that an attack by the Iraqis could find American women in the thick of the fight. It was an issue as sensitive as any in the theater of operations.

"The fact I'm a black woman doesn't enter into the equation, sir?" Now it was Argonne's turn to be wry.

"It doesn't hurt, Lieutenant. I'll get on the horn and see if I can get you approved. The fact that you have flown into Iraq to extract an American soldier does help your case."

"How long before you'll know, sir?"

"Give me an hour. No promises, but it could work out for you."

She saluted and returned to her tiny quarters. The

minutes ticked away interminably until it was time to report to Whitpan. She found him at his desk wearing a
Cheshire grin.

"Gear up, Lieutenant. You've been approved. But remember, this is an assignment, not a vacation."

"I know, sir."

She called Jerome Moody. Twenty minutes later she
was aboard a Blackhawk making one of the many daily
runs to Camp Eagle II.

49

Argonne Sharps reported to the public-information officer at Camp Eagle II, and to her surprise found Jerome Moody. He extended his hand. "This must be my lucky day. I never thought it would be possible to get together."

"You made it sound urgent."

Moody glanced around; the office was manned by a specialist who was on the telephone. He guided her through the door and into the blazing heat. "I can't say much, except that I will be leaving in three days."

"Back to Kuwait?"

"Sorry. I can't discuss it. I hope you understand."

At that moment the specialist said, "Lieutenant Sharps, you can see Major Wilson now."

She looked at Moody, and said, "I don't know how long this will take. Why don't you go to the officers' club. I'll join you there when I'm done. I'll call on the way out."

He took her hand. "I'll be waiting."

Major Barry Wilson sat behind his desk, reading from a single sheet of paper. "Have a seat, Lieutenant."

Wilson was quick to get to the point. "Lieutenant

Sharps, I'm sure you know that the political front is as important as the combat front."

She nodded politely, although to her, politicians were more of a royal pain than a necessity.

Wilson continued, "I read the report on your mission into Iraq. Most commendable. The fact you are a woman—and African-American—makes this assignment all the more important."

She bristled slightly. "I don't think either is important, sir. I'm a soldier. I do my duty to the best of my ability."

Wilson let the comment go. "I see Major Whitpan has put you in for a citation. Most commendable. And, very significant for this assignment."

He leaned back in his chair and perused her for a few moments. "Public opinion is always a major factor in a war. How we are perceived in the field is as important as our readiness to fight. You can be a great help during this assignment. One of the congressmen—rather, congress-woman—" He paused, shuffled through some papers. "Congresswoman Hart, from New York, is a strong ad-vocate of women in combat. Be advised, she will try to play you for all it's worth. You know the military's policy on this matter. Answer what you can, but don't offer up any personal views. Is that clear?"

"Very clear, sir."

"The delegation is billeted at the Dhahran Interna-tional. At the airport. You and several others selected for this assignment will be billeted at the same hotel." He grinned. "Have you been to the International?"

"Haven't had the pleasure, sir. I've been in the field practically every minute I've been in-country."

"Then," he said, "you can look forward to two luxu-rious Arabian nights." He handed her orders for the assignment. "I'll be there myself. We'll meet in the dining room at seventeen hundred hours. You've been requisi-tioned a Hummer." His voice dropped to a near whisper. "You know the situation between the Coalition and the Saudis regarding women."

"Yes, sir. Their culture is very clear on the role of the woman."

"Prehistoric, I admit, but, it's their country. They call the music. However, the International does have a looser atmosphere."

"So I've heard, Major."

He stood and extended his hand. "I'll see you for dinner. Wear your Class-As."

She saluted. "I will, sir."

Major Jerome Moody sat anxiously at the bar, his eyes fixed on the front door. When he saw her enter, he was out of his chair in a flash. She sat on a barstool and began waving her hand in front of her face.

"Oh, my God. I had almost forgotten what air-conditioning was like."

"How about a cold drink?" he asked.

"Orange juice will be fine."

He ordered two glasses; the tinkling of the ice in the glasses made her smile. "I almost feel guilty. My comrades are burning up in a snake-infested hooch and here I sit in a cool room drinking cold orange juice."

He tapped his glass to hers. "Don't feel bad. You've earned the break." There was a question that hadn't been answered yet. "Why are you here? I know it's not leave time you're on."

She explained the situation with the congressional delegation. "They want to trot out a woman. A black woman at that. I'm supposed to conduct myself like a good little girl. Polite. Quiet. Don't make waves. You know the Army, say all the right things or say nothing."

Moody said, "I don't know you that well, but I would hazard a guess that will be impossible."

"Just ask my father. He always said I was the outspoken one in the family." She drank some juice. "What is your situation? How much time do you have?"

"Three days, but I have to report back tomorrow night at midnight."

Argonne found Moody exciting and special. She was not going to play coy. In war, there is no time for shyness and silliness. "Can you get off base?"

"I can get some time off, but I'll have to stay in touch with my unit. I could be called back at the drop of a dime. There's a lot going on right now. You can feel it in the air. It looks like this situation is getting close to coming to a head."

She understood and told him about the hush-hush operation going on with the Apache helicopters she had seen at FOB Oasis. "Come to the International with me. You can join us for dinner, then we can take it from there."

"Take me to my billet. I'll throw my gear together. Dhahran Airport is about an hour away," he said.

They left minutes later. The clock was ticking and time was against them.

50

* * *

Arriving at the International was similar to going from Hell to Heaven. Ornate decorum, personalized service, air-conditioned rooms, the elegance designed for royalty. Both found rooms on the same floor. Moody had the first suggestion on arrival: "Let's get our gear unpacked and go swimming."

Argonne had other plans. "Not so fast. I've thought of only one thing since we arrived in September."

"What's that? Moody asked.

"A hot bath. I want to soak for an hour, and scrub all the sand out of my pores. Wash and dry my hair. Get a manicure. But first, I'm going to buy some trinkets at the gift shop."

Moody could see there was no persuading her otherwise. He said, "OK, but when you're ready, give me a call. I'll be by the pool. Capisce?"

She squeezed his arm, and started toward the gift shop. She didn't see him go to the front desk and talk quickly to the hotel manager.

*   *   *

Nearly an hour had passed when she reached her room. The view from the balcony was stunning; the desert met civilization before her eyes. She pulled back the spread on the bed, ran her hands along the cool, crisp white sheets, fluffed the pillows, and dove headlong onto the bed, feeling as though she had landed on a cloud.

She called the front desk, requested laundry service and a pitcher of iced tea. Then she opened her bag and removed her only full-dress uniform. It was wrinkled, but she knew it would look pristine for the evening.

In the bathroom, she opened up the spigots in the large tub and cracked the seal on a bottle of newly purchased bubble bath. She poured, then laughed as the bubbles foamed quickly, and was about to toe-test the water when a knock came at the door. She opened it to find a bouquet of roses in the hands of one of the hotel employees.

"For you, mademoiselle. From a gentleman."

She took the flowers, gave him a tip, and handed him the laundry bag with her uniform and a pair of low-quarter shoes. "Do you have shoe-shine services here?"

He nodded politely, took the bag and shoes, and left.

In the bathroom, the tub was overflowing with bubbles. She stripped and stepped into the water.

The tingle of the bubbles, sting of the hot water, and the sound of soft music playing from the radio on the nightstand made the moment perfect.

For the first time since leaving Fort Campbell, she felt luxury.

At four o'clock, Moody was waiting anxiously by the pool, waiting for Argonne's call like a young boy on his first date. Moments later he saw her approaching along the edge of the pool.

She didn't walk; rather she appeared to glide, like an ebony goddess, her hair sparkling like black diamonds in the Arabic sunlight. She wore a complimentary robe supplied by the hotel, as did he. Her facial makeup was not heavy, and he could see she didn't need more than her natural beauty. A light coat of pink lipstick highlighted her lips.

"Hi, soldier." She winked at him. "Want some company?"

Before he could say a word, she tossed the robe aside and stood in a pink two-piece swimsuit that fit her body like a second skin.

Moody said nothing; he could barely breathe.

51

Congresswoman Rachel Hart was more beautiful than she appeared on television, thought Argonne. She was tall, ebony-skinned, lithe, with the movement of a high-fashion model. She wore a poplin jumpsuit and hiking boots, and looked ready to trek into the desert aboard a camel.

In her crisp Class-A uniform, Argonne approached the stunning woman. "Good evening, Congresswoman."

The politician eyed her carefully. "Good evening, Lieutenant." She motioned to the two men sitting at her table. "I believe you know Major Wilson."

Argonne nodded at him. "Good evening, sir."

The PIO raised a glass and said, "You look refreshed, Lieutenant."

"Very refreshed, sir." She turned her eyes to the other man. He wore a business suit, appeared too large in the neck for his shirt.

Hart introduced the man. "This is Congressman Dilford. He's a part of our congressional fact-finding team." She smiled wryly. "He doesn't like the heat."

"God-awful heat," Dilford moaned.

"So we've found out, Congressman." Argonne turned to the man standing beside her. "This is Major Jerome Moody. Tenth Special Forces. I hope you don't mind that I invited him to join us for dinner."

Hart motioned them to the table. "Not at all."

During the dinner the talk was mostly time-killing conversation, with the three soldiers being careful of every word spoken in regards to their current mission. Finally, the congresswoman zeroed in on an issue of particular interest to herself. As expected, her focus was on Argonne. "Lieutenant Sharps, as a woman in a combat theater, what are your thoughts on women being excluded from combat?"

"I don't think it matters one way or the other, ma'am. Gender seems to be important to those who aren't going to be near combat. Those of us who feel it is our duty have nothing to say about the issue."

"Would you clarify your answer, Lieutenant?" Dilford asked smugly.

"Be glad to, sir." She had expected this from the moment she left FOB Oasis. "I joined the military to serve my country. Not for my country to serve me. Before I attended West Point, I felt that women can handle any combat situation presented to men. That includes physical hardship, stress, and the daily rigor of military life."

"Even fighting men who might be larger than you in size?" asked Dilford.

"Size doesn't mean a thing to a well-equipped, highly trained soldier. Regardless of gender. The only difference is that a bigger person might take just a tad longer to hit the ground after he's shot by a small woman."

Congresswoman Hart laughed heartily. Even Wilson was obviously pleased by her answer, and Moody broke into a large grin.

Dilford wiped a handkerchief at his forehead. He didn't appear amused. "What about the more brutal aspects of war, Lieutenant?"

"Nothing can be more brutal than combat, sir," she replied.

He shook his head. The heat, and her coolness, was raising his irritation level. "You know what I mean. Rape! If our women are captured you can be damn sure they'll be physically sexually abused in the most horrible ways."

She was fully prepared for the question. "Of course they will. But Congressman, rape and sexual abuse is not a special treatment by the enemy that is reserved for women. In most wars, especially in the Middle East and Asia, men who are captured are systematically raped. It's no secret the Russians did it to German men—soldiers and civilians—for revenge for the rape of Russian soldiers and civilians. It's another tool in subjugating, breaking down the resistance of the captured soldier. Our pilots were raped in Vietnam periodically to break their will."

"That's absurd," stormed Dilford.

"I'm afraid she's correct, Congressman," Moody said.

Dilford stared hard at the Moody. "Would you, as a man, allow that to happen to you? My God, you're a Special Forces soldier. You'd fight to the death before you'd allow that sort of treatment."

Moody's eyes were unflinching. "I like to think I would. But the reality of war doesn't always offer a soldier the option. Wounded. In pain beyond imagination. There's no control in some instances."

The congresswoman asked, "How do you feel about women in combat, Major?"

He looked at Argonne, and without a note of apology in his voice, said, "I'm opposed. We don't need to send women into battle. Look at Israel, other countries. They have women in uniform who serve an important—but, noncombative—role."

"Roles?" Argonne said icily. "What do you think our role should be, Major? Women are *tired* of *playing* roles!"

Wilson finally came alive to head off the confrontation. "Lieutenant. Major. I think your views have been heard."

It took all of Argonne's strength to hide her feeling of betrayal.

She stood. "Excuse me. I think I could use a breath of fresh air."

Moody sat looking foolish; Dilford was enraged; but, the Congresswoman wore a smile of victory.

In her room, the phone rang continuously, as though set on automatic, yet she refused to pick up the receiver. Only when there was a soft rap at the door did she move from her bed, where she had sat simmering since leaving the dining room. She went to the door and opened it slightly, and saw a young Arab man holding what appeared to be a dozen roses.

The words on the card had been written hurriedly, saying, "Please open the door."

Argonne thought for a moment, then went to the door of the adjoining room.

"I'm here and unrepentant," Moody said.

She motioned him to enter.

It was the first time she felt his strong arms around her. They kissed lightly, then with more passion. He picked her up and carried her to the bed.

That night, the two sat on the balcony overlooking the swimming pool. The moon shone brightly; stars filled the sky. It was perfect, thought Argonne. But she knew it was like living on the edge of the Earth.

"When are you leaving?" she asked him again.

He noticed the edge in her voice. "Tomorrow night."

"I had hoped we would have more time together."

Moody rose and leaned against the railing. "Maybe you don't want to spend too much time with me. We are in a bit of a quandary here."

"Men and women have formed relationships before

during times of war. I don't see any reason that we should be any different." She paused, then added, "If you are of the same mind."

"I am. But, you know the risks involved. I can't even guarantee that I'll come back alive."

"I'm not looking for guarantees. I just want to be certain of your emotions."

"My emotions are solid. You're the only person I want in my life."

She stepped to him, kissed him lightly, then started unbuttoning his shirt. "In the meanwhile, let's make the most of the time we have left before you have to leave."

52

William O'Kelly had immersed himself in the Sharps
family history, gleaning the story through the journals and long discussions with Franklin and Dolores, and
he had even felt a spiritual connection with their ancestors. Now it was time to return to Washington, and prepare for his trip to Saudi Arabia.

Since he had an early flight the next morning, he
planned to leave shortly after noon for the drive to Tucson. Dolores had prepared a picnic lunch, and the three
sat under the cottonwoods at a long wooden table.

A light wind rustled the tops of the trees, and the temperature was mild, a perfect setting for his last day.

"It's certainly been a pleasure having you for a guest,
Bill," Franklin said with a tinge of sadness.

"It's been a thrill, one I will always cherish." He
checked his watch, glanced down the road.

"Mr. Crowley said he'd be here shortly after noon,"
said Franklin.

"Come on, let's eat." Dolores was holding a large bowl.
"This is the Sharps favorite family meal. Rabbit stew. The
recipe was invented by Selona back in the late eighteen-

hundreds." She began dipping portions and passing the plates. Boiled ears of corn, fresh home-baked bread, and an apple pie filled out the menu.

"When will you be leaving for Saudi Arabia?" asked Dolores.

"In about a week," O'Kelly said. "There's a lot to do before I leave."

"What about the book? Any idea when you'll get started on that?" asked Franklin.

"I'm going to start on the outline when I get back. There won't be much time for anything else. But I think once I get to the Mideast I'll be able to spend some time on it each day." He glanced to the road. "What about you, Franklin? Any idea when your group is leaving?"

"The first group leaves next week. The advance team. My group will follow near the end of November."

"Then you'll be home for Thanksgiving."

"Yes. That's a big day for our family." He looked at Dolores. "I'd be risking life and limb if I wasn't here for that holiday."

"Bad enough you might not be here for Christmas," Dolores said.

"I'll be here. Maybe Argonne can come too." Franklin glanced toward the road. "Here comes Mr. Crowley."

All turned to see a black hearse approaching. The vehicle pulled into the front, where two men got out and walked toward the cottonwoods.

Frank Crowley, in his fifties, wore a Stetson hat, Western boots, a dark suit, and a string tie. He looked nothing like the morticians of the Old West. With him was Lloyd Bentson, a minister at the Baptist Church of Bonita. He was tall and gangly, with a pronounced limp.

Franklin and O'Kelly approached and shook hands. The five talked at the table while the noon meal was finished.

An hour later the men stepped to the rear of the hearse. Inside, a copper coffin rested on metal runners. The undertaker released the securing fasteners and slid the coffin into the waiting hands of the others. Followed by Dolores, the pallbearers carried the coffin to the cemetery, where a freshly dug grave waited.

The remains of Marcia O'Kelly had been brought from the graveyard at Fort Grant for this, her final resting place. Boards lay across the grave, the casket placed squarely, then ropes ran under and over the copper coffin.

Reverend Bentson read from the Bible and without further ceremony, the casket was lowered. The men shoveled dirt into the grave until it was filled, and patted the soil with the flat of the blades.

For William O'Kelly it was not as somber as he had anticipated. He had done what he thought was the right thing: seeing to the proper resting place of a distant relative.

When the funeral was over and the hearse departed, the reporter loaded his rental car and prepared to leave.

"Safe journey, my friend," said Franklin, his hand extended.

"And you as well. I'll stay in touch and keep you informed. I'll look you up in Saudi Arabia. I'm looking forward to meeting Argonne."

He kissed Dolores on the cheek, then slid into the driver's seat. At the front entrance he stopped for a moment beneath the shiny cavalry sabres. He glanced back through the rearview mirror, saw the Sharpses on the porch, waving farewell.

PART 5

LAST FLIGHT

53

As Thanksgiving neared, Dolores knew there was no dissuading Franklin from joining the volunteer physicians preparing to leave their lucrative practices to travel to Saudi Arabia. It was easy for her not to complain once she accepted the fact that he had made a commitment. With that, she set about making certain that their days before his departure would be spent in a comfortable setting.

She made a call one afternoon to Virginia. "Hi Poppa. How's the weather in the D.C. area?"

"Cold," Samuel Sharps said.

"How would you feel about coming here for Thanksgiving? It'll be much warmer than in Alexandria. The children will be here and it'll give you the opportunity to spend some time with Franklin before he goes to the Middle East."

"That sounds like a wonderful idea. When is he leaving?"

"Around the first of December," she said. "His team will meet in New York and fly directly to Saudi Arabia."

"How do you feel about this trip he's making?"

There was no hiding her concern. "I'm not thrilled one bit. Especially with all this talk about the possibility of chemical or nuclear warfare. But, you know how he is when he sets his mind to something."

Samuel knew all too well. "I think he gets that from his mother."

Dolores chuckled. "I doubt that's the only person he gets it from."

54

Franklin eased back the throttle of his aircraft, set in flaps, and descended for the final approach at his airstrip at Sabre Ranch. He pressed the switch to lower the landing gear and listened for the electrical whir, then the thump of the wheels locking down. There was no whir, only the steady drone of the engines. He tried the gear switch again. Once again, there was no sound of the gear going down to the locked position.

Damn! Then the engine went silent. Franklin quickly grabbed the microphone and declared an emergency over the radio. His mind tuned in to the mental discipline of preparing for a possible crash landing. He trimmed up the nose and held the aircraft at an airspeed above stall and began looking for a spot to land.

The rugged terrain offered little opportunity—he was too far from the ranch. His only choice was a dirt road. Working the controls, he guided the aircraft toward the earth, his breathing heavy but steady.

When the airplane touched down, the sounds of the props tearing into the ground and the undercarriage making contact was ear-shattering. A cloud of dust boiled up, he heard the sound of shattering glass, felt a hot, searing pain through his upper torso.

The Cessna came to rest near a clump of cactus.

Franklin, his eyes clouding, sat motionless, pinned to the seat by a piece of the sheared propeller that speared his chest.

55

Argonne had been at Camp Eagle II three days, getting a needed breather from the relentless training at FOB Oasis. Every bone in her body ached; she felt as though she had aged twenty years. At least, she thought, climbing into her bunk, it had kept her mind off Jerome Moody. There had been no word from him in the several weeks since his return to Kuwait City.

She was about to drift off to sleep when a young enlisted woman entered her tent.

"Lieutenant Sharps, there's an emergency phone call for you in the orderly room."

Argonne pulled on her gym shorts, sneakers, and T-shirt. Each step of the way she was haunted by the terrible thought that something had happened to Jerome. She spoke nervously into the TACSAT telephone. Unexpectedly, the voice of her mother came over the satellite linkup.

"Argonne, I have some terrible news." Dolores explained the circumstances of the airplane crash and death of her father.

The words crackling from the other side of the world numbed her to the very core.

"Did he suffer?" were the only words she could utter.

"No. He died instantly."

She felt the orderly room begin to spin; the phone fell from her hand as she collapsed into a chair.

When Argonne regained consciousness, she was staring into the face of Whitpan. He was holding a wet towel to her forehead. "Sit tight. You fainted."

When she recovered her senses, she looked at the TAC-SAT telephone. "May I call my mother?"

"I told her what happened. She is waiting for you to return her call." He turned to the clerk, saying, "Get her a linkup."

Minutes later she was again talking to her mother in Bonita.

When finished, she looked at Whitpan. "What do I do now, sir? I need to have emergency leave."

"I've already contacted the Red Cross representative. You should be on an airplane sometime later tonight."

She went to her quarters and began packing. All of her gear had to be stored with the supply sergeant. It took nearly two hours, but she was finally transported to the terminal at King Fahd Airport for the first leg of her journey home.

56

The trip to the United States was nothing like the journey to Saudi Arabia. There was no sense of excitement, nor of mystery, only sadness, the emptiness wrought by the loss of a loved one. Argonne immersed herself in thinking of the life she had known as the stepdaughter of a good, decent man. She remembered the first time he bought her a horse, remembered birthday parties and her first airplane ride.

Upon arriving at Boston's Logan International Airport, she collected her luggage, went through Customs, then hurried to a pay telephone and called her mother.

"I'm catching a red-eye out of here in an hour, Mom. I should arrive around four in the morning. I'll rent a car and drive home. I should be there about seven-thirty."

"I'll be happy to pick you up, Argonne."

"That won't be necessary. Really. I think I'd prefer to see you when I get home. Not at the airport."

She started to say good-bye. "Where's Daddy?"

In the living room at Sabre Ranch, Dolores glanced toward the coffin mounted on two wooden sawhorses.

"He's right here, baby. You can see him when you get home."

Dolores hung up and walked to the bronze coffin, draped with an American flag. It was the second time in her life she had stood in this living room staring at a coffin bearing the body of her husband.

"Was that Argonne?" a voice called from the darkened hallway.

Her son, Jacob LeBaron Sharps, had flown home immediately from medical school upon learning of his father's death. She looked at him as he stepped into the light, tall, like Franklin, she thought, with the same trim build. "Yes. She'll be here around seven-thirty."

"Want me to pick her up at the airport?"

"She wants to rent a car."

They looked at the casket, folded the flag back, and opened the top. Franklin lay dressed in a dark suit—and a turtleneck, since he hated neckties.

"At least he didn't feel any pain," Jacob said.

"Thank the Lord for that."

He touched his father's lapel. "Mr. Crowley did an excellent job on his face." There had been a deep gash over the left eye when Franklin slammed into the yoke.

"Crowley always does good work. His family has sure had plenty of business from this family over the decades."

He ran his hand over the flag. "There's just one thing missing." He left and returned a few minutes later. He pinned a miniature set of paratrooper wings on his father's lapel. "There you go, Pop," he said. "You'll have your jump wings on when you get to Heaven."

"You did a fine job on digging the grave, son."

"Keeping with tradition, Mom." There was anger in his voice. Then he said, bitterly, "Why him, Mom? Why now? He was doing so well. Everything was going so good for him."

She didn't understand either. "It was just his time." She

didn't want to think about it any further. "Come on, let's get some sleep. We've got a whole lot of family coming tomorrow. Argonne. Your grandfather. Uncle Kevin. We'll have a houseful."

Jacob looked around. "Where are we going to put them all?"

"We'll make do," she said, as she closed the coffin, and rearranged the flag, then went to bed.

When she had left, Jacob noticed in the kitchen, she had turned on the archway light at the entrance to the cemetery.

Another family tradition.

57

In Kuwait City, Major Jerome Moody sat in a vacant apartment overlooking the Persian Gulf. It was dark, but he could see almost perfectly through the sighting aperture of a laser and night-vision device designed to guide "smart" bombs to their target. When the war started—if it started—the device would allow pilots to drop their weapons from a high altitude and home in on the laser beam, guiding the bomb with pinpoint accuracy to the target. Or, so was the plan.

The city was in a constant state of turmoil, with reprisal murders by Republican Guard soldiers a daily, brutal ritual. The Iraqis had shown no mercy for the underground's guerrilla war against their invaders. He had personally witnessed dozens of summary executions on the spot with no trial and often not speedy. The enemy was enjoying their stay in the seaside city; young women were the top prize of the occupiers. Rumor ran high that many young Kuwaiti women had committed suicide following hours of brutal rape at the hands of the Republican Guard.

Troops had poured into the city believing that the attack—if one came—would come from the sea and the

coast of Saudi Arabia, directly to Kuwait City. Moody
could see they sat waiting for the "mother of all wars."

His mind was tightly focused on the mission, his men,
and the constant threat of being discovered. All movement
was by night, made more difficult by the burgeoning numbers of Iraqi soldiers. It was obvious the Iraqis were preparing to fight on three fronts and determined to hold
Kuwait City or burn it to ashes.

The familiar sounds of Kalashnikov AK-47s echoed
throughout the day and night in the tiny capital, always
bringing Moody to full alert. He never let down his guard,
knowing that one slight lapse in discipline could be fatal.
He tried to not think about Argonne, though her face did
slip into his mind; as did recollections of her scent, her
laughter, and her temper. The woman could stand her
own ground, no doubt about that.

He had been given the word that the Coalition forces
were increasing in strength and numbers along the Saudi
border; that a counteroffensive by the Iraqis was no longer
a real threat. The Navy had sealed off the Persian Gulf;
the air forces ruled the sky; the Army had built a formidable defensive fence along the Iraqi and Kuwaiti borders.

All was in place for the shooting to start.

58

Argonne arrived later than expected. She wore her uniform and appeared exhausted. Dolores and Jacob embraced her on the front porch and the three went inside. The casket commanded the center of the room; family members stopped their conversation and stood. She walked past them, stood at attention in front of the flag-draped casket, and saluted smartly.

Argonne leaned forward and kissed her father's forehead. "Hi, Daddy," she whispered. "I'm home." A hand touched her shoulder, and she turned to face Samuel. "Gramps," she said softly, folding into his outstretched arms. He held her long and tight, felt her chest heave and heard her sniffle as the tears she had been holding back finally flowed freely.

Dolores took her hand. "You look exhausted. Why don't you go to your room and get some rest."

She shook her head. "I'm all right. And just too tired to sleep." She picked up her luggage, went to her room, and returned after a moment.

The kitchen and dining room were filled with food

brought by friends and relatives. "You could feed an army, Mom," Argonne said.

"That's about what we're going to have here tomorrow," Dolores replied as she answered the telephone. After several minutes she hung up. Looking at Samuel, she said, "That was Bill O'Kelly. He wants to come but can't get away. He's sending flowers."

"That's very thoughtful. I'm sure he's as shocked as the rest of us."

Argonne recognized the name. "He's the writer that's doing a book on our family?"

Dolores told Argonne about his visit to the ranch and his book plans. "He is going to try to reach you in Saudi Arabia when you return. You'll like him. He and your father became friends at once."

Samuel motioned for her to join him on the couch. "How about giving your Gramps a briefing on what's going on in your theater of operations."

She told him as much as she knew, pointing out the problems that plagued the forces in coping with the desert. "The heat is the worse, but it's starting to let up a little. If only the sand would behave we might not have so many mechanical problems."

"Well, you won't be alone," Samuel said. "You can bet the Iraqis are up against the same obstacles. And their equipment is not as good nor maintained as well as ours. I saw that on a tour I made of Iraq during their war with Iran. Poor maintenance, from the soldiers' individual weapons, to their armor and aviation assets. That will make a big difference if the pot boils over."

She agreed. "That's already become obvious. Quite a few of their soldiers have surrendered and our intelligence people are confident that the average soldier doesn't want to fight us."

"Lord, I hope not," Dolores said. "This family has gone through enough fighting for other countries. I don't understand why we have to always be the first one the world turns to when the world goes crazy."

"The price of freedom," Samuel said.

Dolores shook her head and looked at the coffin. "I don't think he would agree. You know his feelings on Vietnam. All those boys killed, and for what? For nothing at all."

Samuel said, "I don't agree. I like to think that my son died for something important. Just like the troops in Saudi Arabia are there for a good reason. The world has to stand up to the tyrants. If we didn't learn anything else in World War Two, we certainly learned that painful lesson."

Dolores glanced at Argonne. "Well, I just pray that this foolishness stops before our children have to get into harm's way. I've got a daughter living like an animal on the other side of the world, facing the fourth-largest army in the world. This won't be like Grenada or Panama. This is going to be bloody for both sides." She patted Argonne's hand. "This child hasn't even had the chance to get married and have children."

With that, Argonne found the opportunity to defuse the tense situation and to tell them about someone special in her life. "I'll have children one day, Mother. Matter of fact, I've met a man I've become quite fond of."

Dolores's and Samuel's eyebrows suddenly rose curiously. Her mother asked, "And who might that be?"

She told her about Jerome Moody, and both appeared delighted. "Well now," said her mother, "it's about time you came home with some good news. Are you able to see each other often?"

"Not as much as we would like." She explained about his classified work inside Kuwait City.

"Good God," Dolores exclaimed, "that man is in the worse place any soldier could be."

"He definitely has a front-row seat in the theater. Are you able to communicate while he's in the field?" Samuel asked.

"No. That would be too dangerous."

"That's true. But it would be too dangerous."

Dolores shuddered. "Just when I think there might be hope for you finding a husband, you go and spoil it with this revelation."

Before Argonne could answer there was the sound of a car driving up in the front. The three hurried through the door and onto the porch. Two small children rushed from the car, shouting, "Grams!" Dolores knelt and caught the children in her arms. "Mmmmm. How are my babies?"

A voice came from a man standing at the driver's side of the car. "A handful, Momma." Kevin Sharps stood watching as his grandchildren Tiasha and Edora hugged and kissed his mother.

Argonne raced to him. "Uncle Kevin!" The two embraced; then Kevin walked to Samuel, and the two hugged one another. "Hi, Pop," he whispered. Samuel said nothing. His cheeks were wet with tears and he felt weak in the knees.

"Sorry the others couldn't come." He apologized for his two sons. "Their commitments wouldn't allow it." His boys were divorced, each having a child by their former marriages. His eyes went to the house and suddenly appeared saddened.

"I understand," Samuel replied in a choked voice. "Come on . . . let's go see your brother."

The family walked into the house, arms linked, silent, but together.

59

The mood on the morning of the funeral was somber as family and friends gathered at the ranch to bury Franklin LeBaron Sharps. An honor guard arrived from Fort Huachuaca. Samuel wore his uniform, as did Argonne. Both stood at attention as the casket was carried to the fresh-dug grave site.

A minister said a prayer, and then the honor guard fired a twenty-one-gun salute; the shrill of "Taps" followed, its eerie sound echoing through the air. Then the body was lowered and the mourners walked past the grave, each dropping a rose onto the coffin. The line extended almost to the cottonwoods, and when the last person had passed they gathered at the picnic tables that sat filled with food, while the Sharps men took up shovels and began filling the grave.

The initial shovels made a crushing sound, which gradually faded to a soft patter as the hole began to fill. Sweat poured from the faces of Samuel, Kevin, and Jacob, who labored metronomically, until, finally, the task had been completed.

The family stood in silence as the patting-down of the

earth was done. Flowers were used to cover the grave, and one by one they walked to the cottonwoods. Except Franklin's father, wife, brother, and son and daughter. They stood with arms joined, each in private thought.

Not a word was spoken. Finally, they walked to the cottonwoods.

That evening the Sharpses were again alone, talking quietly in the living room, except for Argonne. She was in her bedroom, packing for her return to Saudi Arabia. Dolores came in to help, but seeing the chore was nearly finished, she sat on the bed.

"I wish you could stay a few more days," she said to her daughter.

"I do too. But that's the Army way. Bury the dead and get on with life."

" 'The Army way.' Look what it's done to my family. Killed your father. Nearly destroyed Franklin, your uncle, and grandfather. Now, you're packing your bag so you can return to war. I'm afraid I'm not too impressed with 'the Army way.' "

Argonne closed her suitcase angrily. "I don't need to hear this right now, Momma. I really don't."

"I'm sorry. I just hate the thought of being alone. I've been through this before. I never expected it to happen again."

Argonne sat beside her mother and took her hand. "I've been thinking about that, Momma. Why don't you close down the house, hire a caretaker, and move to Atlanta."

She didn't like that idea. "I could never leave here. Not permanently. Besides, there's the restaurant."

"Sell it," said Argonne. "Go and find a new life. You're still a young woman. Who knows, there might be another fine man out there."

Dolores smiled. "I'm not lucky with men. I'm beginning to feel like a black widow. Literally."

"That's not true, Mother," Argonne replied. "You're

forty-six years old. That's too young to become a recluse. In Atlanta you can get involved with dozens of projects that can give you a quality of life you've never known. And, you'll be close to the babies. I know they'd love to have their aunt Dolores around to spoil them."

A distant look came over her face. "That would be nice. Something to think about," she said in a fading voice.

After that, Dolores went to the living room. It was getting late and the family retired to bed. Before she turned out the living-room light, she went to the kitchen and turned on the light that always burned above the archway.

Tradition.

PART 6

NORTH TO THE EUPHRATES!

60

On January 17, 1991, at two remote Iraqi radar posts near the Saudi border—code named White Site and Blue Site—eight AH-64, Apache Longbow attack helicopters, operating in two groups from the 101st Aviation Battalion, struck the first blow against Saddam Hussein's army. Led by battalion commander Lieutenant Colonel Richard Cody, the two teams from Task Force Normandy struck with precision and deadly accuracy at 0237, knocking out the Iraqi radar fence, and opening a giant blind hole for attack aircraft to fly unsuspectedly to their targets.

Task Force Normandy was the tightest-kept secret of Operation Desert Shield. Only required personnel were privileged to the secret operation, including members of Cody's battalion. Training had been conducted under the canopy of security deep in the desert, away from observation of Coalition forces. A mock replica of the two targets was constructed and the training began with an intensity none of the pilots had known before.

While there had been rumors, troopers of the 101st knew to keep their eyes and mouths closed, in order to insure there would not be a leak. And there wasn't. The attack came off with surgical precision, and the gate was opened for Pave Low helicopters to begin jamming the Iraqi radar sites, and allowing the strike and missile forces to reach their targets with devastating efficiency. In the air, fighters from all the Coalition nations quickly chased the Iraqi air force from the sky, and for over a month the Stealth and B-52 bombers had their way while suffering few losses.

In the early phase of Operation Desert Shield, the greatest fear was that the Iraqis would attack Saudi Arabia, a persistent nightmare of the Coalition. Images of thousands of tanks and a half-million ground troops crossing the line haunted every commander and soldier. On the beginning of what was now called Operation Desert Storm, Saddam Hussein had been blustering and bluffing, never believing he would be attacked for fear of astronomical casualties.

The madman from Iraq had blinked; his bluff was called. The Persian Gulf War had started off with stunning success for the Coalition forces.

61

* * *

Aboard CV-67, the USS *John F. Kennedy* aircraft carrier, naval Lieutenant Jonathan Sharps Bennet stood on "vultures' row," an observation area high above the deck of the massive supercarrier. It was late in the evening and the ship was alive with activity. He stood cross-armed, his teeth clamped around the chewed remains of his last Cuban cigar. He was twenty-five, trim, and muscular, and walked with the practiced swagger of a U.S. naval fighter pilot.

The carrier—"Big John," as it was affectionately known—was over three football fields in length, carried an average of seventy-eight aircraft, ranging from Strike Fighters to air interceptors, AWACs-capable aircraft, light bombers, air refuelers, counter electronics, and an array of helicopters. Over five thousand sailors and Marines were stationed on the huge fighting ship, which carried enough firepower to attack and defend whatever waters it sailed. Based out of Mayport, Florida, CV-67 sailed to the Middle East in September, and was selected as the flagship for the Battle Group Red Sea Battle Force.

Now, in mid-February, as the air war continued, the

ship buzzed and shook with the frenzied activity of men preparing for battle. To the flight deck from the hangar deck below, the four elevators whirred without stop, raising the fighting birds from the bowels to the tight formation topside where each aircraft was armed and ready for the moment to catapult into action.

Jonathan Sharps went below to his quarters and dropped into his bunk, ragged from the full day of work and the gnawing agony of waiting to go again into battle. He stretched each muscle that ached from the constant jolts and g forces from launching and the sudden crunch of "trapping" on one of the ship's four arresting cables.

A single light burned above the sink in his quarters, which was no larger than a prison cell. Windowless. Gray. A lonely cubicle. A place to come to for the bodily necessities such as sleep, showering, and solace.

He tried to grab a few hours of sleep but due to the fatigue could only lie staring at the ceiling, where a *Playboy* pinup smiled down from above.

He glanced at the bulkhead opposite the sink, at photographs depicting the life experiences that shaped him into what he was: a fighter pilot.

A destroyer of men and their machines.

One photograph of his Arizona childhood captured him at twelve, standing with his cousin Franklin, clutching a brace of prairie chickens he had shot while hunting. On that day he realized that he loved the thrill of the hunt.

Though he was not a Sharps by name, he was by blood. His great-grandfather David had been killed in the Great War in France. His mother, Theresa, had stayed in Arizona, and his grandfather Jonathan had been killed in World War II, while serving in the Navy. His father, Robert, had served in Vietnam, and now it was his turn to go to war.

He would hunt in the skies, pushing the outside of the envelope in search of the enemy.

Another was of his great-uncle Samuel, kneeling by his P-51 Mustang at a forward air base in World War II Italy. The third was him seated in his F/A-18 Hornet Strike Fighter, the day he arrived aboard Big John.

Gradually, his eyes began to close. Drifting off, he felt himself in flight.

He was alone, soaring through the sky like an eagle. Just before the curtain of sleep closed around him, he saw, on the horizon, another eagle approach.

A thin smile crept across his lips; his eyes tightened beneath the brow. His finger began closing around the trigger, when—suddenly—a sharp, metallic voice shrieked over the MC-1 intercom. "All pilots report to your ready room! I repeat . . . All pilots report to your ready room! On the double!"

The ready room of the *Kennedy* was not as plush as the briefing rooms of the newer carriers, but it served its purpose as a combination tactical discussion center, general hangout area for the pilots, and trophy room.

The floor was carpeted in blue; brown, contoured leather chairs sat in neat rows. The front wall of the room was lined with banks of television screens plugged into a variety of communications systems ranging from cable television to surveillance satellites roaming the sky above the Earth.

A commotion from the rear interrupted everyone's thoughts.

All eyes turned to the CAG—commander of the Air Wing. He wore a blue baseball cap emblazoned with the gold letters TOP GUN.

He entered with the arrogant swagger of the fighter pilot, flashing a confident grin. He paused, studied his men, understanding what they were thinking.

He wore "speed jeans," inflatable pants that lit up with high-pressure air on the lower torso, preventing the blood from pooling in the legs during high-g maneuvers. The nylon pants prevented unconsciousness; with each step there was a *zing* where the nylon fabric rubbed at the inseams.

An hour later, Jonathan Sharps sat in the cockpit of his fighter, helmet and oxygen mask tightened over his head and face. He stared at the catapult officer, waiting for him to point. When his finger snapped forward, Lieutenant Sharps saluted smartly, felt the sudden lurch of the aircraft hurtling along the "cat." Within seconds he was free from the carrier and climbing into the darkness above the sea.

Glancing at his HUD—heads-up display—a hologram-like system which provided complete readouts of his instrument, he banked toward the north. He was joined by his wingman, and in the distance he could see the lights of Kuwait City. That had been one of his primary bombing missions since the beginning of the war.

He recalled his first combat mission: He had not been scared, but aware of the threat that awaited him over the sky of the enslaved city. He flew three sorties that first day, attacking the airport with his Mark-82 bombs, then the beachfront defenses; then a squadron of Republican Guard tanks on the outskirts of Kuwait City.

There had been dozens of sorties since then, and he knew there would be more.

62

Jerome Moody had watched with childlike delight when the first Navy fighter-bomber struck the airport at Kuwait City at the beginning of Operation Desert Storm. He loved every earthshaking moment, watching the Iraqis scurry for their bunkers from their bonfires, which gave inbound attacking aircraft a well-lit target.

Fire and screams rose into the early-morning air; the earth, buildings, fleeing soldiers, and frightened Kuwaitis felt the shock waves tear through the city as tanks, parked airplanes, and fuel depots exploded.

The following weeks proved busy. Raids began in open force, the guerrilla forces primed with weapons, training, tactics, and hatred. Harassment operations had begun throughout Iraq, with the Kuwaitis in their country, and Kurds in Iraq. The Coalition's lethal and relentless assaults had deadly effects on the enemies' resolve.

Thousands had begun throwing down their weapons and surrendering en masse to the Coalition. Saddam had been kept on the move and was using look-alikes to confuse the Allied intelligence sources. Baghdad was in near ruin and certain panic from the outset, which was re-

ported for a while on the spot by CNN television news
from their perch atop a hotel in the center of the capital
city.

On January 19, 1991, the Iraqis had fought back with
their only offensive weapon, the deadly Russian-built Scud
missile. Israel was under constant barrage but was gritting
its national teeth and not retaliating, which could have
threatened the Coalition. Patriot-missile units were having
success shooting down the incoming Scuds, but a few got
through and caused damage, including one that was dis-
abled over Dhahran, but fell and exploded in a U.S. barracks, killing dozens and wounding scores.

Moody took the radio and whispered, "Green One, this
is Hardcore." He waited for the reply. "Move your team
into position and prepare to attack when I make my
move."

The voice of one of his Green Beret soldiers replied,
"Roger. Good luck."

He called back to the American—"Remember, we only
have a thirty-minute window before the bombing re-
sumes."

Moody stood within the shadows and removed a black,
flowing Arab robe. Beneath, he wore the uniform of an
Iraqi Republican Guard colonel. He had the dead officer's
clothing, weapon, papers, and even his BMW automobile.
All were courtesy of the underground fighting organization.

By the time he climbed into the car, the bombing had
stopped, but the streets were in chaos. He began driving
along Rashad Street, toward the center of the capital, ne-
gotiating the gauntlet of roadblocks established by the
army, reaching the headquarters of the Republican Guard
General Command, which was in so much confusion that
he was not checked for identity. Which he had counted
on.

He had checked his watch, eased the car to a stop in

front of a roadblock at the headquarters building, and removed a large satchel when three soldiers approached brandishing AK-47 assault rifles. They looked haggard, dirty, and scared out of their minds.

Recognizing the rank on Moody's Iraqi uniform, one soldier, a swarthy sergeant, stood at attention and saluted. *"Salaam Alaikum."*

Moody only grunted as he handed the dead officer's papers to the soldier and scanned the defensive positions on the boulevard.

Looming from behind a necklace of sandbags, a Soviet 2S1 SO-122 Gvozdika self-propelled, medium-artillery, armored vehicle sat beneath camouflaged netting, its massive 122mm howitzer gun extending from the turret. One of the crew sat straddling the barrel; intermittently, the brightness of a cigarette glowed from above the gun.

Again he scanned. Thirty meters from the Gvozdika, an Uragan BM-27 rocket-launcher vehicle was nestled with similar sandbags and camouflaging. Soft, Arabic music drifted from behind the sandbags. Christ, Moody thought, how could these clowns ever hope to survive—listening to music in the middle of a battle.

He made a mental notation of the emplacement, recalling how the two weapons were not there yesterday afternoon when he returned to Mustafa's secret command bunker in the dead man's shop.

"You may pass, Colonel." Moody took his papers and nodded. He went inside headquarters, which had once been an elegant hotel. He started up the stairs, knowing the elevators were out of order. After a few steps he heard footsteps behind him. An officer, young and appearing exhausted, was walking behind him. He was in a hurry and rushed past Moody, muttering his excuses. The Green Beret only grunted and continued up the steps.

At the fourth floor he opened a door allowing him entrance into the headquarters' communications center. He found sheer chaos and walked unnoticed to the main entrance, where he again presented his papers. He said nothing and was passed through. Once inside, he melded into the confusion and spotted a desk, where he slid the fifty-pound satchel into the chair opening.

He lit a cigarette, scanned the center, and once outside, knelt and tied his shoes. He tossed his cigarette toward the Gvozdika emplacement. The sentries did not see the black locating device that was being tracked by GPS from a Keyhole-12 satellite miles above the city.

The sirens began to blare. Moving fast, Moody checked his watch. Two minutes.

From another pocket he removed a pack of cigarettes and stripped away the wrapping, revealing another black device. This one was a transmitter, its frequency set identically to the detonator inside the satchel. He pressed the red button, a muffled explosion followed, then a red-orange fireball tore through the outer wall of the building. Debris fell in large chunks, raining down on the front entrance, burying the sentries beneath the rubble.

He began running to where the others waited in a bombed-out store a hundred yards away. His legs churned as the whine of the fighter—the unmistakable burner sound of an F-18 Hornet—could be heard. Diving through the windowless front window, he rolled to where one of the Berets was holding a laser sighting device. It was angled up, toward the roof. He held it steady, then . . . an explosion the likes of which he had never seen. With the center of the building damaged by his explosive satchel, the impact of the Mark-82 laser-guided bomb did the rest of the job.

They watched as the building completely collapsed. Seconds later, another Mark-82 hit the transmitter, destroying the Gvozdika and Uragan positions.

Moody quickly stripped off the uniform, revealing his black military fatigues. He was soaked in sweat.

Moody looked at his sergeant. "Let's get it on!"

From the torn-up building, captured RPG-7 rocket launchers erupted, slamming into whatever Iraqi forces had survived. The rattle of their AK-47s echoed through the street; more RPG-7 explosions followed as the entire area was reduced to death and rubble.

The fight was vicious and short, the way Moody had planned it. Once satisfied that they had done enough damage, and bludgeoned the Iraqis, he pulled his men back, slipping away through the chaos.

63

In February the final ultimatum to Saddam Hussein had been made: "Get out of Iraq . . . or die where you stand!" The madman ignored what he called empty threats, despite the fact that the "air campaign" had annihilated his command-and-control capability, air force, armor, and hundreds of thousands of ground forces. All he had to do was watch CNN and see the hundreds of thousands of Coalition ground forces arrayed along his border.

There had been much criticism of the idea of a "ground campaign." Many analysts believed the war could be won from the air in relentless bombing of Iraq. Neither General Powell nor General Schwarzkopf spoke in open agreement to the media regarding what the plan would be, which led Saddam into a deeper sense of security.

By saying nothing, the two commanders had a plan few would know until it was too late to stop.

The 18th Airborne Corp was ready and champing at the bit. It was composed of the 101st Airborne, 82nd Airborne, and the 24th Mechanized Infantry. These three divisions were primed and ready to charge at a moment's notice. But as the political thermometer changed, the troops were dug in and waiting for the balloon to go up.

The division was now up "on the line," that invisible demarcation that separated the Coalition from the Iraqis. The enemy was close enough to see, hear at times, even smell when the wind was right. Tactical Assembly Area Campbell began to assemble on January 23, 1991, with the arrival of the 3rd Brigade, followed by the 1st Brigade three days later, and the 2nd Brigade on the twenty-ninth. It was a sight to behold, and the first time the full division had been assembled to launch a full-scale attack since World War II.

This massive deployment required 358 flights by Hercules C-130s and 1,900 vehicles, some rented from Saudi businesses, moving in convoys. On many occasions, when the drivers saw bombing in Iraq, the trucks and vans would pull over and wait for the attacks to stop.

TAA Campbell was a maze of tents, reinforced bunkers, camouflage, and miles of razor-sharp concertina wire that formed a defensive perimeter. The camp was positioned on a range of scattered dunes where camouflage netting covered artillery batteries, helicopters, vehicle motor pools, and Humvees mounted with TOW anti-tank missiles. This gave the camp the appearance of a military Barnum and Bailey circus, and required a full day to drive from one end to the other.

At G minus 1 and holding, the 101st Airborne/Air Assault Division was dug in, primed, and itching to get into the fight.

64

Argonne had toughened in the months since returning from her father's funeral, and felt as though she had brought a part of him with her, always beside her, whispering encouragement in her ear. And now, more than ever, she would need to rely on that toughness in order to survive what lay ahead.

The only luxury she allowed herself was the time to think about Jerome Moody, and to worry about his safety. On countless occasions she had tried to find out what was going on but always hit the wall of "Classified." She was a soldier and understood the need for secrecy in his mission; as a woman, that was entirely different. He couldn't know about her father, or the emotional pain she was facing along with the stress of preparing to go to war. And there was no doubt that the 101st was going into actual down-in-the-dirt, kick-ass combat.

"Interested in some chow?" asked Monty Ohlhauser. He had come to her tent bearing gifts. In his hands he held a large box.

She was sitting on her bunk, dressed in her flight suit,

boots on but not laced, a "ready to go in a moment" preparedness.

"Sure. I'll take a New York steak, medium-rare, baked potato, Caesar salad, and a bottle of Mouton."

He sat the box on the bunk. "How about a fruit cup, candy bar, and sunflower seeds?"

She laughed. "That sounds even better."

He opened up the care package sent by his wife and started shelling out the goodies.

They sat in a silence interrupted only by the sporadic cracking of the seeds, crunching of the bars, and the occasional slurping from the small fruit cans.

"Delicious. My compliments to the chef."

"I'll see that she's informed."

An uncomfortable silence fell over the Kiowa crew. They would glance sheepishly at one another, then turn their eyes away as though the other might connect on their central feelings and thoughts. After several minutes Argonne said, "I feel like I'm at the Last Supper."

"Sorry 'bout that. Didn't mean to get you down."

"You haven't. I think it's good that we talk. God only knows, I sure need someone to talk to right now."

A boyish smile came over his face. "You know," he said, "I don't really know much about you except that you're a fine officer, great lady, terrific pilot, Point graduate, and from Arizona."

She chomped into a candy bar. "That's me in a nutshell. The all-American girl. Come to think of it, I don't know much about you except you're a great pilot and weapons officer, married, kids, and have been a good strong source of support when I needed it."

"Yep. That's me."

Another long stretch of silence followed; then Argonne asked, "Monty, are you as scared as I am?"

His lips pursed, and then he said, "Only for my family. I guess that's selfish, but I can't stand the thought of dying and me not being there with them. Missing the ball games, first dates, barbecues." His voice trailed into silence.

She reached over and patted his hand. Then she sat back and said, "It's really going to happen, isn't it?"

"Yes. Both sides have come too far to back off now. Saddam doesn't care about his people. Only his personal pride and safety. If he backed down, his own Republican Guard would kill him."

She began clearing the cans and wrappers and dumped the refuse into a trash can. She straightened and with a tough edge to her voice, asked, "Are we 'Air Assault' ready?"

Monty stood and extended his hand. "Yes, ma'am. We damn sure are ready!"

She looked at her watch. "I've got a few letters to write, then grab some sleep. I have a feeling it's going to be a long day tomorrow."

Ohlhauser left. She sat on her bunk and wrote her mother:

Dear Mom,

Well, here we are, a few hours before the beginning of G-Hour. The troops are excited, morale is high, and we've trained so hard I see nothing but success for the operation and the conclusion of this war. I know you've heard a lot of propaganda spinning out from the Iraqi government regarding how there will be tens of thousands of casualties on the side of the Coalition. That is absolute bovine manure.

We are the finest army assembled since the D-Day invasion. We are highly trained, motivated, and equipped with the finest equipment of any fighting force in history. We are ready! We are professional, and each man and woman is here because they want to be, not because they were forced against their will.

Unlike, I might add, the Iraqis. I truly believe that the great majority of them do not want a fight. That is clear through the tens of thousands already deserting and crossing our lines to surrender. And the shooting hasn't even started.

With that said, I want to thank you for being my mother. I got lucky in the draw and had you and Pop for parents. You loved me, cherished me, and never for a moment made me feel that I wasn't special.

You were more than parents. You were a Godsend. I'm the luckiest child ever born.

I know it's difficult for you right now, and I'm glad that you're in Atlanta with family, and I hear your prayers.

Well, guess I better go. Like the Sergeant Major always said . . . "When the bugle blows . . ."

I just wanted to tell you that I love you very much, and you are in my thoughts.

Love,
Argonne

With that she rolled onto her cot, closed her eyes, and for the first time since childhood cried herself to sleep, knowing that soon she was going to war!

65

For the 101st Airborne Division, OPLAN 90-5, code-named Desert Rendezvous II, was the boldest, most intricate "behind the lines" assault in the history of warfare. Division Commander Major General Binsford Peay II had told the troopers that the road home led through Baghdad. And that was where they were going.

Or damn close.

General Norman Schwarzkopf, the CINCCENT (commander-in-chief, Central Command), had been pulling back on the reins with the bearish strength of his nickname. Despite pleas and urges from commanders in the field, there would be no aerial reconnaissance by helicopters of western Iraq until G minus 7, seven days before the ground campaign would begin. And that day would be decided by President Bush, Secretary Cheney, and Chairman of the Joint Chiefs General Colin Powell.

His reasoning was simple and sound: to make the Iraqis think the primary assault force would come from the sea, directed at liberating Kuwait City, which was what Saddam Hussein believed. His troops were amassed near the city, anticipating that very move.

At 0530, February 24, 1991, other than the commanders, William O'Kelly had been, without a doubt, the most frustrated man in Saudi Arabia. He had spent most of his stay since arriving sitting on his butt at boring pool briefings, and watching television. Although he was *Army Times,* he was required to follow in lockstep with the other reporters. Sensing the ground campaign was about to "jump off," he devised a plan that would get him close to the action, and possibly in the stockade, or killed.

O'Kelly had arrived at TAA Campbell wearing desert camouflage, a helmet with the illuminating tape on the crown that would signal to others he was American, a subdued Screaming Eagles patch, the rank of major on his collar, a fresh airborne haircut, and a holstered pistol on his hip.

He had acquired the equipment illegally, at the hotel, by paying an employee for doing the service, which was thievery, and not unknown in the Arab world. Afterward, he merely hopped aboard one of the many convoys moving north and eventually wound up at TAA Campbell. From that point he blended in, eating MREs, sauntering about, never being asked to identify himself. After all, he was an American, wore the uniform, and knew enough about what to say that he went unnoticed.

He had become, in effect, a journalistic spy.

And he had seen Argonne Sharps, which now brought him to the 2/17th tarmac at TAA Campbell. She had not been hard to find, being the only black woman helicopter pilot, and was standing by her Kiowa, reading from a single sheet of paper. She saw him approach and snapped to attention and saluted. "Good morning, sir."

He returned the salute, saw the smile on her face, and asked, "Good news this morning, Lieutenant?"

"Very good news, sir." She handed him the paper. O'Kelly read:

SUBJECT: MESSAGE TO ALL SCREAMING EA-GLES
   1. *DIVISION OPORD 91-1 IS EFFECTIVE FOR EXECUTION UPON RECEIPT OF THIS MES-SAGE. G-DAY H-HOUR IS 240600C FEB91.*
   2. *THE DIVISION'S NEXT RENDEZVOUS WITH DESTINY IS NORTH TO THE EU-PHRATES RIVER. GODSPEED AND GOOD LUCK!*
   3. *AIR ASSAULT! SIGNED MG PEAY*

Rendezvous was a buzzword for the Screaming Eagles. In 1942, when the division was activated, its original commander, General William Lee, wrote his men that they had no history, but a . . . "rendezvous with destiny." That phrase became the title for a book relating the 101st's exploits in World War II.

He looked at her. "Wow! Looks like this is it."

She nodded, then looked at him warily, and asked, "What unit are you with, sir?"

"Whichever one you can get me into, Lieutenant," he said. He was too close now to back out of the charade. Then he added, "I knew your father, and I know your mother and grandfather."

"How—"

"I'm William O'Kelly. I'm a reporter with the *Army Times,* and I've got to get a front-row seat in this fight. Can you help me?"

She was flabbergasted. "My mom and dad told me about you. But this is unbelievable! Are you insane?"

"Perhaps, but it's the only way I could think of getting to the action." He told her about his odyssey from Dhahran.

"Well, you're certainly determined, but you can't fit in my Kiowa." She scanned down the tarmac. Blackhawks were lined up like roaring hornets; troops were formed at each chopper, ready to board. "I don't know you, Mr. O'Kelly, but my family trusts you. I guess that's good enough for me." She pointed toward the Blackhawks. "That's the First Brigade. If you're brazen enough to get this far, I'm certain you'll be able to find your way aboard one of those choppers."

He turned and saw another pilot approaching. It was Monty Ohlhauser. He saluted, saying, "Good morning, sir. Great day for a war."

O'Kelly returned the salute. "I'm Major Jensen. From G-three. I just wanted to be here to see this fabulous armada take to the sky. Something I can tell my grandchildren about."

"You'll have a lot to tell them about this day, sir," Ohlhauser said.

O'Kelly looked at Argonne, extended his hand, and said, "Good luck, Lieutenant. And Godspeed." They shook hands, and he started away, then turned and said to her, "I'm certain your great-great-grandparents would be very proud of you." He winked, then disappeared toward the line of Blackhawks.

Ohlhauser only looked at her quizzically.

66

The early-morning darkness along the Tapline highway erupted with the roar and thunder of the ground campaign pushing forward. Where in the past there had been distant rumblings, now there were the distinctive sounds of crashing artillery, armor fire, bombs, and the MLRS (multiple launch rocket system) launchers spitting forth their weapons of destruction. It was, to Mickey Martinson, the most dramatic sight of her entire life.

She sat at the front edge of the perimeter, M-16 in hand, watching as the darkness turned brilliant from an explosion, then receded to black.

The Iraqis were to the front, and though a support unit, her detachment had been moved onto the line to provide precious water to the troops advancing into Iraq.

Mickey stared to the front, wondering what would happen in the minutes or hours ahead. Trucks were pouring out of the detachment area, moving north to follow the advancing troops. She was required to stay to the rear in support, as was the policy of the army, and though she didn't like it, she obeyed orders.

Overhead, the sound of aircraft seemed to shake the

heavens; the very ground on which she lay dug in trembled as the massive armor units from the 24th Mechanized Infantry Division pushed toward the enemy emplacements.

She saw Captain Crager approach. Her CO was geared up for combat, wearing everything but the chemical suit too hot to wear despite the fear of biological warfare that had terrified the soldiers. While the Scuds had not yet delivered a chemical payload—to their knowledge—there was always that possibility. When fighting a maniac, nothing is unsuspected.

"Morning, ma'am."

Crager knelt beside Mickey and nodded at the two soldiers in her bunker. "Keep alert, guys. I don't need to tell you that the wire is tightening."

She was going from hole to hole, checking on the troops, the way a good commander operates. It was starting to become light, and the sounds of the heavy stuff seemed close enough to touch.

"I wonder what's happening out there," asked Mickey. "If any of our guys have been hurt or killed."

"It's heating up," the captain replied. "I've been listening in on the radio. The initial assaults are pouring through Iraqi lines as though they aren't even there. So, keep your eyes and ears on. It's going to be a long day. I'll rotate you to the company area in a few hours."

With that she moved on to the next bunker, leaving the three soldiers to themselves.

At daylight, Mickey spotted movement to the front. At first she thought her eyes were deceiving her; then she saw another, then another form moving, their shadows preceding them on the sand.

Korppert, a college kid from Hatton, North Dakota, eased his M-16 over the sandbagged position and set his sights on the first of the advancing Iraqis to come clean and clear in his vision. "I've got a target," he whispered.

"So do I," said Mickey. She switched off the safety to

single shot, the best mode of firing from distance.

"I've got one," said Templer, a mini-mart manager from Fargo. "He's coming straight at us."

The three soldiers, along with the others on the perimeter, sat breathlessly, their sights set on the chests of the enemy advancers.

"Wait till they're closer," said Mickey.

Their breathing was heavy, then began to calm as the enemy closed on them one step at a time.

"Ready . . . aim . . ." Mickey stopped. She saw something in the hand of each man. "Wait. Don't fire." She pointed at one of the soldiers. He was carrying a white cloth.

"They're surrendering," she said. At that moment she felt a combination of relief and disappointment. She looked at Templer. "Go get the captain."

The private popped up and hurried away. The two kept their weapons trained on the Iraqis, which she estimated numbered around fifty. *Hell,* she thought, *with the guys gone in the trucks they damn near outnumber us!*

Mickey and Korrpert rose carefully, keeping their weapons trained on the advancing soldiers. Both switched to the automatic mode for more effective fire in a close-in situation.

She raised her rifle up, then again, indicating for the soldiers to drop their weapons and raise their hands. *Amazing,* she thought, as they complied. One by one the Iraqis laid their weapons down.

Mickey whispered, "The sonsabitches are surrendering without a sound!"

An hour later the troops were still in a state of shock at what they had seen. They began hearing reports from other units along the line, and from the battle area. The Iraqis were not fighting except in small pockets. They were literally throwing down their weapons and walking toward Coalition lines.

Mickey watched a squad of MPs process the prisoners. A complete frisk, removal of boots, then binding their hands and feet. They were then placed in an isolation area, awaiting transport to an EPW (enemy prisoner of war) camp, where they would be fed, watered, and given better care than the Iraqis gave Coalition pilots shot down during the air campaign, or any other prisoners.

Thinking of that, she felt a momentary anger, wanting to kill them all. Then she settled, realizing who she was and why she was here.

She was not a murderer.

67

Moody had gotten the word only hours before G-Day was authorized, and that made sense. His position was too critical. Should he be captured and that information extracted, it could have taken some of the edge off the sharpness of the bayonet now aimed at the heart of the Iraqi army.

He was at Mustafa's vault, sitting with eight leaders of cells he had formulated into a fierce and terrifying guerrilla fighting force. Their eyes were cold, but there was a glimmer of hope in them.

"The Iraqis have taken the bait. Our forces are now crossing into Iraq, and the southern border of your country. They are en route with the most destructive fighting force ever assembled," Moody told the others.

Suleiman, the old man, wiped his sleeve at the tears rolling down his cheeks. The others sniffed, dabbed eyes, and praised Allah.

"The time is ours," Moody said. "The Coalition is moving north, toward the Euphrates. Saddam's troops are caught in the crossfire. There will be no invasion onto the beaches of Kuwait. It was a ruse. One the Iraqis fell for.

The war of liberation of your country has begun in full force. Now, you must disrupt the internal structure of the Republican Guard here in Kuwait."

He paused, then said what all the guerrillas savored: "Kill them all!"

68

In Atlanta, Dolores Sharps sat spellbound as the news from CNN began to roll and show the unfolding of the ground campaign in Iraq. She immediately went to the telephone and contacted the only man on Earth who might console and inform her about what was happening.

"Samuel, have you seen the news?" she said, voice trembling.

In his office at home, General Sharps turned down the blaring news from the Persian Gulf and settled back in his chair. There was an eight-hour time difference from the East Coast to Iraq, and he knew when Saddam Hussein had refused the final ultimatum that there would be a ground war.

"There's nothing to be concerned about, Dolores. She's in support, and that won't put her near the front lines." He knew the lie would not work.

"She flies a Kiowa. That's a scout helicopter! I don't think that means she'll be delivering flowers to Schwarzkopf!" was her heated reply. She was nearly at the end of her emotional string. "First Franklin, now this. I just don't know how much more I can stand."

The only thing he could do was to be strong, and re-assuring. "She will be fine. You have to believe that. We all do. We are not the only people going through this. There are millions throughout the world, and she is not the only one that is facing danger." It was cold, harsh thing to say, he knew. But, it was the reality of the moment. The die had been cast. Now, all they could do was wait.

"I know you're right." There was a sound of apology in her voice.

"They are the finest-trained fighting force in the world. There is no doubt in my mind that everything is operating 'as planned.' "

"They're so young."

"What do you think governments do? Send old people to war? It's the old that start the wars . . . the young who fight them."

Dolores knew that, and his words were reassuring, but still there was the fear. "I just can't see her doing this."

"Then don't," he replied.

"How did Shania stand all those years of you being at war, and then Franklin?"

He didn't have to give it a thought. "She understood that we did what we had to do. Franklin made his choice initially based on anger for what happened to Adrian. I made my choice based on patriotism. Then I saw a larger picture."

"What do you mean?"

"The role of the black man in our society. There was so much work to do. Not just the fighting, but the pres-ence. The purpose of who we were and how we would fit into the fabric of this nation. That is what Argonne is doing. She's not just fighting for America in a time of war, she's fighting for those who will follow. She's a black woman in a white man's army. I thought I had it rough. Damn. Her job is a hundred times tougher than mine could have ever been. For that, I'm very proud of her com-mitment."

Dolores then said, "I've never thought of it that way. I guess I'm being selfish."

"You're not being selfish. You're being human. You're being a mother."

69

On G plus 2—the third day of the ground campaign—
the 101st was pushing hard through Iraq on the
ground and in the air. Forward operating bases (FOBs)
were the priority as the division began to push through
the enemy on the west flank in what Schwarzkopf called
"the Hail Mary," the football term designed to describe a
last-ditch effort to win the game in the final seconds.

That was far from the case.

Major General Binsford Peay II, 101st Airborne, Commanding, had told the troopers, "The road home is
through Baghdad."

Now it was time to light up the highway!

The Iraqis had taken the bait hook, line, and sinker. Convinced the Coalition would attack from the sea, the pil-
lagers of Kuwait had dug in expecting the Marines to
come ashore from the Persian Gulf. That did not happen.
Coalition armor forces rolled north, meeting resistance
that broke and ran at the firing of the first shot.

The dreaded minefields and petroleum-filled tank traps

proved to be nothing but minor inconveniences as the armor divisions punched huge holes in the enemy defenses, churning up ground and crushing the fighting will of the enemy forces.

The capturing of prisoners took on a bizarre, almost comical look. On more than one occassion, Cody's Apaches and Blackhawks hovered over hundreds of surrendering soldiers, raising an unanticipated question: How does a helicopter crew handle hundreds of captured prisoners?

The scene was ludicrous.

At the advance FOB called Viper, troops were mounting up, helicopters were refueling, and more supplies rolled in as the division pushed toward the Euphrates. The FOBs became FARPs (forward area refueling points), where precious fuel would be needed to keep the advance moving forward.

Trucks had brought fuel through an ancient trail called Wadi al-Batin, a wicked traverse through desert and rocky hills once traveled by Muslims on their pilgrimage to Mecca. Fuel trucks, called "blivets," rolled hour after hour toward the FOBs; giant Chinooks brought fuel as well, to be used until the trucks arrived.

"Keep the pressure on" was the order of the moment. The goal was Highway 8, on the Euphrates River, where the 101st would block any effort of the Republican Guards' retreat from Kuwait City. It was looking more like shooting fish in a barrel than a turkey shoot.

70

Argonne Sharps and Monty Ohlhauser were out front, furiously flying reconnaissance and reporting back to headquarters. Surrendering Iraqis could be seen for miles as they threw down their weapons and raised their arms, clenching the surrender leaflets dropped by air and artillery.

"I've never seen anything like this, Monty," Argonne said. "My God, there's hundreds of them."

"Maybe more," he said. "Our guys are kicking some major ass." There was an almost giddy sound to his voice.

Approaching one wadi, a dry streambed in the desert, she saw hundreds of Iraqis waving, when suddenly, machine-gun fire could be seen spewing from a bunker concealed inside the hill. Soldiers were falling all over, as uninterrupted fire swept them down.

"Good Christ! They're killing their own people!" Ohlhauser yelled above the carnage.

Argonne flicked off the safety cover, armed a Hellfire missle, took a breath, and sighted the bunker. Her finger closed on the trigger; the missle launched and screamed forward.

Momentarily, there was impact as the brown earth heaved upward, forming a gray-black cloud shaped like a mushroom.

"Wa-hoooo!" shouted Ohlhauser. "Great shooting, Six Gun! Great damned shooting." Argonne's hands were trembling; there was a copperish taste in her mouth.

The shot set most of the Iraqi soldiers to flight; scores fell to their knees in prayer, facing Mecca. The guns from the wadi fell silent and off came the soldiers' shirts, which they waved frantically at the Kiowa.

"Poor bastards," Argonne said. "They don't have a bit of fight left in them."

"Can't say I blame them," Ohlhauser replied.

The landscape looked like the surface of the moon. Craters pocked the earth where cluster bombs dropped by the B-52 Stratofortress had rained steel onto their positions since the beginning of the air campaign. Now the ground forces were sweeping in and cleaning up.

The radio was filled with the same reports. All along the push the Coalition was meeting little, if any, resistance.

Argonne flew lower, noticing that many of the soldiers—if they could be called that—were old men and young boys. Saddam had emptied the cities and villages of men, passing out AK-47s and ammunition and giving no training.

As they hovered over a bunker they could see it was nothing more than a reinforced foxhole. Six dead bodies lay inside it in a heap.

Argonne pointed at the black cloud over the hole. "Even this far out in the desert, the flies still find the dead."

She peeled away and the Kiowa took more reconnaissance photographs of the battlefield, then headed for the FOB.

71

Lieutenant Jonathan Sharps Bennet sat in the cockpit of his fighter, the F-18 locked into the shuttlecock and ready for the catapult launch. The blast deflector shield rose behind the two firetails streaming off the Hornet's GE-404 engines. Forward of his cockpit, the launch officer knelt on the deck, checking his flaps, ailerons, and launch bar. When certain all was ready, he pointed down the "cat track."

In the "bubble," the cat operator watched as the pressure reached the right setting on the massive pistons operating the catapult, and when satisfied, pressed the Fire button.

Steam streaked from beneath the track as the Hornet lurched forward. In the cockpit, Bennet was slammed into his seat by the transverse g's working on his body.

Less than two seconds later the Strike Fighter was screaming off the deck.

Passing the end of the bow, he pushed the throttles through military power into "zone-five afterburner," and raised the nose to begin climbing.

The aircraft was designed as both a fighter and a strike

bomber. He was in the bomb mode, carrying Mark 82 laser-guided ordnance, 20-millimeter uranium-depleted tank-killing ammunition for its six-barreled chain gun, and two heat-seeking missiles in the unlikely event he encountered enemy fighters.

Below, and to his front, the blue of the Red Sea turned brown where it met the desert of western Saudi Arabia. His target was Kuwait City, which he had hit on many occasions since the beginning of the air campaign. Now, with ground forces—whose armored columns he could see to the west—driving the Republican Guards out of their hiding spots in the city, they were easy targets for every type of Coalition aircraft. Especially for the A-10 "Warthog," a pure tank-killer. Hundreds of tanks had been destroyed and there were more fish to fry.

As he neared the city, his wingman peeled off and began a run toward the airport while Bennet flew north.

"Red Wolf One, going onto target," the pilot reported.

He watched the F-18 streak toward the airport; skeletons of bombed-out Iraqi airplanes littered the field. For all practical purposes, there was no air force, and little of an airport. Initial bombings had blown large craters into the runways, denying Iraqi aircraft takeoff or landing. What few Russian-built Hind-mil 23 helicopters the Iraqis had were now burned-out hulks. The only way in or out of the city was by boat, or ground transport along Highway 8, now known as the "Highway of Death."

Jonathan watched the Hornet open up with his Vulcan .20mm guns, sending a radar-guided burst that shredded a TU-72 tank that was caught in the open. The turret blew straight into the air; then, as the metal-searing projectiles ignited the tank's arsenal, there was a voluminous explosion.

"Another dead kitty," the pilot said.

The bombing had almost become boring in the past month. Sortie after sortie, bombing, strafing, no air combat since the first week and he missed all that action. What had been exciting had evolved into tedium.

He rolled onto his target, a mechanized infantry platoon racing to the west. Probably Republican Guards, he figured. They were about the only ones who were fighting, and doing that for self-preservation. It was obvious that the Guard was trying to get back to Iraq with all sides closed off.

"Good luck," he whispered as he armed one of his air-to-ground missiles. At that moment he saw the four vehicles break formation and begin to scatter.

He sighted on one vehicle, a half-track loaded with troops. When he got lock on the target he fired his missile. The contrail snaked for a few minutes, then took a steady path toward the half-track. He watched on his FLIR (forward-looking infrared radar) as the deadly device found its mark.

He rolled out and gradually eliminated the other three and turned back toward the carrier.

The initial jubilance of arriving in the Middle East was gone. Now everybody wanted to finish off the bastards and go home.

72

What had become known as "the *shamal* from Hell" had struck FOB Cobra on G-2, and it had looked as though the assault would stall out just short of the Euphrates. The "brownout" slowed the incredible advance, but it allowed the commanders to consider their next moves. There had been talk of a "Baghdad Sequel," and that the Screaming Eagles would be the vanguard of the attack on the capital.

That was not to be, however. By G-3, the weather had cleared and the 101st was sent from newly formed FOB Viper to attack bridges and other positions along Highway 8 between An Nasiriya and Basra. The Iraqis were running for home and the Screaming Eagles were waiting for them.

Argonne had been relegated to a rear position, since Viper was now the main fighting platform from which the rest of the lightning war would be fought. The three brigades had taken all their positions along the highway, destroyed bridges, trapped fleeing Iraqi convoys in the middle, and the flyboys were having a feast on the Highway of Death.

To the west and south Argonne saw billowing black smoke, and the word went out that Saddam's troops had blown the Kuwaiti oil fields in their hasty retreat.

The terrain had changed from the customary harsh desert as the division attacked Iraqis along the Euphrates valley. The Coalition saw lush, green farmland, marshes, and for the first time inside Iraq began to see a civilian population. This became a serious matter, for the Coalition did not want to kill civilians.

Argonne Sharps and Monty Ohlhauser were given the least palatable mission in the campaign: to cruise a corridor south of the highway between Basra and An Nasiriya, to search for straggler units trying to slip in behind the Coalition as they pushed north in the desert.

After hours of flying, they realized that there was nothing for them to do but fly and search and listen to the radio, knowing they were now no longer a part of the fight. It was disappointing, and they felt left out, but it was an order and she would follow it despite her feelings.

"Looks like it's going to end before it really gets started, Buckaroo," she said into her mike.

"From the sound, it's already over," Monty said.

The desert was strewn with scorched and burning remnants of what had once been one of the world's largest armor threats.

And there were the EPWs. Everywhere they could see massive gatherings of Iraqi troops waiting in the desert for Coalition forces to steer them to prison camps.

"Looks like the war is over," Argonne said.

She couldn't have been more right.

What was left of the Iraqi army had been annihilated in the Euphrates valley, caught on the highway by aviation forces from all the nations and services joined in the fight to drive Saddam Hussein out of Kuwait.

Behind the scenes the political back channels were burning red-hot between the Middle East and Washington. It was finally agreed that on the following morning at 0500, the advance would stop and there would be a cessation of fighting.

Iraq had agreed to accept the terms of all the United Nations resolutions.

The Persian Gulf War was over.

EPILOGUE

★

GOING HOME

On February 24th, the phone rang in Atlanta and Dolores Sharps answered. Her sister, Renee Bennet, had watched nervously throughout the war, beginning with the air campaign, knowing her son Jonathan would be among the first in the fight.

"Is it true? Tell me it's true, Dolores."

"Our babies will be coming home soon, sis," Dolores said tearfully.

After she hung up, Dolores called Samuel. He was sitting in his study, watching the celebration unfolding throughout America on television. He felt a mixture of joy and sadness. He had known this jubilation at the end of World War II, and the bitter disappointment at the end of the fighting in Vietnam. When he hung up, he walked to the back and took his nine-iron. With a crisp swing he drove a golf ball to the driving range.

He put the club back in his bag and returned inside, wearing a pleased smile.

*   *   *

In the desert of Saudi Arabia there was jubilation, but the 101st Airborne Division's departure would be just as arduous as its arrival had been.

Argonne was required to prepare her Kiowa for transport to the port for shipment to the United States. The same was required of the North Dakota Quartermaster Detachment that had supplied the vital lifeline of precious water. It was at the staging area that Lieutenant Argonne Sharps once again crossed paths with Specialist Fourth Class Michelle Martinson.

Argonne saw the enlisted woman, smiled, and waved. Mickey saluted; then, like sisters who had endured both a nightmare and an adventure, they embraced.

"I thought of you often after the ground campaign jumped off," Mickey said. "I followed the progress of your unit as close as I could."

"It all happened so fast, I was barely able to keep up with what was going on. Still have plans for flight school?"

"Yes, ma'am. I'll go to college this summer and fall, graduate around Christmas, and hopefully, be accepted."

Argonne gave her her phone number in Clarksville. "If you need a reference, I'll be proud to write one for you."

"I'll call you when I get back to the States." A sergeant called to Mickey from a nearby truck. The two women saluted and shook hands and Specialist Four Martinson hurried off to join her unit.

Argonne finished with the paperwork on her Kiowa and caught a bus that took her to King Fahd. There was someone else she wanted to see while she was in the area.

The ride to SOCCENT headquarters at King Fahd took several hours and Argonne arrived dusty, sweaty, and tired. She had prepared by bringing along a suitcase and found her way to quarters that had been set up for female personnel. She took a long, hot shower, then hurried to the secret facility on the base. At the ribbon-wire gate she was stopped by a sentry, who refused her passage. It had been three weeks since the end of fighting and she hoped Moody had returned—and that he was safe.

"I'm sorry, ma'am. You can't enter without authorization," he said.

She understood, and had expected as much. She handed him a note and asked, "Will you pass this to your commanding officer. It's for Major Jerome Moody."

The soldier took the note, stepped through another secured fence, and handed it to another sentry, who disappeared into the building. She left for the officers' club. She had told Jerome she would wait two hours. If he didn't show she would understand and hope to hear from him later.

William O'Kelly was sitting in the bar when he saw Argonne enter the club. "Hi. Remember me?"

His hair had grown, but she recognized him. "Mr. O'Kelly . . . or, should I say Major Jensen?"

"Call me Bill. The major has moved on to a new assignment," he replied.

Both laughed. "Where did you wind up after we met?"

"I got the story. I crossed the Euphrates with Task Force Rakkassans. Quite the adventure."

She was amazed. "And you never were found out?"

"In all that confusion? I just acted like I didn't know what I was doing. I fit right in." His eyes gazed past her.

She turned and rushed forward into the arms of Jerome Moody. They held each other, he kissed her forehead and her cheeks and tasted the salty wetness of her tears.

She introduced Moody to the reporter. O'Kelly, sensing he was intruding, quickly excused himself. He said, "I'm leaving tomorrow. When is your unit going home?"

"I think in a few weeks. There's still a lot to do before we ship out."

"I'll call your mother and grandfather when I get to Washington," O'Kelly said. "I still want to talk with you about the book. You've added a new chapter." He looked at Moody. "I hope there'll be another generation of Sharpses one day."

Argonne smiled. "Perhaps."

He shook hands with them and left. The two soldiers sat at a table and talked, then walked into the moonlit night to stare up at the stars. "We first met on a night like this," he said.

"I remember." There was so much she wanted to tell him; to ask him. Instead of talking, they laced hands and walked, not noticing the sounds of the base, the hustle and bustle of vehicles.

They could talk later. For now, they just held hands.

1992—The Monument

On July 25, 1992, thousands of Americans gathered at
Fort Leavenworth, Kansas, amid a sea of blue cavalry hats and tunics; children ran and played on the grass
and steps while old soldiers lounged on the benches, shar-
ing decades of memories. Some good. Some bad. Most
were real.

They stood on hallowed ground, where ancestral and
spiritual descendants mingled with ghosts from the past.

They had come to dedicate a monument to the memory
of men and women who sacrificed in order that others
might enjoy what they had fought so valiantly to build
and protect: a nation.

One only had to see the monument to understand the
price they paid.

They were called the buffalo soldiers.

Upon entering the Buffalo Soldier Monument, which
rises above the once mosquito-infested site where the 10th
Cavalry established its first headquarters on the Western
frontier, the visitor passed a three-flag rostrum where Old
Glory fluttered between the regimental colors of the 9th
and 10th Cavalries. A path wound toward what appeared

to be a descending figure eight, the upper circle a natural pond surrounded by prairie grasses and wildflowers, to the stairs that led to the lower elevated circle, a reflecting pond. Between the two ponds a mounted Negro trooper sat poised on his horse on a pedestal of hand-cut stones, his Spencer rifle gripped in one hand, the reins of his horse gripped in the other, his kossuth hat pushed back at the brim. Benches surrounded the reflective pond, allowing the visitor a place to sit and enter into the solitude and dignity of history.

Suddenly, a jolt of excitement threaded through the crowd as a tall man dressed in an Army uniform approached the podium. He was recognized at once, and was greeted by applause that was long, loud, but polite.

General Colin Powell, the highest-ranking African-American in the history of the United States military, and Chairman of the Joint Chiefs of Staff, stepped to the podium, waved to the crowd, basking in the specialness of the moment, then began to read from the farewell speech of Colonel Benjamin H. Grierson to his troops of the 10th Cavalry Regiment.

" 'The officers and enlisted men have cheerfully endured many hardships and privations, and in the midst of great dangers, steadfastly maintained the most gallant and zealous devotion to duty, and they may well be proud of the record made and rest assured that the hard work undergone in the accomplishment of self-improvement and valorous service to country cannot fail sooner or later to meet with due recognition and reward.' Benjamin H. Grierson, Colonel, 10th Cavalry."

Powell went on:

"And now, one hundred and four years later, on July 25, 1992, his dream of recognition and reward has finally come true. And so has my dream.

"Beginning with the buffalo soldiers in 1866, African-Americans would henceforth always be in uniform, challenging the conscience of a nation, posing the question of how could they be allowed to defend the cause of freedom,

to defend the nation—if they themselves were to be denied
the benefits of being Americans?

"The great liberator Frederick Douglass made the same
point. Douglass said . . . 'Once let the black man get upon
his person the brass letters of "U.S.," let him get an eagle
on his buttons, and a musket on his shoulder, and bullets
in his pocket and there is no power on Earth which can
deny him his citizenship in the United States of America.'

"So look at this statue. Look at him. Imagine him
in his coat of blue . . . on his horse . . . a soldier of the
nation . . . eagles on his buttons . . . crossed sabres on his
canteen . . . a rifle in his hand . . . a pistol on his hip. Cou-
rageous iron will. He was every bit the soldier that his
white brother was. He showed that the theory of inequal-
ity must be wrong. He could not be denied his right. It
might take time—it did take time. But he knew that in
the end he could not be denied.

"The buffalo soldiers were not the only ones in this
struggle . . . the 24th and the 25th infantry regiments . . .
the 92nd and 93rd infantry divisions . . . the high-flying
Tuskegee Airmen . . . the parachuting triple-nickels . . .
our navy's Golden Thirteen . . . the Montfort Point Marines . . . and thousands of other brave black Americans
have gone in harm's way for their country since the days
of the buffalo soldier. Always moving forward and upward . . . step by step . . . sacrifice by sacrifice.

"But we are not here today to criticize an America of
a hundred and fifty years ago, but to rejoice—to rejoice—
that we live in a country that has permitted a spiritual
descendant of the buffalo soldier to stand before you today as the first African-American Chairman of the Joint
Chiefs of Staff.

"And I am deeply mindful of the debt I owe to those
who went before me. I climbed on their backs. I will never
forget their service and their sacrifice. And I challenge
every young person today . . . don't forget their service
and sacrifice . . . don't forget our service and sacrifice and
climb on our backs to be eagles.

"And so the powerful purpose of this monument must be to motivate us. To motivate us to keep struggling until all Americans have an equal seat at our national table. Until all Americans enjoy every opportunity to excel . . . every chance to achieve their dreams . . . limited only by their imagination and their own ability.

"We will leave this beautiful monument site today knowing that caring Americans made a modest dream come true. But let us also leave, my friends, determined, that the most important dream in the world—the American Dream—of progress and full equality has gained today with this monument a new vision.

"A new strength.

"And a new tomorrow . . ."

Samuel, Dolores, Argonne, and Jerome had sat in silence, listening to the words from a man who personified their family's history. Words that they felt had been directed to them personally. In reflection, they measured their lives by the values embodied in the statue: strong, resilient, and perennial, like the prairie grasses surrounding the mounted trooper.

They walked away, arms linked, their thoughts private, but each knew what the other was thinking:

It was a good day on the eve of a better tomorrow.

Afterword

The writing of The Black Sabre Chronicles has been a once-in-a-lifetime thrill and adventure. When I began the project, military service to the United States by African-American servicemen, servicewomen, and their families was a darkened corner of American history.

I hope some light has now been shed to illuminate the tremendous contribution, service, and dedication to our country and its people by these extraordinary Americans, and the white soldiers and their families who stood beside them as friends, neighbors, and in the harshness of battle and the home front.

While the scales of equality are not yet balanced, there is progress.

I'm proud to say that The Black Sabre Chronicles is being used as a teaching tool in primary, secondary, and college education to provide insight into the African-American experience in the United States military service.

Buffalo Soldiers was selected by the U.S. Army Center for Military History to present to General Eric K. Shinseki, the U.S. Army Chief of Staff, as one of forty writings for his Recommended Professional Reading List.

The Stone Ponies brought another accolade to myself personally as Airborne Author of the Year, from *Static Line,* the worldwide paratrooper newspaper.

In this last book of the series, I think it is important to remember a man—a buffalo soldier—of the 10th Cavalry, who, on December 7, 1941, while stationed at Fort Riley, Kansas, volunteered for the flight program at Tuskegee Institute. He would become a member of the famous 99th Pursuit Squadron—the Red Tails—known today as the Tuskegee Airmen. He fought with the heart of a lion and was a gentleman in the highest meaning of the word.

He is Lieutenant Colonel James Hurd, Sr., who passed away during the writing of this novel. He was deeply loved, and will be greatly missed.

Additionally, I would thank the men and one woman who graced the covers of three of these novels: Nasby Wynn of the Tuskegee Airmen, John Hughes of the Airborne, and Sheila White of the Air Assault.

In my own military service, in Vietnam, I learned lessons that assisted me in writing of the men and women of The Black Sabre Chronicles.

I have learned that to be afraid is not shameful . . . so long as you do not shame yourself.

That where you are going is not as important . . . as the journey.

That courage is found not in the rifle; rather, in the heart.

I learned that freedom is a gift too often unappreciated. **God Bless America! And Perdition to our enemies!**

TOM WILLARD
May 2002
Bismarck, North Dakota